Norma Ackroyd is the quintessential English country rose – pretty and rather innocent. But on the day her path crossed with that of the notorious womanizer from London, George Laxton, fate itself seemed determined to shatter her previously sheltered life.

For Norma fell hopelessly in love with Laxton and chose to ignore or disbelieve all the bad things she heard about him – to the intense chagrin of her family. They knew that many of the stories were true and that Norma was courting almost certain disaster. But she was determined to let heart rule head, and who knows, maybe leopards can change their spots?

This delightful story, which twists and turns like the vicissitudes of love itself, will appeal strongly to all readers of romantic fiction.

The Black Sheep

***

Ruby M. Ayres

HODDER PAPERBACKS

The characters in this book are entirely imaginary,
and have no relation to any living person.

This book is sold subject to the condition that it shall not,
by way of trade or otherwise, be lent, re-sold, hired out
or otherwise circulated without the publisher's prior
consent in any form of binding or cover other than that
in which this is published and without a similar condition
including this condition being imposed on the subsequent
purchaser

Printed in Great Britain for Hodder Paperbacks Limited,
St. Paul's House, Warwick Lane, London, E.C.4 by
Cox & Wyman Ltd, London, Reading and Fakenham

ISBN 0 340 14811 X

CHAPTER ONE

A CLOUD of dust, the sound of grinding brakes, and a woman's shrill scream.

The grey Jaguar came to a skidding standstill, and the man at the wheel half-turned in his seat to see what had happened.

'You might have killed me,' said a shaking, angry voice.

The young man looked relieved. 'Oh, well, as long as I haven't!' He stepped out into the roadway. He was a tall, thin young man, angry and impatient.

The girl who had flung herself back against the bank bordering the road to escape being knocked down by the car looked at him with flashing eyes.

'It's disgraceful, racing about the roads like that!' she said. 'The police have no right to allow it.'

The young man's rather harassed face broke into an unwilling smile.

'I didn't know there were any police in this Godforsaken hole,' he said. 'But I must admit I was driving rather too quickly; as a matter of fact, I'm in a hell of a hurry.'

The girl glanced down at her wrist with resentful eyes; it was torn by the brambles and bleeding slightly.

'Don't let me detain you,' she said frigidly.

The young man frowned.

'I'm sorry if I frightened you,' he said, with a touch of impatience. 'But I don't see how I could have known that you'd be walking right in the middle of the road.'

'You ought to have been more careful,' she told him severely, but now there was a little gleam of amusement in her eyes.

'That's a fine car,' she said, a shade enviously.

His face brightened.

'Yes, isn't it . . . Can't I give you a lift anywhere? I'm going right through to Lumsden — if that's your way.'

She looked at him and hesitated; then she looked at the car and hesitated no longer.

She climbed in without further invitation.

The man had given his invitation impulsively. He had not the least desire for her company. He thought she might have had the decency to refuse to accompany him, seeing that he had already told her he was in a hurry.

He climbed in beside her with faint interest.

She was very plainly, almost cheaply, dressed; that was the first thing he noticed, before his eyes wandered to her face, to the slightly tanned skin and round chin. She wore a blue beret, very much the same colour as the April sky above them, and beneath it her hair was blown into little loose curls about her ears and temples.

'Red,' the man beside her told himself curtly. He hated red-haired women. But, as a matter of fact, it was not red at all; it was only just where the bright sunshine touched it that the copper-brown waves took a brighter sheen.

He was a man who judged very largely from externals. He was used to driving with women who wore expensive clothes. He maintained a sceptical silence.

Presently she spoke, but only to criticise his driving. He did not like having his driving criticised. 'I have never been in these parts before.'

His voice added gratuitously that he did not care greatly if he never came again.

The girl looked faintly surprised.

'I've lived here all my life,' she said. 'I should think I know every tree and stone for miles round.'

They had turned a corner at the top of the hill now, and were passing some wide iron gates through which a carriage drive, some half a mile in length, led away up to a white stone house faintly visible against a background of trees.

The man glanced at it as they passed.

'Do you know that place?' he asked.

'Of course I do!' She leaned forward a little and looked interestedly towards it.

'That's Barton Manor,' she explained. 'It's been empty for years, but the new owner is just coming to live there. We're all most frightfully interested in him,' she added naïvely. 'He's a sort of black sheep, I believe.'

'Indeed.' He did not sound particularly interested, but the girl went on.

'He's a nephew of the late owner, and his name is George Laxton ... Of course, I don't know anything about him really — I've never seen him, but everyone says he's an awful rake ... most Georges are, don't you think so?' she asked.

6

'I can't say I've noticed it particularly.'

'I have,' she maintained. 'I had a cousin named George, and he was a fearful trouble to everyone; he ran away to sea and was drowned.'

'And then everybody was pleased, I suppose,' he submitted drily.

She laughed.

'Well, I don't think they were very sorry,' she admitted. 'And then the Vicar had a son named George, who nearly broke his mother's heart by going on the stage.'

'What a tragedy!'

She looked up quickly.

'I suppose you're laughing at me,' she said. 'I don't mind if you are. When you've lived down here in the country for as long as I have —'

'Which God forbid!' he interrupted.

'Oh, it's not so bad when you're used to it,' she said cheerily. 'We have quite a good time in our own way, though I daresay we should all seem very narrow-minded to you. You'd be surprised if you knew what excitement there is over the new man coming to Barton Manor, for instance. Just at present people can't talk about anything else.' She gave a little chuckle. 'Poor man, I should think his ears are burning.'

'What's he like – young or old?'

'Oh, he's young, of course, and unmarried! — which is a great thing. There are very few men here, you know — marriageable men, I mean; and all the mothers are getting quite excited about him, I can tell you.'

He looked down at her.

'Have you got a mother?'

Her bright face changed suddenly. She shook her head.

'No.' There was a little silence. 'She died three years ago.'

The man looked uncomfortable.

'Well,' he said at last awkwardly, 'I never knew mine at all; she died when I was a nipper — fortunately for her, perhaps,' he added rather bitterly. The car stopped.

'I'm sorry — but I shall have to drop you here,' he said, with a touch of constraint. 'Of course, you know we're just outside the village. I'd have taken you on, only ... well, I've got to meet someone at the station.'

He got out and stood in the sunshine, stretching his legs as if they were rather cramped.

7

The girl scrambled out too. The man noticed that she wore no gloves, and that her hands were slightly brown, like a boy's.

'Thank you for bringing me,' she said. She was quite at her ease. She looked up at him with a friendly smile. 'Well — good-bye.'

'Goodbye ... and let the black sheep down lightly when he comes.'

'The black sheep?' she echoed, not understanding.

'Laxton,' he explained.

'Oh — George!' She made a little grimace. 'Everybody round here calls him "George" you know! Oh, yes, I'm quite prepared to like him myself ... He'll break the monotony, anyway. Good-bye.'

She walked away towards the village through the sunshine.

The man climbed back into the car; he gave a little impatient sigh and started the car again. He passed the girl just as she reached the village; she waved her hand to him as he went by.

'Wonder who she is,' he thought, and then forgot all about her as he turned and drew up at the kerb outside the little station.

He dreaded the next hour or two; if only the sun had not been shining it would not have been so bad; but on a morning like this, when the world was looking its loveliest in its new spring dress of tender green, it was an appalling tragedy to think of having to say goodbye to all hope of happiness for the rest of one's life.

The train clattered into the station and the tall young man swallowed a nervous lump in his throat and moved slowly forward.

The window of a first-class carriage was opened, and a girl stood there looking out. The tall young man took a quick step towards her and wrenched open the door.

'You've come then.' He took her hand to help her to alight; he kept it in his own as they walked from the station.

He was no longer pale; there was a nervous flush in his harassed face. He hardly took his eyes from the girl at his side.

'I hardly dared hope you would come,' he said.

They were out in the sunny road again now, standing beside the car.

The girl looked up at him.

'You knew I'd come if I could. It was difficult — I believe mother guessed something — but ... here I am.'

He helped her in carefully and got in beside her carefully; he asked half a dozen times if she were comfortable. 'It isn't far;

but — but I wanted you to see the old place — before . . . well, of course, you know it's got to be sold.' He was not looking at her now; his voice sounded strained and hard.

She nodded.

'You told me . . .' She bit her lip. 'Oh, I think life is so horribly unfair,' she broke out; there were tears in her voice.

The man kept his gaze steadily before him; there was a fierce look in his face; he drove slowly back along the road, the way he had come; but now when they reached the wide gates of Barton Manor he turned the car in at them and drove up the smooth, wide drive to the white house amongst the trees.

There were men at work in the garden and there was a general air of disuse and neglect everywhere, which was very depressing.

'It had to be done,' Laxton said. 'It would never have sold as it was.' They had left the car now and were standing together on the wide terrace steps looking up at the big house.

'It would have been a fine home — eh?' the man asked, with a sort of rough anger.

She slipped her hand into his.

'Oh, if we only could . . . if we only could . . . Isn't there any — any possible way, George?'

He shook his head; he laughed mirthlessly.

'Only if some philanthropist chose to come along and adopt one of us,' he said. 'But those sort of things don't happen nowadays, do they, Laurie?' He walked on a step ahead of her. 'I think the door is open.'

They went in together. The wide hall was dim and cool; it was oak panelled and lofty; the floor was polished so that it reflected the quaint old suits and helmets of armour that hung on the walls. Laxton closed the door behind him and, turning, took the girl in his arms.

Pretty enough to satisfy the soul of the most exacting man! Golden hair, brown eyes and a small mouth that just now trembled a little as the brown eyes looked up into the man's passionate face.

'Oh, I think it's so unfair — so unfair . . . There isn't any happiness in all the world!' she broke out.

He kissed her passionately. He said that he would give his life to make her happy. He'd work his fingers to the bone if only she would marry him. Nobody could ever love her so well as he. They could go away together somewhere — just he and she . . .

9

They would be so happy ... What did it matter if they were poor if they had each other? He kissed the tears from her eyes; he kissed her pretty, useless-looking hands that tried to hold him back, to stem his headlong passion.

'You wouldn't be any happier than I should. You love money as much as I do.'

'I don't care if I never have another shilling in the world if I've got you.'

She shook her head; she smiled through her tears.

'You'd soon be tired of me if I couldn't always dress as well as I do now — if I had to work and spoil my hands.' She shivered daintily. 'Oh, George, we should both so hate to be poor!'

His arms fell from about her, he looked somehow beaten; when he spoke again his voice was dull and expressionless.

'I don't know if you care to see the rest of the house ... It's supposed to be very fine.'

She broke again into petulant tears; she had not wished him to get too much out of hand, but this change was too sudden to meet with her approval.

What was the use of showing her the house if she could never have it, or live there? she asked, sobbing. He could not really love her or he would never be so cruel as to suggest it. She wished she had not come; she had run dreadful risks to do as he had asked; if her mother found out there would be a dreadful scene; the least he could do was to be kind to her while she was here; they would probably never be alone again in all their lives.

He drew her down to a high-backed oak settle and kissed her again and again.

Anyone who only knew him casually would have been amazed at his tenderness; even his face seemed changed; in its hopeless unhappiness it looked much younger, much softer.

'I love you better than anything in the world,' he said hoarsely. 'I shall never care for another woman as long as I live ...'

She condescended to look at him then; she knew that she was a woman to whom grief was becoming; she said that she would never love anyone else either; that no matter whom she married ...

He broke out into frantic protestation. 'Don't say that ... I can't bear to hear you say that.'

He walked away from her down the long hall; there was something very tragic in his face; during all his years of industrious wild-oat sowing he had never imagined that there could be such pain in the world as that which he was suffering now; he did not go back to her till he had got control of himself once more; then he sat down beside her once more.

'I'm sorry — I didn't mean to be unkind ... Of course, you'll marry — I hope you will ... I only want you to be happy.' His voice broke. 'But he won't love you as I do ... no matter who he is — he could never love you as I do.'

She looked at him from beneath her wet lashes; somehow she had never realised that he cared so deeply; she had liked him for his headlong, impetuous love-making; she had never before met a man like him; there had been something of romance, too, in the stolen meetings and secrecy which had been necessary.

But now she was getting a little afraid. She told herself that things had gone far enough; that it was time to draw back — that if she kept Ryan Hewett waiting much longer he would probably grow tired. And Hewett was rich — and she loved money and the many things it could buy far more than she loved the black sheep whose heart she had so successfully wrested from him.

She was conscious of a little stab of pain. Was this really good-bye? Sudden dread filled her heart.

With all his faults, Laxton was a man. He made her feel weak and dependent, and women love to be made to feel that. For an instant her courage failed; for a tiny moment she asked herself if, after all, it might be worth while; if the love of this man would make up for the many other things she would have to lose.

She rose to her feet.

'It's getting so late. I ought to be going home.'

He broke out agitatedly —

'I can't bear it ... I didn't think it would be as hard as this ... I can't say goodbye to you ... Laurie, Laurie, say that you love me! ... Say that you love me!' ...

She said it easily enough; she even managed to shed some more tears as she stood within the circle of his arms, her face half-hidden against his sleeve.

'I do love you — you know I do,' she told him in a stifled voice. And at that moment she really did.

There were some minutes to wait on the platform for the London train; they paced slowly up and down in the sunset glow.

At the end of the platform a girl was waiting with a grey

sheep-dog on a leash; as they neared her Laurie touched Laxton's arm.

'George — do you know who that girl is?'

Laxton glanced apathetically.

'No.' The denial had sprung to his lips before he had recognised her; he hastily and rather furtively saluted her.

'You do know her?' Laurie's voice was jealous now; she flushed angrily.

He explained laconically.

'I don't know her — I nearly ran her down with my car this afternoon when I was coming to meet you; I had to stop and apologise, that's all.'

'Oh!' She was mollified; her brow cleared.

'Well, she might be worth cultivating,' she said deliberately; she could not resist the opportunity to probe his love still further. 'She might be a very suitable wife for you, George, if you cared to follow the acquaintance up. She's rich enough to buy Barton Manor half a dozen times over ... She's Norah Ackroyd. I went to school with her, but I didn't know she lived here.'

The name conveyed nothing to Laxton; he said so curtly. The train was arriving now, and with the knowledge that this was their real parting, his self-control broke.

'Laurie ... Laurie ...' He could only stammer her name; the girl with the big sheep-dog was too far away to hear what he said, but she saw the agitation in his face, and she glanced curiously at his companion. Laurie had got into the carriage now; Laxton followed her.

'I'll come up to town with you,' he said impulsively. 'Let me — I can get a ticket the other end.'

'No, no ...' She looked round wildly for an excuse. 'You can't ... George, you mustn't ... Supposing — supposing someone comes to meet me in London.'

She tried to speak naturally, but something in her voice roused his jealousy.

'Nobody will meet you — how can they if you haven't told them where you've been and what train you're coming by? You ...' He broke off, he caught her hand. 'Laurie ... you don't mean ... that awful Ryan ... you've told him ... he's coming to meet you ...'

The guard's whistle broke the stillness of the spring evening. When she looked up again Laxton was striding away down the platform; he did not once look back.

He went out of the station walking blindly; hardly knowing what he did, he started the car; as he reversed in the narrow road a big woolly sheep-dog ran towards him barking.

'Friday, Friday, come here!' A girl's voice called to it imperatively; she caught the dog by its collar and held on with both hands; she looked at Laxton laughingly.

'First you try to kill me, and now my dog,' she said. 'Have you got a grudge against us?'

Laxton laughed recklessly; his whole body was throbbing with miserable jealousy; something in the friendly tone of this girl's voice and the open regard of her eyes was comforting.

'On the contrary,' he said; he half-turned in his seat, leaning an arm on the low door to look at her. 'I wonder if I may introduce myself . . . introduce myself properly this time, I mean. I'm George Laxton — the Black Sheep.'

CHAPTER TWO

IF Laxton had expected his companion to be in the least confused by his abrupt confession he was disappointed.

She laughed, though the flush in her cheeks deepened a little.

'How mean of you not to have told me before,' she said. 'I might have told you all manner of awful things about yourself.'

'I am flattered, Miss Ackroyd.'

She looked up quickly.

'How did you know my name?' she asked amazed.

He answered at once.

'I was with a girl on the platform just now who — who went to school with you. She told me.'

'Went to school with me! Whoever was it? Do tell me! I didn't recognise her.'

She might truthfully have added that she had only glanced at Laxton's companion; all her attention had been centred on Laxton himself.

He told her calmly enough.

'Her name's Laurie Fenton . . . perhaps . . .'

She interrupted him with a little exclamation.

'Laurie Fenton! And I never recognised her! How very

extraordinary. I'd love to have seen her again, though I don't think she liked me very much when we were at school,' she added doubtfully.

'No!'

'It was rather a — snobby school, you see,' she explained rather hesitatingly. 'And most of the girls were — well . . .' She laughed rather embarrassedly. 'Well, they thought themselves better than I was, you know,' she added.

'Indeed!' A gleam of interest filled his sombre eyes.

'Yes.' She nodded her head with a little confiding gesture. 'I daresay they were right too, but I hated it at the time — it made me feel dreary and out of everything.' She laughed suddenly. 'But it didn't really matter, and I should have been pleased to see Laurie again — she was so pretty — quite the prettiest girl in the school.'

'Yes.'

Norah glanced at him interestedly; she was at a loss to know what to say next. The dog stretched and yawned wearily.

'Well, I won't keep you any longer,' the girl said. 'I shall tell them at home I've seen you.'

A faint smile crossed his face.

There was something very young about her, something that attracted by its very unconventionality.

'I suppose you won't let me drive you back again?' he asked hesitatingly. 'I'll be very pleased if you will — and I'm not in a hurry this time,' he added, with a tinge of bitterness.

She looked down at the dog. 'I've got him now, you see,' she said.

'Well, there's room for us all.' He called to the dog: 'Good boy, come on.'

The dog needed no second invitation. He jumped in at once.

Norah laughed. 'Well, that settles it,' she said, and the next minute they were speeding off again down the road.

'You're staying at Barton Manor, of course?' she said presently.

Laxton shook his head.

'No, I'm not; it's being done up.' It was on the tip of his tongue to add that he was hoping to let or sell it, but he checked the words. After all, it was no concern of hers.

'It looks a stunning place,' Norah said enthusiastically. 'I've very nearly trespassed dozens of times,' she added laughingly.

The wide gates were in sight now; Laxton slowed the car.

'Would you like to see it?' he asked. He turned the car in at the gates without waiting for her to answer him and drove slowly up the drive.

The girl looked about her eagerly. At the velvety lawns and beds of daffodils; at the belts of dark trees that screened the garden from the road and the winding pathways that led away through clumps of flowering shrubs.

'It looks much nicer than it did when Mr. Snowden lived here,' she told him at last. 'It always looked so gloomy then, didn't it?'

'I don't know. It's years since I was here till the other day. Snowden was my mother's brother, you know. He hated me like the very devil,' he added laconically.

Norah looked up at him.

'Why?' she asked bluntly.

'Why? Oh, I really don't know. He hated my father, so perhaps that accounts for it.'

'Oh!' Norah tried to think what it was she had heard about this man beside her; there were so many different stories, and each one had been seized upon and eagerly discussed by the people who were interested in the newcomer. She had discussed them herself with Rodney, lots of times. She glanced at Laxton furtively; he wouldn't be bad looking, she thought, if only he didn't look so unhappy; she wondered what was the matter with him. He stopped the car.

'If you'd like to walk round the grounds there'll just be time before it gets too dark,' he said.

She scrambled out, followed by the sheep-dog, barking joyously.

'What's his name?' Laxton asked; he was not particularly interested, but it was something to say.

'We call him Friday,' she told him, laughing. 'It was my idea — Rodney gave him to me on a Friday you see.'

'Is Rodney your brother?'

'No, my cousin. I haven't any brothers.'

'Oh! And no sisters either?'

'No.' She looked up at him interestedly. 'Have you?'

'No.'

They had reached the back of the house, where a terrace walk ran round it some ten feet above the level of the wide lawn below. Laxton stopped.

'This is what I wanted you to see,' he said.

They stood silently looking at the wonderful view before them.

Fields and trees seemed to stretch away as far as the eye could see against a background of sunset sky; a thin ribbon of water threaded the way through its foreground.

Norah drew a long breath.

'I had no idea it was so lovely as this,' she said. 'It must be wonderful to have such a home.'

Laxton turned sharply away.

'Wonderful,' he agreed mechanically.

He wondered what she would say if he told her what an empty inheritance it really was; if he told her that beyond the value of the estate itself there was not a shilling in the wide world with which to keep it up, or pay the mountain of debts which weighed upon him in nightmare reality — the smallest expectation which he might throw as a sop to the man from whom he had borrowed the money on which he had lived during the past two years, and which had got to be repaid, cent for cent.

He wheeled round suddenly and looked at the girl beside him.

'Rich enough to buy Barton Manor half a dozen times over . . .'

It was Laurie who had told him that; Laurie who had made such a pretence of grief, and who had gone back to London and to Ryan Hewett . . .

Norah turned slowly; her eyes looked dreamy and far-away.

They walked back to the waiting car; Friday had rushed on in front and taken his seat.

'I always take him with me,' Norah explained. 'He's such a dear . . . Do you like dogs?'

'Very much.'

'I don't think I've ever seen anything more lovely.'

'You must tell me which way to go,' Laxton said.

'Are you going to live here, after all, then?' she asked.

'Yes — why?'

'I thought you said you hated the country. I'm sure you said so when I met you this afternoon.'

'Did I?' he laughed. 'I don't remember what I said then; I was in a bad temper,' he admitted.

'I thought you seemed rather cross,' she agreed calmly. 'We have to turn to the right here.'

He swung the car about.

'That's our house at the top of the lane,' she explained. 'It isn't like yours, but it's quite nice, and I'm fond of it.'

Laxton glanced at the square, rather ugly building.

'We built it ourselves, you know — or, at least, my father did,' she told him. 'It's much nicer inside than you'd think.'

'I like it,' he told her hastily. 'It's — uncommon.'

'Hideous' was the word in his mind.

He drove the car up to the front door, and Friday scrambled out.

'Father's in London today,' Norah explained, 'and so's Rodney. But there'll be plenty more chances.'

'I shall meet them later on.'

'You're sure to, of course; everybody knows everybody else here.'

He looked at her whimsically.

'You don't even bar a black sheep?' he asked.

She coloured a little.

'It was your own fault I said that. You ought to have stopped me. It's a good thing I didn't say anything worse.'

'But you said something better — something which I hope you haven't quite forgotten,' he reminded her. 'You said that you were quite prepared to like me.'

There was a little silence.

'I hope you're not going to take that back,' Laxton said.

Norah raised her eyes; she was smiling.

'No, I don't think I'll take that back,' she told him.

CHAPTER THREE

THE London train was late. Norah Ackroyd paced up and down the platform impatiently.

It was a dull, showery morning, two days after her chance meeting on the road with George Laxton. Norah felt somehow depressed as she paced up and down, waiting for her father and Rodney. Suddenly as the train approached her face brightened. She eagerly scanned the carriage windows as they slowly drew level with the platform. After a moment she ran forward.

'I thought you were never coming, Rodney — the train's very late.'

The man to whom she spoke dropped his suitcase with a little thud to the platform and stooping, gave her a hearty kiss.

He was a very plain young man with red hair and a freckled face; but there was something kind in his nondescript eyes, and his voice was decidedly attractive.

'We were late leaving. Have you been waiting long?'

'Ages. And — where is Father?'

'He's coming on later . . . had to stay and see to some business at the last moment. I offered to wait, but he wouldn't hear of it. Well, and how are we?'

He looked down at her affectionately as they left the station together. A great many people in Lumsden took it for granted that Norah and Rodney Ackroyd were brother and sister; they had been brought up together from childhood, and it was only a few intimates who knew that Rodney was Norah's cousin, and fewer still who guessed that he would like to be something much nearer and dearer.

Norah herself had never dreamed of such a thing; she was very fond of him, but she would have been highly amused had any one suggested that red hair and a freckled face sometimes go with a romantic disposition.

She chatted away to him eagerly as they walked down the road together. He slipped an arm through hers. 'And what other news is there?' he asked. 'I seem to have been away for ever so long.'

'Only four days! And, anyway, there isn't any news. Nothing exciting ever happens in a place like this, except — oh, yes! — I almost forgot! I've had an adventure.'

'An adventure?'

Norah laughed excitedly. 'With George Laxton! The new man at Barton Manor — he nearly ran over me in his car — the day before yesterday, it was; and, of course, he stopped and apologised, and so I had to speak to him, and he's really rather nice.'

Rodney's face changed a little. 'So you've seen the black sheep?'

'Yes . . . and, after all, I don't believe half the silly stories people have been telling about him.'

He glanced at her quickly. 'Why not?'

'Oh — well,' she hesitated. 'I can't explain why exactly, but — well, I don't believe them.' She looked up a little flushed. 'He knows Laurie Fenton — she was with him down here one day, and she saw me and told him she was at school with me.'

'Oh.'

'Of course, I know she didn't like me,' Norah went on

thoughtfully. 'And, of course, I know she thought father wasn't a gentleman, and — and all that. I told him so.'

'You told Laxton?'

'Yes . . . but I didn't tell him that Laurie's hair never used to be blonde in those days,' she added with a chuckle. 'I did think about it, but I changed my mind.'

Rodney laughed. 'Very noble of you, I call it. Most women would have jumped at the opportunity.'

'Would they?' Norah looked grave. She was remembering the tone of Laxton's voice when he had spoken of Laurie, and for the first time she wondered a little. 'She was the prettiest girl in the school, anyway,' she added generously.

'When you weren't there, of course,' said Rodney.

She squeezed his arm. 'So he's coming to see us — you and Dad,' Norah went on, blissfully unconscious of the emotion in Rodney's heart. 'And I'm quite sure everybody will like him,' she added confidently.

Rodney was not so sure. 'There's never smoke without fire, you know,' he reminded her sententiously. 'And after the rotten stories we've heard about him . . . Norah!'

She had torn her arm angrily from his. 'It's most unfair to talk like that,' she said hotly. 'You condemn him when you've never seen him or spoken to him.'

'I wasn't condemning him; I merely reminded you of what we have heard . . .'

'A lot of scandal which nobody in their senses would listen to!' she declared scornfully. 'I don't care what people say — I like him.'

'You've said that before,' Rodney told her jealously.

'And I shall probably say it again lots of times,' she answered defiantly; then suddenly she laughed. She changed the subject, and Laxton was not mentioned again between them till the evening, at dinner.

Mr. Ackroyd was there then, and Norah was bubbling over with delight at having him home again. She adored her father, though to a disinterested eye there might not have been very much in him to adore. He was a tall, rather heavily built man with hair as red as Rodney's, and a loud, rather swaggering voice.

But he had a heart of gold, and there were many people in the world besides his daughter and Rodney who had discovered it.

In manner he was rather rough, and he did not always speak quite grammatically or remember his 'h's'.

'I'm a self-made man,' he would say to anybody who showed the least interest in him. 'I've nobody but myself to thank for my money and I don't owe anybody a penny.'

How he had made it, or when, nobody seemed to know: the fact that he had made it and still possessed it probably being enough for most people.

'And what have you been doing with herself while I've been away?' he asked, looking at Norah.

He was leaning back in his chair contentedly; he was always glad to be home, though he seldom stayed there for more than a few days at a time.

'The same as usual!' she told him, laughing. 'Oh — ' she broke off, 'I've had an adventure, but Rodney doesn't approve of it, so I don't know if you will.'

Mr. Ackroyd glanced at his nephew.

'Rodney doesn't approve — eh! — it isn't often he disapproves of anything you do, my dear.'

'He thinks this is dreadful, though,' she declared. 'But I'll tell you all the same, and you shall decide . . . Well, I've made friends with the black sheep — he nearly ran over me in his car, so we spoke, and I thought he was nice, and he's coming to see you.' She spoke rather quickly, as if not quite sure how her news would be received.

Mr. Ackroyd laughed, and held up his hand.

'Not so fast — not so fast! . . . I can't follow you . . . The black sheep — now, first of all, who is the black sheep?'

Rodney glanced up; his eyes looked somehow angry.

'Norah means Laxton — Laxton of Barton Manor,' he said shortly.

'Laxton!' Mr. Ackroyd echoed the name sharply. 'That fellow! . . . You've made friends with him, and he's coming here!' He brought his fist down heavily on the table. His kind face was scowling, the very tone of his voice had changed. 'I'll take good care he doesn't come here,' he thundered. 'He's an absolute young blackguard! . . . I won't have the fellow in my house, and you can tell him so, or I will — if I ever meet him.'

Norah stared at her father in utter amazement; he had never spoken so roughly to her before; the hot colour rushed to her cheeks.

'Father!' she said breathlessly.

Mr. Ackroyd pushed back his chair irritably and rose to his feet.

'I mean what I say,' he said curtly. 'I won't have the fellow here; you've no business to have allowed him to speak to you; if he'd been a gentleman he wouldn't have done it.'

She broke in then: 'He only apologised for almost running me down; he wouldn't have been a gentleman if he'd driven on and said nothing. I think you're most unjust — you haven't even seen him.'

'There are some people it isn't necessary to see,' he interrupted grimly. 'I know quite enough about the young man to know that he's no fit companion for you; so don't let me catch him hanging round here. I mean what I say, mind.'

He opened the door and went out of the room.

There was a little silence.

'Well!' said Norah indignantly. She looked across at Rodney for sympathy, but he did not raise his eyes. 'Of all the mean, unjust things,' she went on hotly. 'Talk about women being spiteful to each other — men are a thousand times worse.'

Rodney shrugged his shoulders. 'Everyone knows what Laxton is. All these things wouldn't be said about him if there wasn't some truth in them.'

'And what *has* been said?' she demanded angrily. 'I haven't heard anything so dreadful! Just that he's a spendthrift, and things like that — nothing worse.'

Rodney made no reply.

'I suppose you're going to side with Father,' she accused him; there were tears in her eyes now; tears in her voice, too, for that matter; young Ackroyd looked up quickly.

'Norah — you're not crying over that fellow?'

'Of course I'm not crying,' she said indignantly, 'but — but Father's never spoken to me like that before.'

'Which is all the more reason for listening to him now. You know your father never says a thing like he has just said without a good reason. You're generally eager enough to do what he wishes.'

'But this is different — somehow,' she declared, though for the life of her she could not have said wherein the difference lay. She got up and walked over to the window; it was quite dark now, and there was a pleasant smell of damp earth and flowers.

She looked away towards the village and the direction of Barton Manor, and her heart beat a little more quickly as she thought of the man who was there in the great house alone.

Behind her Rodney spoke suddenly.

'Don't be silly, Norah; what does the fellow matter to us? I don't suppose he'll stay here long; from what one hears he hates the country.'

He came behind her and laid his hands on her shoulders.

Norah did not turn. 'I hate injustice,' she said in a stifled voice.

The hands fell from her shoulders; there was a little pause, then —

'You seem to forget that a week ago you were talking about him in the same way as everybody else,' said Rodney constrainedly. 'You've changed your opinion very quickly.'

'I suppose I may if I like.'

She moved past him to the door. He looked after her. 'Where are you going?' he asked sharply.

The door banged by way of answer.

Norah went out into the garden. It was much warmer than it had been in the morning; the chill breeze had dropped to sleep, and through the scudding clouds a pale moon was visible now and again.

She walked on and into the lane without realising where she was going.

It was all a very absurd fuss about nothing.

'Absurd!' she said aloud angrily.

'What is absurd?' someone asked through the darkness.

She started violently.

'Oh, is it you?' she said, with a laugh. 'You frightened me.'

'I'm sorry. I could see you against the light from the house, so thought you could see me.' Laxton fell into step beside her. 'Where are you going?'

'Nowhere in particular. Where are you going?'

'With you, if I may. I came up here to see if I could see anything of you.'

She did not answer; her heart was racing again now, her pulses felt jumpy.

He sauntered slowly along beside her; he was smoking a cigar that smelt expensive. She glanced up at him timidly.

Now her eyes were growing more accustomed to the darkness, she could see the outline of his tall figure distinctly. He walked with his hands in his pockets.

After a moment he spoke. 'What did you say was absurd?' he asked.

She laughed nervously. 'I was only thinking aloud. I didn't know you were anywhere about. I felt angry.'

'With whom?'

'Everybody,' she told him laughingly.

'Not including me, I hope.'

'Of course not. Why should I be angry with you?'

'There's no reason I know of; but women are so funny — they often get angry with a man when there's no reason.'

'Do they?'

'Don't they?'

She laughed. 'I don't know; I hardly know any men — except, Rodney.'

'And Rodney is a cousin, and so he doesn't count — eh?'

She frowned in the darkness. 'He does count — sometimes,' she answered. 'But tonight he was so silly — oh, I felt so angry with him.'

'You won't tell me why?'

'I'd — I'd rather not.' There was a little silence.

'Perhaps I can guess,' said Laxton quietly; she knew that he was looking at her now; she could feel his eyes upon her through the darkness.

'He was talking about me,' he said again.

She was startled. 'How did you know? How could you know?'

He laughed rather mirthlessly. 'Oh, a sort of instinct, I suppose. Well — what did he say?'

She was silent; presently, 'Mr. Laxton, will you let me ask you a question?'

'A dozen if you like,' he answered lightly.

Norah frowned; she did not like him when he spoke flippantly; it seemed impossible now to ask the question that had been on her lips. He seemed to feel the change in her; he stopped.

'What do you want to ask me?'

'You'll be angry,' she warned him.

'No, I shall not.'

'Well — well ... Are you — are you really a — a black sheep?'

The faintest ghost of a smile crossed his face and was gone instantly. When he answered his voice was quite even and undisturbed.

'That all depends what you mean by — a black sheep.'

He hesitated a moment, looking away from her down the road into the darkness.

'The devil is never as black as he is painted, you know,' he said whimsically. 'Though I admit that he's very black.' He turned his eyes to her again. 'I wonder what you've heard about me?' he said thoughtfully. 'What has Rodney been saying?'

'It wasn't Rodney — it was my father.'

'Whew!' He gave a little whistle of pretended dismay. 'Your father, was it? I suppose I'm not to come to the house — and you're not to speak to me — is that it?'

'Yes.'

He shrugged his shoulders; he walked on slowly beside her. 'I'm sorry,' he said at last.

There was a sort of finality in his voice; Norah's heart gave a little dismayed throb; she broke out impulsively —

'But I'm not a child — I'm old enough to choose my own friends.'

Laxton looked up at the moon. There was a flash of triumph in his eyes, though there was none in his voice when he spoke.

'If that means what I hope it does,' he said, 'thank you.'

They walked a little way without speaking. The man was thinking quickly; trying to look ahead — to calculate his chances.

This girl was so young and unworldly; sufficiently unworldly to take him at her own romantic valuation; to dare hold her own opinion against the sounder one of those older than herself.

And the situation was desperate. Only that morning he had received a threatening letter from the man to whom he owed more money than he could ever hope to repay.

There was one chance left, and one only — marriage with a rich woman.

And yet ... through the darkness the black sheep thought of Laurie.

He had not seen her since that day when he had parted from her in jealous anger. She had not written to him. Was it indeed all over? Did she really care so little for him that she could not face life with him because he was poor?

He had sworn to forget her; never to see her again; but now as he stood there in the scented spring night, with the pale moonlight making a golden ladder down to earth, an almost uncontrollable longing to see her once more took possession of him.

Perhaps it was not too late — perhaps if he saw her again,

pleaded with her once more not to ruin his life ... He caught his breath hard.

The girl beside him spoke suddenly.

'I think I ought to go back home. I didn't mean to come so far.' Her voice was a little nervous and uncertain.

Laxton turned at once. 'I'll walk back with you.'

They retraced their steps almost in silence. It was only when they reached the gate that he said suddenly —

'I may not see you again for a day or two. I go to London in the morning.'

'To London?' She did not know that there was disappointment in her voice, but the man heard it, and a little thrill of triumph went through him.

'Only for a day or two,' he said quickly. 'And then, when I come back — ' He broke off.

'When you come back?' she echoed.

The black sheep groped through the darkness and found her hand.

'I'll tell you the rest — when I come back,' he said softly.

And the next minute he was alone in the night.

He walked back to the village slowly. He was not staying at Barton Manor, as Norah had thought, but at the inn in the village.

He passed the big carriage-gates of Barton Manor and stopped for a moment looking towards the dark face of the great house.

When he reached the inn he turned towards the stairs.

As he did so his eye caught sight of a letter in the rack addressed to himself.

He crossed the narrow passage and snatched it down eagerly.

He went up the stairs two at a time to his bedroom; it was small and poorly furnished, but Laxton never troubled about such things; he had slept in many worse places in his time.

She had written, after all; she was sorry; she wanted to see him again. For a moment his sight was blurred so that he could not read what was written there.

Barton Manor, Norah Ackroyd, everything was forgotten but the memory of this one woman, who alone in all his roving, disreputable life had really had any lasting influence with him.

She had written to him again — she had not forgotten him; nothing else counted at all.

'Dear George — ' She had never begun so coldly before, and

the hammering blood at his temples quieted, the little mist cleared away from before his eyes as he read on.

Laurie Fenton had put it quite nicely. She took three pages to say what she might have said in three lines; but the whole gist of the matter was that she had decided to mend her broken heart by marriage with another man — a richer man — a middle-aged, unattractive creature whose sole claim to adornment was money.

'. . . Try and forget me — though I shall never forget you. Fate is very cruel to us . . . if only things could have been different.'

The black sheep read to the very end, and the fire and eagerness died slowly from his heart, leaving him cold and hard.

She had done with him — done with him; it was nothing to her any more what he did — what became of him.

She did not care; neither, then, would he.

There was still Barton Manor and Norah Ackroyd: Norah, who even at that moment was looking from her window on to the moonlit lane and thinking of the black sheep with a little glow of warmth at her heart.

CHAPTER FOUR

Norah was very quiet at breakfast the following morning. When breakfast was over, and she had gone, Mr. Ackroyd turned to his nephew.

'What's the matter with Norah, Rodney?'

Rodney shrugged his shoulders.

'I suppose she's annoyed about your refusal to have Laxton to the house,' he said reluctantly.

Mr. Ackroyd laughed disbelievingly.

'What utter nonsense!' he said briskly. 'Norah isn't so foolish as that! Why, I tell you that fellow isn't worth discussing.'

Rodney looked interested.

'Do you know him, then?'

'I know of him — good deal of him! He's up to his eyes in debt to begin with; he's been out of England for the past two or three years because he'd made it too hot to hold him. He lives on credit and borrowed money. I'd rather see Norah dead than know she was mixed up with the young blackguard!'

'She seems to have taken a fancy to him,' said Rodney.

26

'Fancy! Rot!' Mr. Ackroyd pushed back his chair so violently that it fell over. 'A man like Laxton always gets on with women,' he said again angrily. 'They make a hero of him; think he's misjudged and misunderstood. You've got to get this nonsense out of the girl's head, and the sooner the better.'

Rodney did not answer.

'I'll have a word with the young puppy myself,' Mr. Ackroyd went on, with dignity. 'I'm not afraid of him if he does own Barton Manor; a fat lot of good it will be to him without a penny to spend on it.'

'It's to be let or sold, so I hear.'

The elder man muttered something unintelligible under his breath. Norah was the apple of his eye. To his way of thinking the man had not yet been born who would be worthy of her.

Rodney rose to his feet, stretching his arms.

'Well, there's no harm done,' he said laconically. 'And Laxton has probably plenty of girls in town to run after without coming down here to annoy us.'

'Annoy us! He won't annoy me!' Mr. Ackroyd asserted loudly. 'He won't get the chance! Impudent young puppy, racing about the lanes as if he's bought the place. From what I can hear he spends half his time in the Connaught Arms — a nice thing for the master of Barton Manor. His old uncle would turn in his grave if he could see him.' He went out into the hall and Rodney heard him shouting for Norah.

After a moment or two she came to the top of the stairs: 'Did you call me, Father?'

Mr. Ackroyd chuckled.

'Did I call you! When I was bellowing like a town bull! Yes; I did call you, my dear. Come down here, I want to speak to you.'

Norah obeyed slowly. She stood on the bottom stair, with her eyes cast down. There was a moment of silence, then suddenly she looked up.

She put her arms round his neck and gave him a hug.

'Is that what you wanted?' she asked teasingly.

Mr. Ackroyd smoothed his hair. 'It was, partly,' he admitted. 'And now get your coat and come out with me.'

'I'm very busy . . .'

'Not too busy to come out with me. Run along.'

He waited for her at the open front door; he was happy again now; he even felt slightly foolish when he thought of the little breeze they had had last night. Norah was a sensible girl; it was extremely unlikely that she would be seriously attracted by a man of Laxton's type.

Mr. Ackroyd was comfortably sure in his own mind that some day Norah and Rodney would make a match of it.

He was quite sure that his determination last night had — as he would have put it — 'knocked all nonsense out of the girl's head'.

He had yet to understand that Norah had inherited a great deal of his own obstinacy, and that as a rule the more people tried to set her against a person the more she clung to them.

'I'm quite ready,' she said demurely at his elbow.

She slipped her hand through his arm as they went together down the lane that led to the main road; Friday, the big sheepdog, was racing ahead of them, barking happily.

'I've been thinking,' Mr. Ackroyd said with elaborate carelessness which would not have deceived a child, 'that a little holiday in Town would do you a lot of good, my dear.'

'I don't think I care very much about London,' she said. She kept her eyes steadily ahead of her down the road as she spoke. 'The country's so lovely at this time of the year.'

There was a pause, then Mr. Ackroyd said 'Humph!' rather curtly. His shaggy brows were frowning again; his arm felt rather stiff and unresponsive beneath her hand.

They were within sight of the village now; a thin church spire stood up above the trees; the roofs of the scattered houses and cottages shone red in the sunlight.

To the right of them Barton Manor rose majestically against the sky; Norah glanced towards the house and quickly away again.

She wondered if Laxton had yet gone to London, or if anything had happened to make him change his plans. Her heart beat a little faster as she thought of what he had said last night —

'I'll tell you the rest — when I come back.'

Something in the tone of his voice had seemed to imply so very much, and yet, of course, it was absurd to imagine for an instant that . . .

And then she woke from her dreaming with a start as she glanced across the road, and saw George Laxton himself. He was coming out of the village post office, a sheaf of letters in his hand.

At the same moment she realised that while she had been dreaming her father had turned into the tobacconist's to get some of his favourite cigars, leaving her to walk on ahead.

George Laxton did not see Norah at first. He shovelled the letters anyhow into the letter-box and turned to cross the road, when he almost ran into her.

'I beg your pardon . . .'

Startled, she began, 'I thought . . .' but he anticipated her reply.

'I'm not going to town, after all,' he said without preamble. 'I wonder if you'd care to come out in the car with me this afternoon; or if you've been forbidden to have anything more to do with me.'

There was something mocking in his voice; a sort of hard unhappiness in his eyes.

'I'm not a child,' she said impulsively. 'I can do as I like.'

A faint smile crossed the sombre face of the black sheep.

'Very well — I'll come along in the car at three o'clock.'

She caught her breath with a little gasp of dismay.

'Oh, not to the house.'

Laxton's mouth twisted a little.

'I thought you said you could do as you liked,' he said impatiently.

'So I can, but . . .' She faltered. 'I'd much rather you didn't come to the house,' she said weakly.

He laughed. 'Very well; I'll wait at the end of the lane. Goodbye.'

He was barely out of sight when Mr. Ackroyd rejoined his daughter; he was smiling and looked well satisfied.

'Sorry to have been so long, my dear, but Anderton was talking about your friend Laxton.' There was a touch of cynicism in his voice. 'Nobody seems to be able to talk about anything else. By the way, if it's of any interest to you to know it, he's engaged to that school friend of yours — what's-her-name! Laura — Laurie something.'

'Laurie Fenton.'

Norah's hands were clenched.

'Yes, Laurie Fenton. Heaven only knows what they hope to get married on — neither of them have got a shilling in the world, have they?'

'I don't know.'

'Humph! Well, Laxton's a fool!' said Mr. Ackroyd bluntly.

'Ought to have looked out for a woman with money. It's his only chance.'

They turned their steps homewards.

She was rather silent for the rest of the way home; rather silent, too, during lunch. Afterwards she went up to her room; it was only two o'clock; she opened the window and looked out down the lane towards the main road.

If Laxton were really engaged to Laurie Fenton she was certainly not going out with him, she told herself haughtily; but she was not sure that she believed it, perhaps because she did not want to believe it.

'I shan't go,' she said aloud.

She went downstairs determinedly; she looked in at the dining-room, but there was nobody there; she looked in at her father's study. Mr. Ackroyd was lying back in his favourite armchair; there was a handkerchief over his face and he was snoring unmusically.

Norah smiled and closed the door softly.

She felt restless; she wondered where Rodney was; she wished he would come and make up her mind for her by suggesting a walk.

She walked to the front door. As she did so Rodney came down the stairs behind her.

She half-turned. He absent-mindedly ran his fingers through his hair and murmured that he had some letters to write.

He waited a moment, then turned and went slowly back up the stairs.

Norah stayed where she was. She was conscious of a little thrill of excitement. Perhaps Rodney had decided for her, after all; perhaps this was Fate.

She went back up to her room, wandered about restlessly . . .

Five minutes to three . . .

He would be coming along the road soon if he were a punctual man; any moment she might see a little cloud of grey dust above the hedge.

If she stayed in she would not be able to settle to anything, and it was such a lovely afternoon.

She opened the window again. The warm spring sunshine beat invitingly on her face. Out in the garden the birds were singing . . .

She caught up a head scarf and crept softly downstairs.

Friday, lying half asleep in the hall, started up joyously;

he was always game for a walk; he began to bark his delight.

Norah caught him by the collar. 'Stay there, Friday — I can't take you.'

From his room upstairs Rodney heard her voice.

'Lie down, Friday . . . you can't come.'

He heard the shrill, excited barking die down disappointedly. Why wouldn't she take the dog, he wondered. As a rule she never stirred without him.

Rodney listened for a moment, then he rose to his feet so hurriedly that he knocked his chair over; he went quickly to the window.

There was a sudden suspicion in his mind; where could Norah be going?

He opened the window noiselessly and leaned out.

There was no car in the drive; he waited — then he saw her running down the lane, tying the scarf under her chin as she went.

Rodney's heart was thumping uncomfortably; he could see no more from this window; he turned impulsively and ran into the next room, from which one he had a view of the high road as well as the lane.

As he looked a grey Jaguar came slowly round the bend, and rapidly gathering speed, disappeared in a little haze of dust.

CHAPTER FIVE

'OF course,' said Norah, 'I know I ought not really to have come, but . . .' She looked up, smiling dubiously, into the face of the black sheep.

They were half a mile away now, and whirling along through the afternoon sunshine.

The black sheep was looking straight ahead of him. 'Why not?' he asked, without turning his head.

Norah shook her head. 'I don't know, but — do you think I ought to have come?' she demanded impulsively.

He now looked down at her. 'I think charming people should do everything in the world they want to do,' he said.

He had made similar speeches scores of times, and he thought he knew to a wearisome degree just how such a speech would be taken: a little simper, a conscious blush, and a swift lowering of eyelids.

But Norah was a disappointment, inasmuch as she did none of these things. Her eyes met his quite frankly and steadily.

'What a silly thing to say,' she said calmly.

The black sheep was taken aback. 'What ought I to have said then?' he asked, with a touch of exasperation.

'You ought to have said just what you think, of course,' she told him. 'And I should like to know what you really do think.'

'About what?' he asked.

'About what I've asked you.'

'I'm afraid I've forgotten what it was,' he admitted.

As a matter of fact, he had. It is difficult to appear interested when the girl beside you is the wrong girl and you are wishing she could be somebody else.

'I asked you if you thought it was wrong of me to have come out with you?' Norah repeated.

'Wrong!' The black sheep knitted his brows. 'I'm only too grateful to you for having taken pity on me. I loathe my own company. I could no more go for a ten-mile walk alone than I could fly; I could no more spend an evening heaped up in an armchair with nobody to talk to than — than — well, than anything,' he finished rather lamely. 'That's why I'm going to fill Barton Manor with people till it's let. I've got to live here till then — or, at least, I've got nowhere else to live — and so I'm going to fill the old barn. I was posting the invitations summoning the guests to a house party when I saw you this morning.'

Norah gave a little protesting cry.

'Oh, how can you call it that? I only wish it were mine!'

There was a little silence; then the black sheep laughed.

'Do you?' he said. 'Perhaps I wish the same.'

He glanced at her quickly to see the effect of his words, but apparently they had conveyed nothing of any importance to her.

'Perhaps some day you will be able to live there,' she told him kindly. 'Perhaps something will turn up. Things do happen like that, you know, don't they? I wish it could for you. Laurie would just love Barton Manor, I know.'

A swift streak of colour tinged Laxton's face. His hands tightened their grip of the wheel.

'What do you mean?' he asked sharply.

She looked at him in surprise. 'Only that I heard you were engaged to Laurie Fenton,' she said faintly embarrassed. 'Isn't it true? — I'm glad — I mean I'm sorry. Oh, dear! I don't know what I do mean.'

She was flushed and distressed, but the man beside her kept his eyes steadily averted.

He drove some little way in silence; then —

'I'm not engaged to anybody,' he said shortly.

They were driving down a gently sloping road now, with high hedges on either side, and tall trees, whose long arms met in an archway overhead. After a while she said, 'And were you abroad very long?'

'Long enough; two or three years. I couldn't come back, you see, or I should have done.'

'What do you mean — couldn't come back?'

He coloured a little. 'Well, daren't, then, if you like, to put it that way. There were a nice little crowd of creditors waiting to seize me if I dared to set foot in London. One chap in particular! Old Devil!'

There was a sort of surly defiance in his voice. He looked at the girl beside him and quickly away again.

'So you see the stories you've been told about me are more or less true,' he went on carelessly. 'I am up to my eyes in debt, and I have got a rotten name. I shouldn't be here now, only the people I owe money to know that Barton Manor is worth a tidy bit. When that's sold they'll come down on me like a pack of wolves and fight for the bones.'

'What a shame!'

'Oh no, it isn't! I've let some of 'em in badly. I'm not at all a figure of romance, I assure you, and if I'm not quite so bad as people make out, it's more luck than anything else.'

She was silent for a moment.

'I think perhaps you rather like to make out that you're a black sheep, don't you?' she suggested. 'Perhaps people have talked about you at one time when you didn't deserve it, and it made you hard and angry, and so now you think you'll be reckless and give them something to talk about.'

She was looking at Laxton with sympathetic eyes. She felt somehow very sorry for him.

A little muscle in his thin face jerked convulsively for a moment. 'That's a kind way to put it,' he said constrainedly. 'That's the kindest thing anyone has said to me for a long time.'

Norah flushed. 'I think it's true,' she answered.

Laxton shook his head.

'You'd find it a hard job to get anybody to agree with you. My uncle — old Snowden, who had Barton Manor before me, you know — was firmly convinced that I was the greatest crook unhanged. If he hadn't died before he had time to alter his will Barton Manor would never have come to me. As it is, I'm the next-of-kin, and so it couldn't be helped. He didn't leave me a penny with it, you know; I haven't a shilling in the world except about a couple of hundred a year, which was my mother's and which he couldn't touch. He hated my father and he hated me, and there you have the whole thing in a nutshell.'

Norah looked puzzled. 'But you can't keep a car like this on two hundred a year, surely!' she said impulsively.

He laughed outright at that. 'I'm afraid I don't,' he said. 'I bought this out of a lucky deal, and I've kept it up ever since on borrowed money. I'm afraid even you would be unable to find any more kind excuses for me if I told you the appalling amount of money I owe to Scrooge and Company.'

'Scrooge and Company?'

'That isn't their name really — they trade under a highly respectable one — but they're money-lenders, or, in other words, daylight robbers who get hold of fools like me and never let go till they've sucked 'em dry.'

He looked down at her with a faint smile. 'I really don't know why I am boring you with all this about myself,' he said apologetically. 'You won't want to come out with me any more, will you?'

She looked up at him; her eyes met his very frankly.

'I should like to come — if you ask me,' she said. 'Oh — ' she broke off with a cry. A big car had swung round the bend in the road without warning of any kind. For a moment it looked as if it must crash right over them. Norah hid her eyes.

It all happened so quickly; the danger was present and past in a flash of time, during which Laxton wrenched at the wheel, turning the Jaguar violently half into the bank, and the other car was brought to a grinding stand-still almost on top of it. Laxton turned and began swearing angrily, then suddenly he broke off, meeting the eyes of a girl who had half-risen in her seat and was looking at him with frightened eyes; it was Laurie Fenton.

CHAPTER SIX

WOMANLIKE, Laurie was the first to recover herself; she laughed lightly and leaning over the side of the big car, held a daintily gloved hand to the black sheep.

The Jaguar was huddled up on the bank.

'We might have had a terrible smash,' Laurie was saying affectedly. 'How did you manage to get out of the way, George? ... and — how strange we should meet on the road like this! We're not anywhere near Lumsden, are we?'

'Yes — no; I don't know.' Laxton was white and incoherent; he passed an agitated hand through his rough hair. After a moment he stepped out into the roadway; for the first time he remembered Norah; he turned to her apologetically, she looked very pale.

'You were frightened; I am sorry — we had a narrow shave. You know Laurie Fenton, I think.'

Laurie Fenton gave a little shrill scream of amazement.

'Why, it's Norah! Dear little Norah! I positively must come and speak to you.

She went across to where Norah was sitting; she kissed her effusively.

'I saw you the other day on the station — did George tell you? I've thought about you ever since; I had no idea you lived anywhere near here. We haven't met for years, have we?'

'No,' said Norah. She felt tongue-tied and unhappy.

'I told you I knew Miss Ackroyd,' Laxton said, rather shortly.

Norah had not left her seat, but Laxton had no eyes for her. His heart was pounding against his ribs. He was cursing his luck that he was not alone. Now he would not have the smallest chance of a word with Laurie.

'I'm just telling Norah that she must ask me to come and see her,' she said, looking up at him. 'I simply love meeting old friends. Now, you won't forget, will you, Norah?'

'Of course I'll ask you, if you'd really like to come; but we don't live in a grand house at all,' Norah said rather constrainedly. 'Nothing like Barton Manor, I mean,' she added.

She was remembering resentfully that this girl had been one of

35

those who had snubbed her at school; who had looked down on her and called her father common.

Laurie sighed sentimentally. 'Dear Barton Manor! There never could be another place like that — could there, George?'

Laxton did not answer.

Laurie kissed Norah again; she called her a dear thing, and assured her that they would meet again soon before she went back to her own car.

Laxton followed her. 'Where are you going?' he asked brusquely.

He leaned his arm on the door; his back was turned to Norah, and she could not see his face at all.

Laurie flushed. 'We're staying with Ryan Hewett, Mother and I . . . You knew he had a house in the country — a little dead-and-alive place called Didsbury.' She raised her eyes with disconcerting suddenness to his pale face. 'It isn't a patch on Barton Manor, George,' she said in a whisper.

He laughed shortly, and the next moment the big car had whirled away in a cloud of dust.

Laxton climbed back beside Norah. 'We might have had a nasty smash,' he said laconically.

'Yes.'

'I'm sorry if you were frightened.'

'I wasn't particularly frightened.'

Neither of them spoke for some minutes.

'Do you know a place called Didsbury round here?' Laxton asked then. 'It's only a village.'

'Yes, I know it very well; it's about ten miles from home.'

'Laurie Fenton's staying there.'

'Yes, she told me.'

Norah's voice sounded a little faint somehow. The black sheep turned his head sharply.

'What's the matter? I . . . Good God — '

He brought the car to a grinding standstill. Norah was leaning back against the cushions, she was white to the lips; she looked as if she were going to faint, but tried to smile.

'It's all right, but — I think I've hurt my arm . . . It was when the car went into the bank — I think my hand must have been over the side . . . I can't remember. It isn't anything much . . .'

She gave a little stifled cry of pain as he lifted her left hand; it was lying helplessly in her lap.

36

There was a second of silence; then Laxton laid the injured hand down very gently.

'It's a sprain — a bad one, too, I'm afraid ... I can't tell you how sorry I am.'

He brought a first-aid box from the boot.

'You must let me do it up for you ... I won't hurt you, but if it's not done it will be much worse ...'

He looked down at the swollen, fast-blackening wrist.

'I shall never forgive myself — it's all my fault.'

'It isn't — the other car was to blame. They had no right to drive so quickly in lanes like this.'

'You told me that the first day I spoke to you.'

He was bandaging her wrist skilfully now. His big fingers worked surprisingly quickly. Norah set her teeth. Every touch was exquisite agony, but she would rather die than let him know it, she told herself fiercely.

He paused a moment and glanced at her.

'Very bad?' he asked sympathetically.

She nodded. 'It is, rather.'

'It's nearly over now. I'll make you a sling out of my scarf. You'll have to go to a doctor when we get back.'

He was thinking what a scene almost any other girl in the world would have made.

'You're almost as good as a doctor,' Norah told him shakily.

'That's the worst,' said the black sheep. 'I had to pull it tight, or it wouldn't have been any good.'

He slipped his scarf about her bandaged arm and knotted it round her neck.

'Comfortable?' he asked. 'Sure it's not too tight?'

'Quite sure.' She looked up at him with an April smile.

'Now you never *will* come out with me again,' he said, 'will you?'

She laughed a little.

'I will if you ask me,' she answered.

But she was wondering with dismay what she would say when she got home. How she could explain a badly sprained wrist and a bandage. She thought hopefully that she might manage to hide it. After all, it was her left arm, and if she were very careful, perhaps nobody would notice it.

But the sprain ached intolerably. Slowly though Laxton drove on the homeward way, every movement of the car was torture. Once or twice she felt almost sick with pain.

When they were a mile from Lumsden, she asked him to stop.

'I'd rather walk home, if you don't mind,' she said. 'I don't want them at home to know that I've been with you this afternoon. It isn't that I mind what they say in the least; but Father — ' She broke off in distress.

'You mean that your father will be more down on me than ever?' he finished for her.

'Yes, and . . . and I don't want him to be.'

Their eyes met. 'And the wrist — how will you explain that?'

She shook her head. 'I don't know. Perhaps they won't notice; or perhaps I'll just tell our doctor — Dr. Bethune. He's known me all my life and understands most things.'

Laxton looked undecided. 'I think I ought to come to the house with you and explain,' he said. 'I don't want your father to think I'm afraid of him. It's far better to tell him straight out what happened. He may hear through somebody else, and then things will be worse than ever. Let me come home with you and tell him.'

But Norah shook her head. 'I'd much rather you didn't,' she said earnestly. 'You don't know how furious he'd be. He — he'd move Heaven and earth to prevent my ever seeing you again,' she added, laughing faintly.

Laxton looked away from her down the road.

'Does that mean that you're going to be kind and let me see you again?' he asked.

She did not answer.

'Does it?' he urged softly. Norah had never heard just that intonation in a man's voice before. She felt as if something had stirred gently against her heart. She was too ignorant of the world and its ways to know that she was but being used as a pawn in a game of which Laxton knew every move by heart. She was too honest and unaffected to think it worth while to conceal the fact that she liked this man, and that she wanted to see him again, many times.

Her grey eyes were like stars as she looked at him; a little smile quivered over her pale face for an instant.

'Of course, I want to see you again,' she said softly.

CHAPTER SEVEN

RODNEY ACKROYD had spent a miserable afternoon. If he had never seen Laxton's grey car vanishing round the bend of the road intuition would have told him where Norah had gone.

For the first time in his life he was miserably jealous. He had always known that she did not care for him in the way he wished her to; but that she should care for any other man enough to think it worth while to steal out of the house without telling anyone where she was going struck him to the heart.

He left his letters unwritten. He felt unable to settle to anything.

Half a dozen times he felt that he must go and tell Mr. Ackroyd, and see that an end was put to this acquaintance with Laxton once and for all; but somehow he hesitated to do so. Mr. Ackroyd was already annoyed with Norah, and Rodney rightly guessed what a towering rage he would be in if he knew that she had been out with the black sheep again that afternoon.

In his silent, ineloquent way, Rodney adored Norah; his was that blind, unreasoning worship that so seldom meets with the return it deserves.

He paced up and down the garden, cursing George Laxton up hill and down dale. He firmly believed that what Mr. Ackroyd and everybody else had said of him was no more than the truth. It hurt him intolerably to think that Norah was being treated as doubtless dozens of other girls had been treated — just a conquest to boast of afterwards.

The hours seemed to crawl: a dozen times he went back to the house to make sure Norah had not returned; a dozen times he left the garden and walked down to the end of the lane to look anxiously up and down the road; but she did not come, and at last he went back to the house hopelessly.

Mr. Ackroyd met him in the hall.

'Where's Norah?'

A dozen times a day he asked the same question. He was never happy unless his girl was with him, he expected Rodney and everybody else in the house to be able to tell him exactly where she was at a moment's notice.

Rodney answered evasively —

'She went out.'

'Where's she gone? I'll go and meet her; it's nearly tea-time, and she's sure to be in for tea.'

'She'll come back through the village, I expect.'

Rodney knew it was most probable that she would come from exactly the opposite direction, but the last thing he wanted just then was for Mr. Ackroyd to see Norah with Laxton. He quite intended to have it out with her himself first; she would tell him honestly where she had been, he was sure; she had always told him everything; as children he and she had never had any secrets from one another, and Rodney was foolish enough to believe that it was still the same. He would ask Norah to marry him that very day.

His heart raced at his own decision; somehow he had no doubt that she would marry him. He had grown so used to the idea. He had not yet come to realise that he had been cherishing a vain hope.

Down in the hall Friday barked shrilly — a sharp, joyous bark that Rodney knew well enough could only mean one thing.

He went downstairs two at a time. He went out bareheaded into the sunshine, his plain face lit up with eagerness.

Friday was at the gate, clamouring excitedly, and Norah was there too: Norah, walking somewhat slowly, as if she were very tired, and warding off the welcoming leaps the dog made at her every now and then.

When she saw Rodney she frowned.

'Did you think I was lost?' she asked.

She slipped her right hand through his arm, and Rodney's heart gave a thud of contentment. Everything was all right, he told himself in relief. It was impossible for him to know that the little movement had only been made in defence, to keep him from touching her other hand.

'You've been out such a long time,' he said.

'Have I? It doesn't seem very long; but I've had an accident, Rodney . . . Look!'

She indicated her bandaged wrist.

'An accident! My dear girl — '

'Oh, please don't fuss. It's nothing. But I've sprained my wrist a little, and so I went to Dr. Bethune and he's bandaged it. I slipped down and fell on it.' She told the lie badly, but Rodney was too concerned to be critical. He asked a thousand questions.

'A sprain is one of the most painful things you can have,' he said. 'You'll have to take great care of it.'

Norah told him not to fuss so much, and then at sight of his hurt face she relented and assured him that her arm didn't really hurt a bit.

'You look pale enough, anyway,' he said bluntly.

He was silent for the rest of the way to the house.

'Your father's gone through the village to meet you,' he said presently. 'Did you come that way?'

'Yes ...' She did not add that she had seen Mr. Ackroyd and avoided him; she had never told a deliberate lie before; she was wishing with all her heart that there had been no reason to tell one to Rodney now.

'What are you thinking about?' Rodney asked her suddenly.

He was standing with his shoulders leaning against the mantelshelf, looking at her with a strange expression in his eyes.

She started. 'Nothing ... isn't tea ready! I'm so thirsty.'

She turned to the door, but he stopped her with a hand laid on either shoulder.

'I want to speak to you, Norah.'

She shrank a little from his touch. 'You hurt my arm,' she said.

'I'm sorry ... Norah, why do you look at me like that? There's something quite different about you today — something ...' There was a little break in his voice. 'Oh, my dear,' he said — and now he was neither awkward nor ineloquent — 'I love you so much — don't you know that I love you — that I'd give my life to make you happy?'

'Rodney!' There was a sort of frightened amazement in her voice. She shrank away from him. 'Rodney, what are you saying?'

'That I love you; that I want you to marry me. Norah, you must have known it. I've loved you all my life!'

'Rodney! Please — please — oh, stop, stop!'

She laid her uninjured hand on his chest to hold him away.

'I never guessed — I never had any idea ...' She was flushed and distressed; there were tears in her eyes.

'I'd be so good to you,' he pleaded. 'I'd make you so happy. Even if you don't love me as much as I could wish, you're fond of me, Norah? We've been everything to each other. Why not marry me?'

'I can't ... I — just — can't ...'

She spoke breathlessly; she looked away from him through the open window to the distant belt of trees that shut out Lumsden Village and Barton Manor. Perhaps a week ago, had he asked her then — She snapped the thought determinedly.

'I can't, dear,' she said again. 'Oh, Rodney, don't look like that!'

He tried to put his arms round her — but she avoided him.

'Let me go — please let me go.' She fled away to her own room.

She shut and locked the door. She could not believe that this thing had really happened; that Rodney — dear Rodney, whom she had known all her life — had said that he loved her and wished to marry her. Surely she must have dreamed it all.

Perhaps he had not been serious; perhaps it was all just a joke ... Joke! — when she recalled his eyes and the passionate tone of his voice.

She shivered. Somehow she did not like this new, strange Rodney. She could never marry him; it was absurd. She only cared for him in a motherly way.

She sat down by the window; her arm and wrist ached; she seemed to be all quivering nerves.

It was comforting to know that she had told Dr. Bethune the truth, anyway: that she had told him exactly all that had happened, and asked him not to tell her father.

And he had pretended to be very shocked, though there had been a twinkle in his eyes all the time, and he had promised that he would not say a word to any one.

'Only be more careful next time, young lady,' had been his parting shot, and Norah had laughed and promised.

But she had told Rodney a lie; not a very big one certainly, but still it had not been the truth; and she knew that Rodney would have scorned to tell a lie to anyone.

Friday came scratching at the door, whining to be let in. She opened it and went downstairs with him.

Rodney was still in the dining-room, standing at the window looking into the sunshine with unseeing eyes.

Norah went over to him and touched his arm.

'Rodney.'

'Yes.' But he did not turn.

'Rodney, if I tell you something ... will you — will you promise that you won't tell Father?'

He half-turned now; his sad eyes searched her face.

'I promise,' he said.

She twisted one of the buttons on his coat nervously; her eyes were downcast, then suddenly she raised them.

'I told you a fib just now,' she said, 'about my arm. I didn't hurt it in the way I said. I — I ... went out in the car with George Laxton, and we — we had a sort of accident.'

The seconds seemed like hours, as she stood there not daring to raise her eyes, waiting for Rodney to speak.

His eyes were fixed on her face, and beneath his gaze she felt herself colouring in confusion.

'I wish you wouldn't look at me like that,' she broke out. 'It's so silly; anyone would think I had done something to be ashamed of.'

'What are you blushing about, then?' he asked shortly.

He moved away from her; he was afraid to trust himself to say more; he walked towards the door.

As he opened it again Norah spoke.

'Rodney — you won't tell Father, will you?'

He answered without turning his head: 'I already told you I won't.'

The door shut. She was a little afraid of this new Rodney; she wished she had not told him about Laxton.

'Oh — dear!' she said, with a little sigh.

This morning it had all seemed such a fuss about nothing, but now the situation had strangely altered. For one thing she had apparently lost the old, adoring Rodney; lost her champion — the man in whose eyes she had never been able to do wrong. He had been angry that first day when he told him about the black sheep, and now he was something more than angry.

From the window she saw her father coming up the garden, and in sudden panic she flew back to her room.

She did not quite know why she was so afraid to meet his kindly, quizzical eyes; she heard his voice in the hall asking for her; heard Rodney answer that she was in, and had hurt her arm.

'Hurt her arm!' Norah held her breath.

'Yes, but it's nothing much — a slight sprain. Bethune's done it up for her. She slipped getting over a gate into one of the fields, or something.'

Norah bit her lip. Somehow Rodney's deliberate championship annoyed her; she hated it because she knew he had meant it kindly; she heard her father coming up the stairs.

'Norah ...' He came into the room all concern and kindly sympathy. 'Poor child! How did you manage it?' He touched the bandage gently.

'It isn't bad, really,' she assured him. 'Only Dr. Bethune says sprains are nasty things, and advised me to keep it tied up. Yes, I know it was careless, but I shan't do it again.'

She reached up and kissed him. 'Now let's go and have some tea; I'm famished, and we've only been waiting for you.'

She talked away incessantly during tea; she felt that if there were a moment's silence questions would be asked and probably something would be said about Laxton.

Rodney hardly spoke at all; when he did, it was only in monosyllables. Norah escaped as soon as she could and left the two men alone. Her arm was aching badly; she would have given anything to go to bed and rest it, but she did not like to.

She knew if she did that her father would be worried and imagine that she was really ill, and she dreaded a fuss.

When she had gone Mr. Ackroyd looked at his nephew.

'What's up between you two?' he asked bluntly.

Rodney coloured and bit his lip.

'I asked her to marry me,' he said gruffly.

There was a little silence; then he raised his eyes. 'She refused,' he added.

'Refused!' There was anger and incredulity in Mr. Ackroyd's voice. 'Refused!' he said again. 'But she mustn't refuse! I want her to marry you. I — I've always looked upon it as good as settled.'

Rodney did not answer.

Mr. Ackroyd slapped him on the back. 'Don't give in because she's refused you once. Women always like to play hard to get — it puts their value up, you know. Why, I asked Norah's mother half a dozen times before she said "Yes" — God bless her!' he added softly.

'Norah said "No", and she means it,' Rodney declared. He rose to his feet; there was a line of pain between his eyes. 'Don't let's discuss it any more,' he said stiltedly. 'It's all done with, as far as I'm concerned. I shall clear off for a bit, if you don't mind.'

'Don't mind! But I do mind! Norah will have to be made to see reason. I consider that you and she are admirably suited. It's — it's the greatest wish of my life. If she doesn't marry you, who the hell does she think she's going to marry, pray?'

Rodney laughed ruefully.

'There are plenty of better bargains knocking about,' he said.

'And plenty of worse, too,' the elder man answered snappily. 'The girl doesn't know when she's well off. I shall speak to her.'

Rodney swung round. 'I hope you won't, Uncle. It will only make matters worse.'

Mr. Ackroyd growled something unintelligible.

During dinner that evening he watched his daughter closely. She was a little flushed, he thought, and her eyes were rather bright, but she made no attempt to avoid speaking to Rodney.

Mr. Ackroyd felt slightly comforted. 'It'll all come right,' he told himself. 'Girls are all the same; a bit shy at first, but it will all come right.'

When she left them early to go to bed, he made no objection. He said he thought it was the best place for her. He said that Bethune must come round in the morning if the arm was not better.

Norah laughed. 'I believe Dr. Bethune thinks it's much ado about nothing,' she said lightly. She dropped a kiss on his rough, red hair. 'Good night, Daddy; good night, Rodney.' But for the first time for years she made no attempt to kiss her cousin. She passed him rather hurriedly and went out of the room.

She was glad the evening was over; it had been an effort to keep up at all: her arm was a great deal worse than she had admitted. When she reached her own room she opened the window wide and sat down beside it in the darkness.

The sunny day had ended in a beautiful starry night, with not a breath of air to stir the sleeping world.

Away in the distance Lumsden Church clock struck nine. The slow, deep gong boomed out through the silence, and died away again; presently, downstairs in the hall, Friday barked sharply.

Norah looked out into the dark garden below.

Friday never barked like that unless there was someone about; she wondered who it could be at that time of night. Her father and Rodney had both gone to the library, she knew, for the game of cribbage which they played every night before going to bed.

Friday barked again — sharply.

There was a step outside now in the darkness; a man's step on the gravel path below the window.

Norah caught her breath. 'Who is it?' she asked in a whisper.

'Who's there?' But she knew before she heard George Laxton's voice come up to her through the warm night.

'It's only me. How are you?' I've been worrying about you all the evening.'

'You!' She hoped he could not hear the little agitation in her voice. She leaned over, trying to see him, but all she could make out in the darkness was a tall black shadow.

'Where are you? I can't see you,' she said.

'I can only just see your outline,' he told her. There was a little pause; then — 'Come down,' he said.

'Down in the garden! I'm supposed to have gone to bed.'

'What does it matter? Come down for a moment. I want to speak to you.'

'You can speak to me here.'

'I can't say what I want to; you're too far away.'

'You must tell me some other time, then.'

'Don't be unkind.'

Norah laughed softly. 'It isn't good for you to have your own way whenever you want it,' she told him. 'And I want to go to bed.'

'How is your arm?'

'It's — rather bad,' she admitted.

'I know; I've been through it. What did they say — your father and cousin?'

'Nothing very much — I told Rodney how I did it.'

'Told him you'd been with me?'

'Yes.'

There was a little silence, then the tall black shadow moved a little nearer to the window.

'Come down for a minute,' he urged again in a whisper.

Norah hesitated. There seemed to be a thousand voices besides Laxton's calling her. The voice of the still night, the voice of youth and romance, and — perhaps strongest of all — the small and as yet uncertain voice of her own desire.

'Just for a moment, then,' she said.

She half closed the window. She crossed the room softly and tip-toed down the stairs. Friday, seeing her, roused himself and thumped the floor with a feathery tail of welcome.

The library door was fast closed; she could hear her father's voice counting a little triumphantly.

'Two — four — and two's six! Got you again my boy!'

He was evidently in a good temper, which meant that Rodney

was losing the game. Norah went on past the door and into the garden with Friday at her heels.

'I've only come for a minute,' she told George Laxton. There was a nervous little ring in her voice. 'I don't know what they would say if they knew.'

'Does it matter what they say?' he asked.

There was a quality in his voice she had never heard before — a quality which she pathetically misinterpreted.

It never crossed her mind for a single moment that the black sheep had come to her that night because he had been driven by desperation.

He was at the end of his tether; the chance encounter with the woman he loved that day had almost broken him down; the strangely dogged obstinacy of his nature made him long to retaliate, to hit back: to make someone else suffer as he himself was suffering.

It would not have needed great insight to guess that Norah liked him, and during the last few hours he had weighed up the whole thing and decided to take the plunge. He would marry her if she would have him; and if she would have him he could keep Barton Manor — it would at least be something saved from the wreckage of all he had ever hoped for.

But he felt horribly nervous.

He had never met a girl like this one before, and somehow he felt that he was taking a mean advantage. She was being led so easily, being blinded so willingly. She was not like the other women with whom he had played his game; she really believed that he liked her.

And he did like her; he liked her frankness and lack of affection. He liked her for the generous way she had tried to put him in better conceit with himself.

She had a thousand times more common sense than Laurie Fenton. She was probably much more unselfish and generous, and yet . . . yet she was not Laurie . . .

He roused himself with an effort, and looked down at her. He wondered why it seemed so difficult to approach this girl — why, even though it was too dark to see her eyes, the knowledge that she was looking at him disconcerted him and tied his tongue.

'I'm sorry the arm is so bad,' he said haltingly. 'You won't be anxious to trust yourself with me again.'

She laughed softly. 'Oh yes, I shall. It wasn't your fault.' There was a little silence, then — 'What did you want to say to

47

me?' she asked. 'Because I really ought to go in: if Father knew I was out here he would be frightfully angry.'

Laxton laughed.

'Would he — who cares! I'm not afraid of your father.'

'No, sir!' said a rough voice from the darkness. 'And neither am I afraid of you.'

Norah caught her breath sharply, and unconsciously she moved a step nearer to George Laxton.

She was not afraid. But she was conscious of excitement.

Someone turned on the light in the drawing-room behind her; the yellow reflection streamed out into the darkness and on to the face of her father and Laxton.

Mr. Ackroyd was purple with rage; his hands were clenched into fists.

He did not look at her; he was glaring at George Laxton as if he could have killed him.

The black sheep himself appeared quite undisturbed, though there was a little gleam in his eyes. He kept his hands in his pockets and waited for Mr. Ackroyd to speak.

He was not kept waiting long.

'What the devil do you mean by coming here? This is my house and grounds, allow me to tell you. What the hell do you mean by coming up here after my daughter? I've already told her that I won't have you in the place.'

'Miss Ackroyd gave me your message,' said Laxton coolly; 'but as neither of us are children, I fail to see what right you have to forbid us to speak to one another. I admit that this is your garden, and I apologise for trespassing; but with regard to your daughter — '

'Leave my daughter out of the question, you young blackguard,' came the roaring interruption. 'By gad, if I were a younger man, I'd do my best to give you the damnedest thrashing you've ever had in your life.'

'And if you were a younger man I'd let you try,' said Laxton coolly, though now there was a hint of rage in his voice, and he took a threatening step forward.

Norah unconsciously laid a hand on his arm to check him, and her father rounded on her furiously.

'You go to your room, and don't touch the fellow,' he thundered. 'I'll deal with you later; sneaking out of here at this time of night to meet a man whose name is a byword in the country.'

His voice had risen; Rodney, who had been lingering agitatedly in the drawing-room, came out into the garden.

'Uncle, for heaven's sake, do you want everyone in the village to hear?' He turned to Norah: 'Come in, dear,' he said. 'I'll see it's all right.' He tried to draw her towards the house, but she resisted.

'I don't want to go in; I'm going to wait. Oh, Rodney, do let me alone!' Her voice trembled a little; she hated it because she knew Laxton had heard that little word of endearment: there was a tiny fear in her heart now — a fear that this was indeed the end of everything; that she would never be allowed to speak to Laxton any more; she made a last appeal to her father.

'Daddy, you don't understand; if you'll let me explain; it's not Mr. Laxton's fault; I — '

'Let you explain! — don't understand! I understand too well, and you know it,' he raved at her. 'You've been going behind my back for the last three or four days. Do you think I'm a blind bat? Do you think I haven't seen what's been going on under my very nose?'

He hadn't; he had never had the faintest suspicion, and it was that knowledge that was adding to his rage. He took a furious step towards her, and, forgetting her injured arm, laid his hand roughly on it.

Norah screamed.

In an instant Laxton had wheeled round; he was white to the lips with rage, he half raised his fist, and let it fall again.

There was a moment's tragic silence, broken only by Norah's stifled sobbing; then Rodney spoke, his voice was very quiet, but it sounded somehow weary.

'You'd better go, Laxton; you can do no good by staying.'

For an instant it seemed as if the black sheep was going to refuse; then suddenly he laughed; he shrugged his shoulders with bravado.

'Very well.' He looked at Norah; she was hiding her face with her uninjured arm; there was something very young and appealing about her as she stood there in the stream of yellow light, with the darkness of the garden behind her.

The face of the black sheep softened wonderfully; for a moment he looked at her without speaking.

'I'm sorry,' he said at last jerkily. 'Try and forgive me.'

He looked at Rodney, and from Rodney to Mr. Ackroyd. Then he turned his back on them both with royal disdain and stalked leisurely away into the darkness.

CHAPTER EIGHT

NORAH hardly slept a wink all night. The pain of her arm, and the excitement of the day, kept her awake; she lay watching the shadows in the room hour after hour. There was an evergrowing dread in her heart.

Laxton would never come back again; something in the way he had looked at her and the way he had spoken his awkward apology had seemed final. He had walked away, not only out of her garden, but out of her life.

She had fled away to bed as soon as Laxton had gone; downstairs she had heard her father pacing up and down and Rodney trying to soothe him.

But the house was quiet now; for hours the darkness had been undisturbed, save when the clock of Lumsden Church chimed the quarters as the long night dragged by.

When at last Norah fell into a doze she dreamed; and, in her dream, the black sheep turned and looked at her and said —

'I never told you what it was that I wished to say, did I? Well, I will tell you now ... I love you — I want you to marry me.'

And then she woke up and found herself in bed, with the morning sunshine streaming in through the window.

She stayed in her room all the morning. She saw her father go down through the garden and out along the lane, but he never looked back at the house or her window.

She managed somehow to dress for lunch and went downstairs. Rodney was alone in the library; he rose eagerly when he saw her and came forward.

'How is the arm?'

'It's all right, thank you.'

She tried not to speak ungraciously. There was a little moment of awkwardness.

'Uncle John has gone to London,' said Rodney constrainedly. 'He said he mightn't be back tonight.'

'Oh!' Norah's heart sank a little. She loved her father, and she had never quarrelled with him before. Presently: 'Rodney, is he mad with me?' she asked wistfully.

He shook his head. 'Not with you — he is with Laxton.'

She flushed. 'How unfair! It wasn't his fault! He's no more to blame than I am.'

'He is, because you are inexperienced, and he is not.'

'What do you mean?'

'You know what I mean,' he answered. 'You know as well as I do the sort of man Laxton is. He's only amusing himself with you.'

'Rodney!'

'It's perfectly true,' he said quietly. 'I'm sorry if you're angry with me; but the fellow's no good, whether you like to admit it or not.'

'I think you're perfectly hateful.'

'I'm sorry.'

She looked at him with burning resentment. 'I never thought you'd treat me like this,' she said, with feminine logic.

She walked to the door.

'Where are you going?' Rodney asked.

She looked back at him. Follow me, and find out if you think it's worth while,' she retorted, in a rage. 'I dare say Father told you to.'

CHAPTER NINE

THREE days slipped away; the workmen had finished their work at Barton Manor; there was a look of new cheerfulness over the face of the old house.

Now and then rumours stirred in the village and took definite form.

Laxton who had been absent, no one knew where, since the encounter with Mr. Ackroyd in the garden, was coming back and bringing a crowd of his London friends with him; Laxton had sent down a *chef* from town; Laxton was going to have a last fling before the house was sold.

Some said the house was already sold; some said that the man who had been financing him, on the strength of his expectations from old Snowden, had stepped in and taken everything.

Norah listened to all the rumours with a little forlorn heart-ache; she was sorry for Laxton; sorry for the hard unhappiness in his eyes when he had told her so bluntly that he was undeserving of her pity.

Rodney avoided her, and she had found it almost impossible to get back to the old affectionate friendship that had existed between herself and her father. The whole world seemed to be turned upside down and refused to be straightened out again.

And then one day when she was wandering aimlessly in the garden, wondering what to do with herself, a familiar car turned in at the gate and from the window Laurie Fenton waved a white-gloved hand to her.

'So I've found you in! What good luck! My dear child! What have you done to your poor arm?'

Norah coloured a little.

'I sprained it; but it's nothing; it's better now.'

'Well, aren't you going to ask me in to tea? I've come all these miles to see you; I'm still at Didsbury, you know.'

'Of course, you can have some tea?' Norah said.

She tried to seem as if she were pleased to see her visitor, but in reality she was not pleased at all.

The sight of Laurie, and the sound of her high-pitched voice, reawakened a little doubt in her heart that had been there since that day when she first saw her with Laxton at Lumsden Station.

Other events had crowded it out since, but now it rose obstinately to the surface again.

People had said that Laurie and George Laxton were engaged to be married; had there ever been any truth in it?

Laxton had denied it, but now she recalled the manner of that denial, a little throb of jealousy stabbed her.

She tried to stifle it as she led the way into the house.

Laurie was looking about her with critical eyes; she thought the place was ugly, but it looked expensive; she knew Mr. Ackroyd was a rich man; she'd never hesitated to borrow pocket money from Norah when they were at school together, even though she had looked down on her and called her father common.

She was wondering if it would be any good attempting to borrow anything now; she was desperately hard up or she would never have consented to marry Ryan Hewett; she shuddered whenever she thought of him; she hated everything about his person — the way he dressed, the way he spoke, and the way he looked at her.

But she loved his money and his house and the many things he could give her.

Norah took her into the drawing-room and fetched tea; she was never quite at her ease with Laurie.

But she made herself quite agreeable during tea; she reminded Norah of their schooldays, and said, with a little remorseful sigh, that she was afraid she had been rather a cat, hadn't she?

Norah was not interested. She merely said that it seemed so long since they were at school, that she had quite forgotten it.

'And do you know many people round here? But of course you do,' Laurie said. 'People in the country always know each other, don't they? It's not a bit like London, where you may live next door to each other for a lifetime and not even know one another's name. I suppose you've all called on the new Lord of the Manor?'

Norah looked up. 'If you mean Mr. Laxton — he isn't here — he's gone back to London.'

'Has he, indeed!' Laurie bit her lip. She had not known this; she supposed it accounted for the two letters which she had written to Laxton at Barton Manor receiving no reply.

'What do you think of him?' she asked pointedly.

'I!' Norah was pouring tea; she did not look up. 'Oh, I think he's quite — nice,' she said slowly. 'But I don't know him very well.'

'I wonder,' Laurie went on – 'I really wonder that a village like this is so eager to welcome poor old George. Of course, you know what a fearful rake he's been? I like a man of his type myself, but down here — ' She paused eloquently.

'I don't think I quite understand what you mean by a "rake",' Norah answered calmly. 'And, anyway, I don't believe all the silly stories one hears about Mr. Laxton.'

'Ah, but then I've known him quite a long time — ' She looked at Norah uncertainly for a moment. 'Perhaps he told you that I was engaged to him once?' she asked with just the right degree of regret and wistfulness in her voice.

'Yes, I heard.'

'I was fond of him — awfully fond of him, too,' Laurie went on sentimentally. 'But he had no money, and one can't live on love, can one? Of course, you don't know what it is to be poor – really hideously poor, like we are – Mother and me. So poor that you have to look at every shilling.'

Norah raised her grey eyes.

She did not think Laurie looked poor; her clothes were

absurdly smart for the country; her hair and make-up impeccable.

'I shouldn't mind being poor if I cared for a man,' she said bluntly.

A little gleam of contempt lit the elder girl's eyes, but was quickly gone.

'It's so easy to say that when you're rich,' she said, sighing. 'But if George and I had married ...' she shivered delicately. 'The poor boy was heartbroken — it was terrible! I can't bear to think of it.'

Norah rose abruptly.

'I think that's my father,' she said. 'If you'll excuse me for a moment, I'll tell him you're here.'

She knew quite well that Mr. Ackroyd was out, but she felt that she must get out of the room for a moment, before she said or did something for which she would afterwards be sorry.

She had never cared for Laurie Fenton, but she felt now that she hated her for her worldliness and heartlessness; and because, after all, it was she who had brought that look of hard unhappiness to Laxton's eyes.

Norah stood for a moment at the open doorway, looking into the sunny garden with eyes that saw nothing.

Her heart was beating fast, and there was a suffocating feeling of tears in her throat.

She knew now what was the matter with her — knew the cause of the restlessness that had fastened upon her during these last few days. She wanted George Laxton - she wanted the man who was broken-hearted because of Laurie Fenton.

CHAPTER TEN

LAXTON stayed away from Barton Manor for nearly a fortnight. 'He'll never come back,' Norah told herself as each day went by, and the old, unlived-in look which had lifted for a little, fell again on the house.

Rodney had been away, too, and Norah missed him horribly.

'I daresay a little absence will do a lot of good,' so Mr. Ackroyd had agreed reluctantly, when his nephew again said that he wished to go away. 'Let her miss you — let her feel thoroughly

54

lonely and neglected, and she'll be glad enough to see you when you come back, my boy.'

He himself went to town religiously every day during Rodney's absence; somehow since the night of that little scene in the garden he had not felt quite at his ease with Norah.

Badly as he wanted to heal the little breach between them, his obstinacy would not allow him to do so. 'Time enough when she says she's sorry,' was the argument with which he comforted himself. 'Confound it all, she's in the wrong — I'm not.'

So he left her alone as much as he could; going from the house early in the morning, and only coming back in time for dinner at night.

He was very gratified to know that Barton Manor was once more closed. Metaphorically he patted himself on the back and considered it was all due to his cleverness. He believed that he had frightened the black sheep away. He was the sort of man who was firmly convinced that blustering and swearing can strike terror into the bravest soul.

But in this instance, at least, he was wrong. Laxton had paid no attention at all to his threats and bullying. He had stayed away because it suited him to do so and because he quite intended Norah to miss him. He had calculated his chances to a nicety.

Barton Manor seemed to renew its life again on a Thursday morning; Norah, walking along the road to the village, saw that the windows were wide open and the gates fastened back, as if arrivals were expected. A little flush dyed her cheeks.

Was Laxton coming back? She longed to know. She went into the tobacconist in the hope of hearing something from Anderton, the local retailer of gossip.

And Anderton did not fail her. There happened to be no other customers in his shop at the time, and he was only too willing to talk.

'We're to have great doings at the Manor,' he said, as he counted Norah's change across the counter. 'I hear there's a whole crowd coming down from London this afternoon.'

'Oh!' said Norah. She was half afraid to raise her eyes lest they should betray her eagerness. 'You mean that this is to be the much-talked-about house-party?'

All the village had heard that the black sheep proposed to fill the house with his London friends; it had been the one topic of conversation since he had left Lumsden.

'Twenty-five expected, so I hear,' Anderton told her. 'And a *chef* coming, too, and a staff of servants. Wonderful how some people manage to see life on nothing a year.'

Norah said nothing. She disliked Anderton thoroughly.

'It's a rare change for Lumsden, that it is,' he went on. 'Old Mr. Snowden would turn in his grave if he could come back and see the goings on that there'll be.'

'Well, it was dull enough when Mr. Snowden lived at Barton Manor,' Norah said sharply. 'Personally, I think a little excitement will do us all good.' She walked out of the shop without answering his mildly amazed 'Good-morning.'

So Laxton was coming back. Her spirits went up like rockets; the burden of depression she had carried during the past week seemed to have fallen from her.

She wondered what Laurie Fenton was doing.

Laurie had not been over since that afternoon, and Norah very shrewdly guessed that her visit then had only been prompted by a desire to hear something more of George.

She had nearly reached home when round the bend swept the grey Jaguar, and she just caught a glimpse of Laxton's face as he raced by.

There was a woman beside him, and behind followed two more cars — large cars filled with people.

They had passed and were out of sight in an instant, and Norah stood looking after them forlornly.

He had got his own friends.

There was a little lump in her throat.

'You're a fool, a perfect fool, my dear,' she apostrophised herself contemptuously.

But for the rest of the day she could settle to nothing. She was afraid to go down the village and yet she longed to. She told herself that she would rather die than let Laxton think she wanted to see him, and yet every time there was a step in the lane or a voice in the garden her heart leapt to the certainty that it must be he.

Evening came, and with it a phone call from Mr. Ackroyd to say he would not be home till the next day, and Norah gave a little sigh of relief. She dreaded what he would say when he knew that Laxton was back again — dreaded the watch which she was sure would be kept on her movements; for one evening, at least, she was free to do as she liked.

It was Friday who finally settled the question. When she took him down the lane leading from the house for his evening walk he turned off towards the village, and obstinately refused to re-consider his desire and come back.

When Norah called to him, he looked round, wagged his tail and trotted on again; he was going to Lumsden, whether she liked it or not, and, finally, she gave in and followed.

She almost ran past the gates of Barton Manor.

If Laxton saw her she felt that she would die of shame. She only breathed freely once more when she was well past the house.

She wondered what they were all doing — that gay, irresponsible crowd she had seen on the road that afternoon. She would have loved to be amongst them. She realised for the first time that her life had been very tame and monotonous.

'I beg your pardon . . .' Someone spoke beside her, and she roused from her dreaming with a start.

A young man in a dusty Mini-minor peered from its driving window.

'I beg your pardon,' he said again, 'but can you tell me if I am anywhere near a place called Barton Manor? — I don't know this road at all, and for the last mile I haven't met anybody to ask.'

Norah's eyes flashed into interest.

'You must have passed it if you've come from London,' she said. She pointed to the red roof of the big house that was just slightly visible through the trees. 'That's Barton Manor.'

The young man whistled softly. 'By Jove! I saw that place, but never dreamt . . .' He laughed. 'Well, old Laxton's done himself well this time.'

She looked at him; he was a very handsome man, with blue eyes and a slight moustache. 'I suppose you don't know Laxton?' he asked dubiously.

'Yes, I do.' She coloured as she spoke. 'Yes, I know him quite well,' she said nervously.

There was a little silence, then the man moved away towards his machine. 'Thanks, very much — perhaps we shall meet again. I'm staying here a week or so. Laxton's got a house-party — but perhaps you know.'

'Yes.'

There was something a little pathetic in the mono-syllable; the man's eyes searched her face interestedly.

'Well, thanks, very much,' he said again awkwardly, driving off. He glanced in the rear-view mirror, but Norah did not turn her head, and he felt somehow piqued.

He knew that he was sufficiently good-looking to interest most women, and he felt that this country girl in the beret ought to have realised the fact.

At Barton Manor George Laxton himself opened the door.

'By Jove! George, you've hit it all right this time,' the new-comer said. He was staring round him with amazed eyes. 'Never thought you'd got a place like this. I passed it once, and never dreamt it was your show. Little girl in a beret told me.'

Laxton wheeled round sharply. He had been leading the way across the hall.

'Girl in a beret? Had she got a big sheep-dog with her?'

'Yes, I believe she had . . . Got her arm in a sling, too.'

'Oh!' Laxton pushed open the door. 'Come in; they're all somewhere about. I've got Mrs. Durrant down to play pro-priety — you know what these one-eyed villages are.'

The other man laughed. 'You and propriety shaking hands!'

Laxton gave his friend a little shove forward. 'Here's the prodigal guest, my friends,' he added to the room.

A girl, who was sitting on the window-sill smoking a cigarette, jumped down eagerly.

She was very pretty in a dolly sort of style, and she was exceed-ingly smartly dressed. She went up to the new arrival and, stand-ing on tip-toe, kissed him without ceremony.

'We thought you'd cried off,' she said.

A comfortable voice said from the depths of an armchair, 'Ah, the prodigal . . . My dear Hal . . . Dolly, do stop smoking ciga-rettes. You'll ruin your teeth.'

Dolly threw the unfinished cigarette into the garden.

'I never thought I was coming to a baronial hall like this,' said Hal Meredith. 'Fancy old George Lord of the Manor!' he chuckled. 'Great Scott, what would Shylock say if he knew!'

'Oh, he knows all right,' said the black sheep bitterly. 'He knows to a penny what the place is worth, you bet your life. If he didn't he wouldn't be lying as low as he is now.'

'Poor old George!' said Dolly Durrant. 'It is a beastly shame! Why don't you look out for a woman with money? There must be heaps of them about.'

The black sheep made no answer.

'Where's everyone else?' Meredith asked. 'And can I have a wash — and what time do we dine in this ancestral home?'

'They're all out in the garden admiring the sunset,' Dolly told him, with a little grimace. 'I'm not so keen on sunsets myself.'

'I'll take you upstairs,' Laxton said. He led the way from the room.

The two men crossed the hall silently. Meredith seemed a little awed by his surroundings; he had known Laxton for years, but he had never connected him with a place like this; any broken-down club or a cheap flat had always seemed more in the line of the black sheep.

'It seems a rotten shame it's all got to go, eh?' he said awkwardly, as they went upstairs. 'Nothing to be done?'

Laxton shrugged his shoulders. 'Only Dolly's way – a rich wife.'

Their eyes met. 'Well, why not?' Meredith asked carelessly. 'Plenty in your place would do it; if you can get hold of a decent girl.'

No answer. 'And it isn't as if Laurie – ' Meredith went on blunderingly.

Laxton cut him short. 'Oh, for God's sake, shut up! She doesn't enter into the question now. You know as well as I do that Ryan ... However, it's no use talking; but don't think I'm crying over spilt milk. I'm not.' His voice was hard and defiant.

Meredith looked up. 'What do you mean?' he asked. 'Not ... another girl?'

Laxton nodded rather shamefacedly, though his eyes were defiant.

'Yes, your little friend in the beret,' he said.

He felt a little ashamed of the premature confession as soon as it was uttered.

'Of course, I don't want it talked about yet,' he hastened to add. 'It isn't officially fixed up, and she's got a fiery old parent who'd raise Cain if he thought there was anything between us; so Mum's the word, there's a good chap.'

Meredith promised; he was feeling a trifle chagrined that the girl who had never so much as cast an interested glance at his own handsome self should have found Laxton worth marrying; however, there was evidently no accounting for tastes.

'Well, I've come down here to enjoy myself, and I jolly well mean to have a good time,' he said. 'Who else is here, George?'

'Oh, the usual crowd,' said Laxton disinterestedly.

'Mrs. Durrant and Dolly, and the Carews, and Bishop and the rest. You'll see them all at dinner.'

*　　*　　*

If noise and hustle are signs of enjoyment, the house-party at Barton Manor had a thoroughly good time.

For the next week the whole village was overrun with little knots of smartly dressed girls and men.

'A perfect scandal, I call it,' so Mr. Ackroyd declared.

It was at lunch-time three days after Laxton's return to the village, and Mr. Ackroyd had come in hot and angry because, as he declared, he had been elbowed out of the post office by a young fool in a pink shirt.

'You'd think the fellow had bought the place!' he declared savagely, as he sharpened his carving knife on the steel as viciously as if he were about to disjoint the owner of the pink shirt. 'I'm told that they turn night into day, and that the champagne flows like water.' He looked at Norah, but the girl did not lift her eyes. 'It's a puzzle to me where that young scamp is getting his money from,' he went on. 'Someone's going to be let in badly.'

Norah moved restlessly; she was looking a little pale and weary. She had not seen Laxton since that day on the road when he raced past her with a girl beside him, and, apparently, he had not the smallest intention of going out of his way to meet her.

The village was rife with gossip; everyone was talking about the doings at Barton Manor, the young people enviously, the old old people with disapproving voices, and a twinkle in their eyes.

There were young and pretty girls at Barton Manor, she knew. She had seen Meredith with one of them. From her window at night she could see the many-lighted windows of the big house, and once she had heard the chorus of a popular song yelled out by a dozen voices.

'Disgraceful!' So her father said fifty times a day, but in her own heart she thought wistfully that perhaps it might be rather fun.

Rodney was still away, and that fact had not improved Mr. Ackroyd's temper. He was fond of his nephew, and he missed his evening game of cribbage. Night after night he complained bitterly that Norah had driven the boy away.

'He told me – yes, I know all about it,' he accused her. 'I can't imagine what you are thinking about. When I look at those young blackguards at Barton Manor, I thank God from the bottom of my heart that Rodney isn't like that.'

'I wish he was, then,' Norah had answered once, exasperatedly. 'Rodney's very good, I know, but he's too good.'

She broke off before the cold displeasure of her father's eyes, and since then she had sat by in silence and let him say what he liked. But today somehow she felt that she could stand it no longer. She was sick to death of the endless talk about Barton Manor.

When at last lunch was ended and Mr. Ackroyd had taken himself off for his half-hour's snooze she went for a walk through the woods. When she was in these moods she found the house unbearable. She struck across some fields into a wood where a carpet of yellow primroses were just losing their first beauty and tiny fronds of bracken were poking curly heads through the moss and dried leaves.

And there she came face to face with George Laxton himself with Dolly Durrant, hatless and beautifully dressed, sauntering at his side.

The encounter was so unexpected that Norah blushed crimson. She hardly glanced at Laxton. She acknowledged his salute hurriedly and went by almost at a run.

But she had seen enough to know that the girl beside him was young and pretty, and that she and Laxton had been laughing and talking together happily.

She went on her way unseeingly. The brambles tore at her dress, but she never stopped till she reached the other side of the wood; till she had put as much distance as possible between herself and those two on whom the spring sunshine had been falling — together!

Rodney had been right after all when he said that Laxton was a man who could amuse himself with any girl who was at hand; her cheeks burned.

The boundary of the wood was marked by a rough fence and a five-barred gate; Norah leaned her arms on top of it, and hid her face. She felt horribly mortified to think that she had wasted a thought upon him; she wished she had never seen him; never heard his name. She was ashamed because she had been jealous of Laurie, and was now jealous of the golden-haired girl with whom she had just seen him.

What did it matter to her whom he knew, or with whom he walked? Her father and Rodney had been right after all — it was she who had been foolish and wilfully blind, she –

'Is anything the matter?' asked a voice, and, raising her head with a start, she found George Laxton beside her.

She made no attempt to answer; she could not have spoken

had she tried; she just stood there dumbly, looking at him.

The whole world seemed to have changed in a flash of time; she felt a little breathless, a little giddy.

Laxton leaned his back against the gate and looked down at her.

'You must have run to get so far,' he said with a faint smile. 'I came after you at once ... What is the matter?' he asked again. 'Tell me.'

She shook her head; she could smile now, a little tremulous smile. 'Nothing is the matter — only ...' She drew a long breath. 'I don't know, but I seem to have had the blues lately.'

'So have I,' said the black sheep.

He looked away from her into the heart of the shady wood with its fading yellow carpet.

'I thought I was never going to see you any more,' he said.

'Did you?' She glanced up at him, and away. 'I've been at home all the time,' she said unthinkingly.

'I've looked for you every morning in the village — you and Friday,' he said. 'Don't you ever go down that way now?'

'I haven't been lately; and I suppose you've been very busy, haven't you?'

He hunched his shoulders. 'I've been very bored.'

'Bored!' She opened her eyes incredulously.

'Frightfully bored,' he repeated; he half turned, and his hand fell to hers as it rested on the top of the gate. 'I've been wishing you were there — at Barton Manor,' he said.

'Laurie Fenton came over to see me last week,' she said, with apparent irrelevance.

She was not looking at him, or she might have seen the little flash of pain that crossed his face, though when he spoke his voice was even, almost casual.

'Laurie Fenton!' he said. 'There's no such person now; she was married this morning to Ryan Hewett.'

Norah echoed Laxton's words in breathless amazement.

'Married! — to Ryan Hewett! She never told me.'

She looked at him with wide eyes. 'I knew she was engaged to him, of course, but ...'

'It was quite a hurriedly arranged affair, I believe.'

The black sheep kept his eyes fixed steadily on the leafy wood. For the moment he had forgotten even the plans he had made for the capture of this girl beside him; forgotten that he was a ruined man, driven to desperation by his own folly and extravagance.

He was just an unhappy lover, cut to the heart by the knowledge that the one for whom he would have given everything in the world had failed him.

'I wonder she didn't tell me,' Norah said again. 'I should like to have seen her married.'

She had forgotten her jealousy of Laurie Fenton now; Laurie was married – she could never again be anything to Laxton.

The black sheep did not answer, and presently he moved. 'Shall we walk back, or would you rather I didn't come with you?'

Norah hesitated; she looked down the footpath along which they had come.

'But you weren't alone,' she said hesitatingly. 'I thought . . .'

'Dolly has gone home,' he said abruptly. 'She only came out with me because Meredith was not available.' He laughed mirthlessly. 'What is Lumsden saying about us all?' he asked. 'We've got an impromptu hop on tonight,' he said suddenly. 'I suppose you . . . but, of course, you couldn't.'

'What do you mean?'

'I mean that I suppose I mustn't ask you to come? There's no one there I care a hang about — and I'm so fed-up. Mrs. Durrant is there – Dolly's mother. It's only a scratch-up sort of affair; nothing formal . . . I suppose it's out of the question?'

'I suppose it is.' She spoke determinedly enough, but her heart gave a little throb of disappointment; how she would have loved to go!

They were strolling on through the wood now; there was a reckless look in Laxton's eyes.

'Do you think a decent girl could ever care for an alleged blackguard?' he asked suddenly. 'The sort of chap nobody will say a good word for — who's up to his eyes in debts and an unsavoury record.'

Norah was brushing back the loose locks of her hair.

'I don't think what he'd been in the past would matter, if a girl really cared for him,' she said haltingly. 'And if he really cared for her, of course,' she added suddenly.

The black sheep hardly seemed to listen. 'A fellow without a pound in the world,' he went on, 'and a girl –. perhaps she'd have money.'

Norah laughed. 'Would that matter?'

'People would say that it did,' he told her.

She lifted her serious eyes to his face. 'She wouldn't care wha'
people said.'

They were standing still now, and all about them the wood wa:
very still. A bird stirred overhead in the branches, and a little way
off some dried leaves and twigs from last year crackled beneath a
footfall.

Why was it, Laxton asked himself, with a sort of anger, that he
could not bring himself to go on with the task he had set himself?
So far he could always go, and then — something in her very
innocence and sincerity struck the words from his lips. While he
stood hesitating the crackling of the undergrowth came nearer,
and Meredith stepped out from the scrub on to the narrow footpath.

'Hullo! I was looking for you,' he said. He glanced at Norah
and his face changed. A little smile crept into his eyes. 'I beg your
pardon; where's Dolly?'

'She's gone home — I left her some time ago.' Laxton's voice
was curt. He hesitated a moment, then, seeing that Meredith
apparently had no idea of leaving them, reluctantly introduced
him.

'Hal Meredith — Norah Ackroyd.'

Norah smiled and nodded. 'I think we've met before,' she said.
'Wasn't it you who asked me the way to Barton Manor the other
day?'

Meredith beamed; it pleased his vanity that she had remembered him. 'Of course, it was,' he said; 'I knew you at once.' He
fell into step beside her, elbowing Laxton aside. 'I say, are you
coming to our hop tonight?' he asked eagerly.

Norah laughed. 'I should love to, but I'm afraid I can't.' She
half glanced back at Laxton, and was surprised at the way he was
scowling.

'What a shame!' Meredith said. 'We really shall have a good
time — eh, George?'

'I hate dancing,' said Laxton briefly.

His friend chuckled. 'It's a recent hatred then,' he said coolly.
'What about last year in town, when Laurie and . . .' He broke
off, silenced by the fury in Laxton's eyes.

Norah broke the awkward silence. 'I love dancing myself,' she
said. 'But, all the same, I'm afraid I can't come tonight.'

They had reached the outskirts of the wood, where the road
led away in opposite directions to Barton Manor and her own
home. She stopped. 'Well, I'll say goodbye. No – please don't

come any further. I hope you'll have a good time tonight.'

She dismissed them with a nod and a smile and turned away.

'Stupid ass, you are!' Laxton said savagely, as soon as she was out of earshot. 'What the devil did you want to come along for?'

Meredith pretended to look amazed, but there was a knowing smile in his eyes.

'My dear chap, I had no idea ... I thought that you were with Dolly—'

'Well, you might have cleared off when you saw that I wasn't,' Laxton said disgustedly.

The other man laughed. 'Spoiling your chances, was I? — when you haven't troubled to go near her ever since we've been down here. Now, it's no use looking so savage; I know perfectly well that you haven't set eyes on her since we all came down from town. It's your own business, of course; but it strikes me you were counting your chickens before they were hatched when you told me that things were fixed up between you. If they are, she doesn't know it, that's all I can say. If they are, why isn't she coming to the hop tonight?'

'I told you that her father — '

'A fig for her father,' said Meredith lightly. 'Don't tell me, with all your experience of women, George, that you don't know better than to suppose that a girl like her is going to do what her father tells her and stay away from the man she ...'

'Oh shut up!' said the black sheep irritably.

Meredith laughed. He liked baiting Laxton.

'Tell you what,' he said, as they strolled on down the road, 'I'll bet you a fiver you can't get her to come to the dance tonight. There now! That's a fair offer.'

'Don't talk rot. She'd come fast enough if I asked her. But she doesn't know any of the crowd up there, and — '

'And any excuse is better than none, eh?' Meredith finished for him with a chuckle. 'All right, my son. It's off! Have it your own way, but don't blarney me.'

'I'm not blarneying you.' Laxton's dark face flushed. 'Don't talk such bilge! ... I'll take your bet — take it and win. A fiver, then, that I get her to come tonight.'

'You'll lose,' Meredith said complacently. 'I hope you've got a fiver to pay with, that's all.'

'I shall have — after tonight,' was the answer.

They both laughed.

They had almost reached Barton Manor now.

'Ackroyd's an uncommon name,' Meredith said suddenly. 'I wonder if she's any relation to an old chap I used to know. Fiery whiskered old blighter — rather inclined to bluster?'

'It's a most excellent description of my future father-in-law,' Laxton said drily; he looked at his friend with sudden suspicion. 'How did you know him?' he asked.

Meredith shrugged his shoulders; he looked rather eager. 'If it is the same chap, my old man once did him a good turn,' he said. 'I've half a mind to go and call on the strength of it.'

'You'd be kicked out!'

'Not me,' Meredith declared positively. 'What is he, by the way? Norah's father, I mean?'

'I don't know; there seems rather a mystery about it; but he's got money, there's no doubt about that; pots of it, I should think.'

Laxton was frowning a little. 'I was asking Bethune — the doctor here — what Ackroyd was, and how he made his money, but even Bethune didn't know.'

'Humph! Well, I shall risk it tomorrow, and call.'

'Don't be a confounded fool!'

Meredith chuckled. 'Jealous, eh? ... Well, you'd better win that bet tonight, or I shall do my best to cut you out; I like blue berets.'

They had reached the house now, and he went on into the hall, leaving Laxton to follow.

He went round the house to the terrace where he and Norah had stood that night and watched the sunset. He leaned his arms now on the low balustrade, and looked into the beautiful garden below with tragic eyes.

This was Laurie Fenton's wedding day, and all day long he had heard nothing but the clashing of the gates that shut him out of her life.

There was nothing left to him now but this last, desperate chance — this final throw to secure something to himself from the ruin. He roused himself with an effort and went back to the house.

He glanced at his watch as he went. Nearly seven already, and the informal 'hop' which Dolly Durrant and her friends had organised for the night was due to begin at nine. That left him two hours in which to win his bet.

CHAPTER ELEVEN

NORAH went home with a feeling of excitement. The weight of depression had gone. She could realise once more that it was spring-time, and that the world was a very beautiful place.

She was greeted in the hall by an irate parent. Mr. Ackroyd had had an urgent message to go to town at once, he said, when he saw his daughter. Where had she been, pray, that he had not been able to find her? She knew perfectly well that he liked her to pack his bag for him.

Presently she ventured to ask when he would be back.

'Goodness alone knows!' was the lugubrious reply she received. 'I may be away some days.'

Norah was not sorry. Fond as she was of her father she had lately found him rather a trial. She gave a little sigh of relief when presently she saw him drive off.

Norah went back to the house; she wondered what she should do with herself for the next two or three days.

She looked out of the window towards Lumsden; soon there would be sounds of revelry up at Barton Manor. How she would love to be going to the dance! She thought of the look in George Laxton's eyes when he had made his tentative suggestion, and her heart throbbed a little faster.

Had he ever really cared for Laurie? Or was it only what Laurie chose to say? Anyway, it did not matter very much, seeing that Laurie was married.

She was glad Laxton had told her of the marriage; glad to remember that there had been not the least emotion in his voice or face when he spoke.

Surely, had he cared, he could not have spoken of it so indifferently!

She propped her chin in the palm of her hand and looked into the garden with dreamy eyes.

How she would love to be able to buy Barton Manor, and give it back to the black sheep, and tell him that he could go on living there if he wanted to, in spite of all the Shylocks who — as he had bitterly put it — would soon come down on him like a pack of wolves to fight for the bones.

It was a very uncharitable world, she thought resentfully; how,

67

for instance, could Lumsden possibly know the circumstances of Laxton's life, or what had driven him to do the many wild and reckless things with which he was credited.

The sunshine had faded; grey shadows were settling down on the warm face of the earth; presently it grew too dusk to even see the spire of Lumsden Church, and through the trees little yellow lights, like bright eyes, peeped out into the twilight.

Norah rose with a sigh; she wondered what they were all doing at Barton Manor — the girl with the golden hair and Laxton and Meredith and all the rest of them.

Dr. Bethune would be there too; what an enviable thing it was to be a man, to be able to do just what one liked and go where one pleased without criticism.

She ate her supper in the twilight; the windows were wide open, and a faint breeze had risen; it stirred the curtains, and the leaves of a magazine lying near the window, but otherwise the world seemed to have fallen asleep.

Friday slept in the hall, with his blunt nose resting on shaggy paws; when Norah went out to him, he thumped a tail in greeting; she stooped and patted his head. She broke off; Friday had raised his head and growled.

The front door was shut, but Friday growled again, and presently he got up and went over to the door, barking.

Norah followed; she pulled back the latch, then she caught her breath with a little gasp of amazement, for the black sheep stood there in the twilight.

'You!' she said blankly.

There was a ring of gladness in her voice, which Laxton was quick to hear.

'Yes, it's me!' he said ungrammatically. 'I saw your father drive through the village just now, and I guessed he was going to the station, so I thought I'd be reckless and come along. Will you come out a moment? I want to ask you something.'

She glanced back over her shoulder into the hall, but there was nobody about, and she went out into the garden, followed by Friday.

'I came away in a hurry,' he said laconically. 'Dinner wasn't quite over. I left them all cracking nuts and stale old jokes,' he added, with a weary sort of mirth. 'And the dance doesn't begin till nine. Dr. Bethune's coming, and a few other people have run down from town, but there'll only be about thirty of us al-

68

together.' He stopped and looked down at her. 'I want you to come, too,' he said.

'Me!'

'Why not?' His voice was low and insistent. 'What's to stop you now that your father's gone away?' He put out his hand and took hers. 'Please!' he said softly.

She looked away from him. Her breath was coming fast.

His fingers tightened their loose grip of her. 'I want you to come more than I can say,' he said again. 'I dare say you'll be angry if I tell you why, but . . .' he broke off.

'Tell me why?' She was looking at him now, and for a moment the black sheep lost his eloquence, and stood silent.

For the first time in his life he was ashamed of the part he was playing. He forced himself to keep his thoughts fixed on the reason for it all; on his own desperate situation; the ruin that threatened him, and he stumbled on again.

'I wanted you to come this afternoon. I told you — but . . . Well, Hal Meredith put my back up — he said you wouldn't come because you thought I was an outsider; because you didn't care to know me, and — '

'He had no right to say so; it isn't true,' she broke out indignantly. 'I should just love to come, only — '

'Don't let there be any "only," he urged softly. 'Just come — to please me.'

Something in his voice seemed to hold her will; her fingers fluttered in his grasp.

'But I — I haven't anything to wear!' she protested. 'I — oh, I couldn't come with all your smart friends there from London.'

'Clothes! What do clothes matter?' he said impatiently. 'It's you I want . . . you yourself . . . Norah!'

He bent towards her, but she drew a little away from him. He let her go instantly; he even took a step backwards; he knew well enough the wisdom of a little self-control.

There was a moment's silence, then: 'I'll wait here for you,' he said.

His voice was quiet, and very gentle; he spoke as if it had all been decided between them. 'How long will you be?' he asked, in his usual voice again.

She laughed then.

'I won't be half an hour,' she said. She turned and ran back to the house.

He was pacing up and down when she returned.

'Already!' he said whimsically. 'I was prepared for at least another twenty minutes.'

'I was as quick as I could be . . .'

A wave of happiness swept through her; for the moment everything was forgotten but this man; there was nothing in all the world but his voice and his presence; she believed in him and loved him, and that was all she cared about.

'You'll let me come back early, won't you? I — I can't stay late — please.'

'You shall come back when you like — I'll bring you myself.' He stopped; he looked back at Friday, who was following faithfully. 'I'm afraid we can't take the dog,' he said constrainedly.

'Of course not. I'll take him back; if I shut him in the yard he won't be able to get out.'

She called to Friday, and ran back across the grass.

Laxton waited impatiently. He felt very nervous himself. It was a relief when she rejoined him.

'All right? Then we'll get along.'

When they reached the main road —

'We'll go in through the grounds,' Laxton said. His voice sounded a little jerky. 'It's shorter than the road, and we shan't meet anyone that way.'

He opened a gate in the hedge. 'You'd better hold my hand — it's dark.'

Her cheeks were burning. She longed to go back, and yet she wanted to go on. This was the adventure of one who looks out of a garden gate into an unknown road, longing to set out on a voyage of discovery, and yet afraid of the darkness. She clung to Laxton's hand like a child, and they went on together through the silent garden.

CHAPTER TWELVE

DINNER at Barton Manor evolved itself into a very noisy affair after the black sheep had taken his departure.

He had made some inadequate excuse, which Harold Meredith speedily proceeded to discount once his host had gone.

There was gossipy discussion of George Laxton's falling for 'the country girl in the blue beret' on the rebound after Laurie Fenton's casting him aside in favour of Ryan Hewett. Then, with an air of mystery, Hal Meredith went on: 'I made him a bet of a fiver that he couldn't get her to come to the hop tonight. He clinched it. So I can only conclude that he's gone off to exercise his powers of attraction.'

'She won't come,' Dolly declared. 'She knows she'd be out of it if she did.'

'Yes, I think he'll lose right enough,' Meredith said complacently. 'My only fear is that he won't have the fiver to stump up with.'

'Poor old George!' said a pale-faced girl opposite. 'It's rather mean to talk like this about him behind his back, isn't it? After all, we're having a good time here, and it's not our business where the money's to come from to pay for it all.'

Meredith looked slightly shamefaced. 'I didn't mean anything,' he said hastily. 'George is all right; he just needs eight or ten thousand a year; but as it is . . .'

'Perhaps the blue beret girl will give it to him,' said Mrs. Durrant, stifling a yawn behind a fat, rather over-ringed hand. 'I always told him he must marry for money, and if he happens to like the girl as well, why — good luck to him!' She raised her glass. 'Here's his health, anyway,' she said heartily; 'and confound his creditors — Shylock and company, whoever they are.'

'You know,' Dolly Durrant said later to Meredith when they were in the drawing-room, 'or perhaps you don't know — that Shylock, as you call him, has dubbed up again on the strength of this baronial hall, and at the moment our George has quite a nice little sum to his credit at the bank.'

'Really! How do you know? Laxton never told you, surely,' Meredith asked interestedly.

Dolly shook her golden head.

'Of course not — but there was a letter lying on his desk, and — well, I read it.'

Meredith was not in the least shocked.

'Well, I'm glad to hear it,' he said. 'It's something to be able to have a last fling before going to the devil, and if Shylock doesn't mind, nobody else need grumble.' He looked round him with speculative eyes. 'Wonder what this place will fetch? he ruminated.

Dolly raised her brows. 'Goodness! I've no idea, but it's sold already, isn't it?'

'I don't know.'

'Well, I know there's been someone after it, anyway. Laurie's been the last straw, of course,' Dolly went on calmly. 'I always knew she'd throw him over; I hope Ryan leads her a dance; serve her right. He drinks like a fish, you know.'

'I hate the chap,' said Meredith. 'I — Oh, Good Lord!' He rose slowly to his feet and stood staring across the room to the doorway, through which Laxton himself had just entered with Norah Ackroyd and Mrs. Durrant.

There was a second of absolute silence; the babel of tongues and laughter ceased as if by magic; all eyes were turned to the three in the doorway.

Norah was all in white, and the dress was very simply made with a full skirt cut rather short.

She looked younger than Laxton had ever seen her, little more than a schoolgirl, as she stood there between him and portly Mrs. Durrant, her cheeks flushed, her grey eyes a little frightened.

Mrs. Durrant was talking volubly. She took Norah's hands and introduced her to a dozen people. She called her 'My dear', and gave the impression that she had known the girl all her life.

Laxton kept close beside Norah. He was rather flushed, and there was a sort of defiance about him. As they turned into the long dining-room, cleared now for dancing, the gossip continued below the sound of the band.

'My word! isn't she keen on him! She's very young and green, or she'd never show it so plainly.'

'Well, if George pulls it off, I should think he'll be lucky. She's quite pretty and presentable.'

'This girl is worth twenty of Laurie Fenton, or I'm very much mistaken. Here they come.'

Dolly Durrant saw that Norah looked happy; her eyes shone, and there was a little tremulous smile on her lips.

She had danced three times with the black sheep — none of the other dances, or her partners, counted at all; most of the men were inclined to consider her dull and too quiet, and to rather pity Laxton. They did not realise that there was only one man in the world who counted in the very least, and that all the rest might not have existed.

She was living in the moment; she never gave a thought to the rashness of this thing she had done, or what would happen afterwards; the present was everything, and she meant to enjoy it to the full. George was content to dance with her and that was all that mattered.

He led the way across the hall now to the closed door of the library. It was a room that was very little used, and it smelt of books and leather, but the furniture was wonderful old oak and the walls were oak panelled, and the whole room had an air of grandeur and dignity.

Norah slipped her hand from Laxton's and went forward, looking round her eagerly. She thought Barton Manor the loveliest place she had ever seen. Each room was a fresh delight; it seemed a tragedy to her that Laxton had got to walk out and leave it to a stranger.

He closed the door and followed her slowly. 'You like this room?' he asked.

'I think it's just – perfect,' she told him breathlessly. 'Oh, George it does seem a shame that you can't live here always. It would just break my heart if it were mine to know I had to go.'

He laughed shortly. 'Hearts don't break so easily,' he said. 'But – I am sorry, all the same.' He hesitated; then added, 'I've had an offer for the place – not a bad one either, I suppose – from – whom do you think?'

She shook her head. 'I don't know any of your friends,' she said.

He made a little grimace. 'I should hardly call him a "friend," ' he said, with faint sarcasm. 'The would-be purchaser is Shylock . . .'

'Shylock! — the man you told me about?'

'Yes. He's written offering to strike a bargain. My debts and a small balance *versus* Barton Manor . . .' He made a sudden passionate gesture. 'My God, if you knew what it feels like to be in the grip of big finance, and with the knowledge that it's all my own fault . . .'

There was a little silence; then he turned to her. He was very pale, but he smiled faintly as he met her sympathetic eyes.

'I'm sorry; I don't often have outbursts like that.'

'Oh, I'm sorry, too!' she said impulsively. 'I know just how you must be feeling. Isn't there anything to be done — nobody who can help you?'

The black sheep took a step towards her; he put his hands on her slim shoulders in their filmy white covering.

'It isn't likely that anybody would want to help me,' he said jerkily. 'Perhaps you won't believe me when I say that there isn't a living soul in the wide world who cares a hang for me or what becomes of me.'

There was a sort of roughness in his voice. Norah lifted her grey eyes to his face. 'Oh, that isn't true!' she said, with impulsive earnestness. 'You know that I . . . oh!'

She broke off in trembling realisation of what her words implied; she hid her burning face.

Laxton's fingers closed about her wrists; he tried to draw her hands away.

'Norah . . .'

She tried to resist him, then all at once she gave in. She looked up at him with tears in her eyes and such unconscious betrayal of what she felt for him in her quivering face that all the black sheep's eloquence vanished, and for a moment he looked down at her, shaken to the depths of his being.

Perhaps for the first time in his life he realised how well he deserved all the hard things that had been said of him, and how little he deserved that this girl should believe in him at all.

And yet in spite of the genuine shame which came to him in that moment he was still fully alive to the fact that this was his chance; this the moment for him to play his winning card.

He turned a deaf ear to the voice of his better nature that pleaded to him that he was not playing fairly, that his experience was no match for her innocence, and with a sudden utter recklessness he bent and kissed her lips.

CHAPTER THIRTEEN

RODNEY ACKROYD came home unexpectedly the night of the dance at Barton Manor.

At Paddington he had run across his uncle. Mr. Ackroyd was in a hurry, but he yet found a moment in which to talk to Rodney and raise his fallen hopes.

'Norah will be glad to see you, my boy. She hasn't been the same girl since you went away. What did I tell you?' He chuckled and poked Rodney in the ribs. 'Quite pale she's been looking,' he declared, with a blissful ignorance of the real cause of his daughter's altered appearance.

'Didn't I tell you things would come all right? You go in and win, my boy. No — I'm not coming back tonight. I shall be home some time tomorrow. Norah will be delighted to see you.'

He chuckled again. 'Walk right in and surprise her,' he repeated, with enthusiasm. 'You'll be home by nine if you catch this train.'

But Rodney paused to ask a last question: 'Laxton — is he . . .'

Mr. Ackroyd laughed contemptuously.

'Oh, there's nothing to fear there,' he declared. 'I've settled his little hash; hasn't shown his face near the house since. I know his sort — off at the first hint of anything disagreeable. No, no, there's nothing to fear from that quarter any longer. He's got a houseful up at Barton Manor, a crowd of his riff-raff friends from London — a perfect scandal, I call it, to come and upset a decent neighbourhood. Well, goodbye, my boy — and good luck.'

There was a sort of infection in Mr. Ackroyd's cheerfulness, and Rodney's spirits went up like rockets as he travelled home.

It was dark when he reached Lumsden, and the night smelt of the country — the fields and the woods — as he walked through the sleepy little village and along the high road, past the sounds of revelry coming from Barton Manor.

This was evidently the house-party of which Mr. Ackroyd had spoken, Laxton's 'riff-raff friends', who were rousing the echoes with their mirth.

He quickened his steps a little. What a crowd for Norah to have got in with — and had things gone differently she might have done. There was something Early Victorian in Rodney's nature; he shook his head disapprovingly.

As he turned into the lane he heard Friday howling mournfully. He wondered a little at that; as a rule Norah never allowed her favourite to be shut out of the house; he went on to the front door.

Rodney's spirits fell; the house was so silent; there was no warm welcome for which he had hoped.

Friday was still howling, and with sudden apprehension he went out again and round to the yard.

As he opened the gate the dog bounded out; he rushed round him in little excited circles, yapping delightedly; then suddenly he made off into the darkness towards the road.

Rodney called to him. The dog came back, looked up at him and barked, and made off once more. His whole manner seemed an invitation, and with sudden impulse Rodney followed him. Friday semed pleased; he ran a little way ahead, and came back to see if he was still being accompanied; they had gone the length of the lane and were out in the main road before Rodney realised how far they had come.

Presently he lost sight of him; he stopped and whistled ... he was answered by a little whine and the sound of scratching at the side of the road — Friday was pawing one of the gates which led into the Barton Manor grounds.

Rodney's heart seemed to stand still. Norah — surely she could not ... He moved forward and tried the latch; it opened easily, and Friday raced on into the shadows, his blunt nose close to the ground.

And now the sound of music was clearly audible once more, and through the trees the brilliant lights from the house shone out invitingly.

Rodney's heart was beating heavily; if Norah had come here! ... Oh, but the thing was impossible; he called to the dog insistently.

But Friday took no notice, and Rodney went on across the wide, smooth lawn till he was quite close to the house.

With each step the conviction that Norah was there, in that crowd of dancers, deepened in his heart; his hands were clenched as he walked.

He had hated Laxton before in a vague, abstract sort of way, but now he felt as if that hate had grown from a dead, slumbering thing to something abnormally alive and virulent, as he walked on like a man in a dream, across the smooth gravel path and up to the big front door.

Friday was already there, wagging his stumpy tail and uttering little cries of excitement.

After a moment the door opened; Rodney supposed that he must have rung the bell, though he had no recollection of so doing. He heard himself asking for Laxton — saw the dubious look which crossed the hired servant's face.

'Mr. Laxton is engaged just now, sir ...'

'Mr. Laxton will see me; I — I have come for my cousin, Miss Ackroyd.'

The man led the way across the hall; the library door was only closed and the man pushed it open, standing aside to allow Rodney to pass.

'If you will wait here a moment, sir —' Then he broke off in dismay.

Rodney stood quite still — staring into the room; he seemed incapable of movement or action of any kind; then, with a smothered oath, he strode forward and caught Norah round the waist, wrenching her away from the man who stood with his arms round her.

Norah gave a little stifled cry, and for a moment there was a tragic silence; then the black sheep moved across to the door and shut it with a little irritable slam.

Out in the hall Dolly and her partner had seen the little episode and were lingering curiously.

Laxton came back with his hands in his pockets, and looked down at Rodney's infuriated face.

'Well, what have you got to say?' he asked.

The unconcern of his voice drove Rodney mad. The cynical smile in his eyes seemed to the other man a studied insult to the girl who stood between them. Half blind with rage and pain, he made a sudden dash forward with upraised fist.

'Rodney!' Norah screamed his name in shrill terror. She rushed in between the two men. 'Don't hurt him — don't! Oh!' the last word was a twisted moan of pain and fear, as the blow which had been intended for Laxton fell full on her upturned face.

In a moment everything was confusion; out in the hall the sound of the angrily raised voices had been heard, and as Norah staggered back into Laxton's arms the door opened and Dolly Durrant burst into the room.

'What is the matter? Oh, dear . . . oh, what's happened?'

Several people had followed at her heels; to Norah, half-stunned as she was, the room seemed full of curious, inquisitive faces. She made a desperate effort to recover herself; she tried to push Laxton away when he would have supported her. 'I'm all right . . . it's nothing . . . Please don't make a fuss.'

But everything was whirling round her.

As in a dream of pain she saw Rodney's eyes, shocked and horrified at what he had done; saw him move towards her, and, half-fainting as she was, a sudden fear for Laxton rushed to her heart.

Rodney hated him — Rodney had meant to kill him; she had read it in his eyes; she must get between them — she must save him . . . She put up her hands feebly.

'Don't hurt him — oh, don't hurt him! — for my sake, Rodney. I love him — Rodney . . .' The last word was a little frightened appeal as she felt everything slipping away; she took a stumbling step forward, and Laxton caught her as she fell.

77

CHAPTER FOURTEEN

As soon as it was light George Laxton got up and dressed; it was a beautiful morning, the grass was still wet with dew, and a bed of wallflowers near the front door scented the air with their perfume as the black sheep passed them and went on down to the gate.

He wondered what had happened at the Ackroyds'.

Poor Norah — twice she had been hurt through his fault . . .

What sort of a wife would she make for a man? he asked himself, in cynical amusement. She was so different from the woman whom he had always believed he would marry, and for a moment his face fell into haggard lines, as he thought of Laurie Fenton and the way she had let him go to the wall.

He walked on with drooping shoulders and down-bent head. He was carelessly dressed and unshaved; his feet were thrust into loose slippers, and he wore no hat.

'Dissipated-looking brute!' was the bitter thought of a man coming towards him down the road, though his voice was quiet enough when he greeted Laxton. It was Rodney Ackroyd.

His plain face looked pale and haggard against his shock of red hair, but his eyes were steady as they met the other man's.

Laxton flushed dully. 'I was coming along to your place,' he said.

It was nervousness that made him speak roughly, but Rodney was not far-seeing enough to guess it, and his face darkened.

'I thought I'd save you the trouble,' he said curtly. 'If you can spare me a few moments.'

Laxton glanced at his companion. 'We'll walk along together. I suppose the old man's been raising Cain, eh?' he asked.

'The old man — if you mean my uncle — is not home,' said Rodney.

He stopped suddenly, and, half turning, looked up at the black sheep.

'For God's sake drop this shilly-shallying once and for all,' he said passionately. 'I was half mad last night, I admit, but when you've known a girl all your life and cared for her . . .' His voice broke roughly, but he struggled on again. 'Look here — I'm willing to forget it if you're going to play fair. I'll — I'll even do my level best to help you with Mr. Ackroyd, if — if . . .'

The black sheep stared. After a moment he laughed drily. 'Rather a change of front, eh?' he submitted. 'Well, I suppose you'll hardly be surprised if I ask you what the devil my affairs have got to do with you?'

'Nothing — except where they concern Norah; if you think I'm going to stand by and see her life ruined by you you've made a mistake.' Rodney's eyes never left Laxton's face; he seemed to be trying to read his thoughts.

After a moment: 'For Heaven's sake, man,' he broke out once more passionately, 'let it be one thing or the other! When you came to Barton Manor it was common talk that you were engaged to another girl. It's no business of mine, I know, but after last night — '

He stopped desolately, with a sudden realisation of his own impotence, and for a moment the thoughts of both men went back to that last scene in the library.

'Look here,' he said abruptly. 'I don't want your damned interference, as I've told you, but I'll do you the credit of saying that I believe you're honest, and if it's the least satisfaction to you to know it, I was going to ask your cousin to marry me last night when you came in and upset everything.'

Rodney was only anxious to do what was the best for Norah's happiness, though there was nothing but doubt in his mind. He knew the reputation Laxton had; knew the many stories that were being repeated everywhere with more or less truth; knew that a few weeks ago he had been engaged to another woman, and he could find nothing to say.

'Perhaps I'd better come after breakfast,' Laxton said dubiously. He glanced down at his slippered feet and passed a hand over his own unshaven chin. 'I look a bit of a wreck now.' He even smiled.

He was so casual over the whole thing; there was nothing of the lover about him — no eagerness; he just spoke as if it were an everyday occurrence to propose marriage to a woman, as perhaps it was with him, Rodney thought bitterly.

'I'll tell Norah you're coming,' he said.

'Very well — thanks.' They looked at one another for a second, then the black sheep turned on his heel. 'Well — goodbye.'

And he sauntered back along the road. He was relieved to have an hour or two's respite; after all, it is only a very eager lover who can propose marriage before breakfast, even when the sun is shining, so Laxton dawdled over his bath and breakfast — stayed to write a couple of letters, and have ten minutes' argument with Meredith before he again went down the road towards the Ackroyds'.

He would not have cared had Norah's father been there; he knew he had got to get the interview over some time or another.

He was whistling a snatch of song as he turned into the lane. Norah saw him coming, and flew upstairs to her room; her heart was racing, and for the moment she dreaded nothing in all the wide world so much as the meeting with this man.

She looked at her face in the glass — one cheek and temple were bruised and swollen, but she had let her hair fall forward to hide it a little, and it did not show so very much, she told herself hopefully.

She supposed Laxton had only come to inquire how she was; it was hateful that she should twice have been hurt while she was in his company.

She went over to the window, standing a little behind the curtains so that he should not see her.

He was not hurrying himself in the least; as he walked he switched at the hedges and grasses with a stick he carried; she could hear the soft sound of his whistling; presently he disappeared round a bend in the garden path.

She moved away then, and sat down on the bed, with her hands clasped in her lap. Probably he would not ask to see her.

The minutes ticked by; presently Rodney called to her: 'Norah!'

She rose then and went slowly downstairs. Rodney was standing in the hall. He avoided her eyes.

She caught his hand nervously. 'Rodney — I don't want to see him ... I — ' The words died away on her lips as she saw that Laxton was in the doorway behind them and knew that he must have heard.

There was a moment's silence; then Rodney went away and left them, and Norah followed Laxton into the drawing-room.

He tried to speak, but for a moment no words would come, then he broke out awkwardly —

'I hope you are better ... I've been worrying about you. I want to tell you how sorry I am for — for last night. I behaved rottenly, but — but ...' He raised his eyes desperately; he had been staring at the carpet. He could have kicked himself for the strange nervousness that had seized him; he had imagined that he would be able to carry the situation with a high hand.

'Will you marry me?' he broke out.

Afterwards he could not believe that he had bungled the thing, or done it so inartistically; but Norah apparently saw nothing wrong with the manner of his proposal; her eyes were like stars as she took a little step towards him.

He seemed so wonderful to her; this tall, rather lanky man with the unhappy eyes; she put out her hand and touched his. 'Do you — really — want me?' she asked him.

It seemed to Laxton that the soft touch of her fingers reached his heart; he jerked his hand free almost roughly.

'Of course I want you,' he said. 'I — I'm not good at expressing what I feel, but . . .' He broke off with overwhelming memory of the day he said goodbye to Laurie Fenton. He had been eloquent enough then; his tongue had not felt as if it were tied in knots.

'You know what it means,' he said rather hoarsely. 'I haven't got any money; you're marrying a poor man. We shan't be able to live at Barton Manor, unless — ' He stopped, wondering what she would say had he spoken the words trembling on his tongue: 'unless your father allows us something.'

That had been the thought in his mind; a mean, pitiable thought enough it seemed beneath the happiness in her eyes.

'I'll do my best,' he added, with an effort. 'And if you feel you care to risk it . . .'

'I don't mind being poor,' she told him. 'After all — ' a little smile lit her grey eyes — ' after all, it would be rather fun having to cook, and mend your things, and see how little we could live on, wouldn't it?'

Laxton caught his breath. If it ever came to this, then goodbye to all hope of happiness for ever, he told himself grimly. He had had enough of poverty and pinching during the last five years to loathe the very mention of 'making ends meet'. The old man would be sure to stump up; Norah was his only child, and he thought the world of her.

'I should hate to bring you down to that,' he said, with an effort.

But she shook her head. 'I should be happy, whatever happened — with you,' she said steadily.

The black sheep flushed crimson; he turned away. 'I — I don't want you to think I'm better than I am,' he stammered out.

'You're too good for me,' he said, stammering a little. 'No wonder your father kicked me out ... Norah — what is he going to say when he knows?'

She shook her head. 'I shall just tell him I love you, and that I'm going to marry you,' she answered simply.

'Will you always love me, no matter what people say or how much they try and set you against me?' he asked.

'Always,' she told him.

'Thank you, dear,' said the black sheep humbly, and bent and kissed her lips.

'I've brought you a ring,' he said presently, with a touch of embarrassment. 'It's quite plain — a single diamond.' He glanced at her with a faintly apologetic smile. 'I meant to have you, you see,' he said.

He did not tell her that it was the ring which Laurie Fenton had refused to wear — the ring which had cost about ten times as much as he was really in a position to afford.

'I don't know if you like diamonds,' he added. 'If you don't I can change it.'

But he knew that she would like anything he chose to give her. He slipped the ring on her finger. Fortunately it was just the right size.

'Perhaps you won't care to wear it till I've spoken to your father,' he said again; but Norah declared she was going to wear it at once and always!

'It's all like some wonderful dream,' she said. 'I never thought when you nearly ran over me that day that — that this would happen. Did you?' she asked shyly.

'I hoped it would,' he answered mendaciously.

He went away soon afterwards. When he got out into the high road he squared his shoulders and drew a deep breath.

It was over; he was an engaged man. The first step had been taken towards the saving of Barton Manor; but there was still Mr. Ackroyd to deal with.

Meredith met him in the hall when he got back. 'Hullo — where have you been?' he asked. 'I've been looking all over the blessed show for you. There's a lawyer chap waiting to see you — in the library.'

Laxton frowned. 'Confound him!' He turned towards the library reluctantly.

A small, nervous-looking man rose from a chair as he entered. Laxton shook hands with him.

'What's the trouble now?' he asked rather ungraciously. 'More debts and dunning letters — eh?'

Mr. Moffat shook his head; he was smiling.

'Not this time, Mr. Laxton — better news this time. I am glad to tell you that I have found a purchaser for Barton Manor — a most generous offer — an astoundingly generous offer; and, bearing in mind what you told me when we last met, I have closed with it — in fact, everything is arranged.'

'You mean you've *sold* the place?' Laxton asked bluntly.

There was a look of shock in his eyes as he looked down at his companion's smiling face.

'I thought you would be astonished,' the elder man said complacently. 'I am free to admit that I had not hoped things would be settled so soon. As I have said before, it is a most generous offer, and one which you will be extremely unlikely to get a second time.'

Laxton looked out of the window to the sunny garden and the sloping lawn, with its shading belt of high trees, and for a moment a little pain gripped his heart.

He had said scores of times that he hated the country; and yet now Barton Manor was to pass from him it gave him a queer little sensation of pain.

'I'm not in a hurry for a week or two,' he said, with rather overdone carelessness. 'You can tell your client, whoever he is, that I shall have to think it over. Of course, I should prefer to live here myself if it's at all possible; it's a fine old place. I should like to keep it if it could be arranged.'

He was thinking of Norah, but it was impossible for his companion to know this; he merely stared at the black sheep with growing displeasure.

'But — but the thing is impossible,' he said at last, with undisguised annoyance. 'You have no idea, Mr. Laxton, what an enormous sum a house like this costs to keep up. And, if you will forgive me saying so, your income — '

'Oh, I know all that; but, all the same, I prefer not to decide anything definitely for the next week or two,' Laxton answered rather curtly. 'Who is your client? Give me his name, and I'll write to him myself if you like.'

'My client does not wish his name revealed. If you have anything you desire me to say — '

Laxton shrugged his shoulders. 'Oh, very well; if you care to make a mystery of it, I'm sure I don't care. At all events, please understand that for the present the whole thing is to stand over. Will you stay to lunch? Oh, very well — if you can't spare the time.'

They parted constrainedly.

'I'll write to you,' were Laxton's last words; he smiled as he watched the lawyer's offended figure disappear down the drive; he realised with a sort of school-boyish glee what a delight it would be to write to him with the information that Barton Manor was not for sale, after all.

Then he went back to the house and hunted Meredith to tell him about his engagement.

At lunch-time the black sheep was treated to a storm of good-natured chaff.

Dolly was inclined to be envious — Mrs. Durrant was obviously delighted.

'You've behaved very wisely — most wisely,' she told Laxton approvingly. 'It would have been a thousand pities if Barton Manor had had to be sold; and as it is . . .'

'It'll have to be sold, anyway,' the black sheep broke in hastily. He looked red and angry. He hated the way in which everyone took it for granted that he was marrying solely for money. He had hoped it had not appeared so very obvious. 'It's quite on the cards that we shall be cut off with the proverbial shilling, and then — '

'Then there'll be no wedding, of course,' said Dolly calmly.

Somebody giggled. Laxton pushed his plate away. 'If you're trying to be funny,' he began, in a temper, but she looked at him with wide eyes of pretended innocence.

'I! Try to be funny! I only meant that of course you can't marry on nothing!'

CHAPTER FIFTEEN

MR. ACKROYD came home that evening; he met Rodney at the door.

The elder man looked red and ill-tempered; he greeted his nephew shortly.

'Where's Norah?' he asked. It was always his first question, and Rodney was relieved to be able to answer truthfully that he did not know.

He followed Mr. Ackroyd into the house. 'You've got back earlier than you expected, haven't you?' he ventured presently.

Mr. Ackroyd grunted. Suddenly he turned round. 'Are you lying to me about Norah?' he asked bluntly.

Rodney stared. 'Lying! ... I don't understand what you mean.'

'Don't, or won't — eh?' was the growling reply. 'Look here, my boy, if you know anything you'd better out with it. You can't go on shielding her indefinitely, you know.'

'I don't know what in the world you mean,' said Rodney flatly, though his heart began to beat a little faster. 'If you mean that I know where Norah is, I tell you I don't. We had lunch together, and I haven't seen her since.'

'Well, I called in at the tobacconist's on my way through the village, and Anderton was there. Now, perhaps you can guess what I'm talking about.'

Rodney flushed. 'Anderton's a lying old scandalmonger,' he said sharply. 'I wonder you condescend to listen to what he says.'

'There's never smoke without fire,' Mr. Ackroyd declared.

Rodney pulled a chair forward and sat down. He lit a cigarette with unsteady fingers.

'Well, and what has Anderton got to say?' he asked casually.

Mr. Ackroyd came to a standstill close beside him. 'He tells me,' he answered, with the calm which, with him, invariably heralded a terrific storm, 'he tells me that Norah was up at Barton Manor last night, dancing with that fellow, that infernal young crook, and his London riff-raff.'

He glared at Rodney as if he were the responsible party, but Rodney did not even look up. 'I promptly called the man a liar,' Mr. Ackroyd went on. 'But, all the same, I am firmly convinced that there's a great deal of truth in what he says; and at any rate, whether it's true or not, the story is all over the village. A nice state of things! A nice — Why the devil don't you speak?' he broke out in fury.

Rodney shrugged his shoulders. 'You're not in a mood to listen quietly to me, whatever I say. I know you.'

'Listen quietly to you!' Mr. Ackroyd raved. 'Listen quietly to a bit of a boy young enough to be my son! If you know anything about this affair, you'd better tell me for your own sake, and — '

Rodney broke in impatiently.

'Very well, then, it's true — most of it, at least. Norah was at Barton Manor last night — and there was a dance! Laxton took her to the house, and I fetched her home.' He looked at his uncle defiantly. There was something sad in his eyes, but Mr. Ackroyd was too intent on his own emotions to be able to spare a thought for those of anyone else.

He began to splutter. 'She was — was she! And you dare to sit there and tell me to my face that my daughter — your cousin . . .' He stopped for sheer lack of breath.

'It's quite true,' said Rodney rather wearily. 'She went to the dance, and as far as I know she danced with Laxton half the evening. Look here, Uncle, you've got to look facts in the face. You must have known from the first, as I did, that Norah was immensely taken with Laxton. He isn't the sort of chap I should have chosen for her. But she didn't ask my opinion, or yours. You took up the wrong attitude over the whole affair — I suppose we both did. She's wilful, and the more we raved against the fellow the more she stood by him. And now — well, she's engaged to be married to him.'

Mr. Ackroyd was purple in the face; he stammered when he tried to speak. 'Have you taken leave of your senses that you stand there and tell me to my face that Norah is going to marry that young — blackguard? Do you know what sort of a record he's got, you young idiot? Do you know that I'd rather see Norah dead than married to him?'

Rodney had turned away and stood looking out of the window. For the present he knew that it was useless to try and say anything; but he was glad that he could bear at least the first brunt of it all for Norah; by the time she came in her father's first mad rage and fury would have worn off.

'His name's a byword wherever he goes,' Mr. Ackroyd went on at the top of his voice. 'It's a scandal that a young puppy like that is outside the law and can't be touched. His debts — he owes more money than you're ever likely to spend if you live for half a million years; if it hadn't been for old Snowden leaving him Barton Manor he'd have been down and out months ago.

'And when that's sold what do you suppose he'll live on? Not borrowed money any more — he's got no further security, not a pennyworth! And this is the man who proposes for my girl! Do you think he cares a snap of the fingers for her? Do you think he'd give her a second glance if he hadn't heard that I was a rich man? Answer me that, sir!' he stormed.

Rodney turned. 'There's no reason why he shouldn't care for her that I can see,' he said agitatedly.

'Oh — you!' the elder man struck in contemptuously. 'You live in a different world to a man like Laxton! Whatever my girl is, she's not the sort that appeals to such a man; if he spoke the truth — which he never will do! — he'd say that he doesn't care a damn for her — that if she hadn't a penny in the world she might go to the wall for all he cared.'

'Uncle!'

'Don't "uncle" me!' Mr. Ackroyd roared. 'I know what I'm talking about — which is more than you do. The man's a — a waster — a — a . . .' He stopped, at a loss for further words; he took out his handkerchief and wiped his hot face. 'He shan't have her — I'll take my oath to that!' he finished more quietly.

Rodney stood immovable.

'Norah must be out of her mind, too!' Mr. Ackroyd went on, when he had got his breath again. 'After the careful way she's been brought up, to look at an outsider like Laxton . . . Going to marry him! Is she . . . is she!' He laughed aloud. 'We'll see about that! I shall have a voice in this matter, I flatter myself.'

'You'll break her heart — she's fond of the fellow.'

'Fond — fond!' his uncle mocked. 'She's a child! She doesn't know what it is to be fond of anybody. You're talking like a fool, Rodney, though you are my own nephew. It makes me sick!'

He glared at Rodney's unresponsive back for a moment, then went out, and a moment later Rodney saw him stalking down the drive. He drew a long breath of weary relief.

He was afraid of what might happen when Norah came in; afraid that if Laxton was with her it would rouse Mr. Ackroyd to the point of violence. He wondered if it would be possible to go along the road and meet them and warn them.

He went out of a side gate and down the road. At any moment now they might be coming along. But though he walked a mile along the road he saw nothing of them, and he went back home anxiously.

But they had not come in — dinner and been served and set back half an hour, by Mr. Ackroyd's orders.

'As if I could eat any dinner with this on my mind,' he said angrily.

But the half-hour ticked away, and several other half-hours followed, and darkness settled down over the countryside, and the stars came out timidly in the clear sky, but Norah did not come home.

To both men it seemed that years instead of hours passed between the chiming of Lumsden clock. Whenever a car sped along the road in the darkness they both turned and looked anxiously to the gate; whenever a footfall sounded they both felt sure that it must be Norah at last.

'I'll never forgive Norah for this,' Mr. Ackroyd broke out presently in rough agitation. 'After all these years ... What is it —'

Rodney had gripped his arm. 'That's Norah's laugh — I should know her laugh anywhere.'

The two men stood in silence, hardly breathing. 'I can't hear anything,' Mr. Ackroyd whispered; they waited a moment, then —

'If Father isn't home I shan't mind a bit.' The words came distinctly through the night, followed by a little laugh, in which Laxton's deeper voice joined.

Rodney moved uncomfortably.

'Hadn't we better go back to the house?'

He felt very sorry for his uncle; he knew how Norah's words must have sounded to him; the two men went back through the garden without speaking.

The front door was open — Laxton and Norah were in the hall together; the black sheep was leaning over a chairback, his arms crossed on the carved bars, his whole attitude that of a man who is very much at home; he was looking at Norah and laughing; a laugh that broke off when Mr. Ackroyd and Rodney stepped into the hall.

But even then he did not look in the least disconcerted; he raised himself slowly and stood waiting for the deluge.

Mr. Ackroyd did not even glance at him — he looked at Norah and pointed towards the stairs.

'Go to your room at once,' he said.

'Uncle —' Rodney tried to interfere, but was cut short.

Norah flushed scarlet. She had always put up with her father's bullying ways with a sort of affectionate resignation, but it was a different matter now to be spoken to as if she were a child before the man she loved.

'I am not going to my room,' she said quietly. 'And anything you have to say will be said before me. You seem to forget that I am no longer a child.'

'Forget . . . forget . . .' Mr. Ackroyd spluttered, then suddenly stopped. He looked at Laxton.

'Very well, ' he said more quietly. 'I should have thought you would prefer not to have heard what I have to say to this . . . gentleman here.' The little pause was a studied insult, but the black sheep took it unconcernedly. He even glanced at Norah with a faint smile in his eyes.

'We may as well go into the library,' Mr. Ackroyd went on.

Unconsciously he had all the mannerisms now of a showman who is arranging to exhibit his wares in the most advantageous manner. When they were all in the room he took the big armchair by the fire and looked at Laxton with a sneer on his flushed face.

'Well, sir,' he said sharply,' what have you got to say for yourself?'

The black sheep shrugged his shoulders. He was looking rather tired. The whole affair was boring him to death. He thought Mr. Ackroyd the most ridiculous picture of an outraged parent he had ever seen, but he answered courteously enough.

'I took your daughter for a ride in my car, and unfortunately the engine broke down when we were some miles away. I did my best to tinker it up, but it was no good, and we had to walk into Didsbury. We got home as soon as we could. I am sorry if you've been worried, but — '

'Worried, sir — worried!' came in a roar as Mr. Ackroyd sprang to his feet. 'What the devil do you mean? I forbade you to come to my house, to speak to my daughter, and here I find you insolently taking her in your . . . in your confounded car.'

Norah broke in. 'I wanted to go — it wasn't his fault, and besides . . .'

He looked at her flushed face and indignant eyes, and his rage broke out in a fresh volley. 'You must be mad! No decent girl would be seen in this fellow's company. I tell you his name is a byword — I tell you he was kicked out of a town in America for cheating at cards.'

The black sheep moved then; his whole lethargic figure seemed to wake to life; he took a threatening step forward.

'That,' he said furiously, 'is a damned lie.' His dark eyes were blazing as he looked at Mr. Ackroyd's red face.

'And I repeat, sir,' the elder man thundered, 'that it is the truth. Unfortunately, I know more about you than I care to repeat at present. I know that you're a desperate man — that you're driven into a corner, and because you have to make a last rush to get out, you're hoping to make it by marrying my daughter. You think she'll be a rich woman; but you've made one mistake — you've reckoned without me. I'm no fool, and I can see your game, and I tell you now, once and for all, that I'd rather see her dead at my feet than married to you.'

He stopped breathlessly, and for a moment there was absolute silence.

Then the black sheep spoke; his voice was a little uneven and breathless, but he had himself well in control. 'If you were any other man,' he said thickly, 'I'd make you eat those words — every one of them; but ... but you're Norah's father, and so ... so I let them pass. I intend to marry your daughter whatever you say — if she'll have me. She knows my position — she knows just how little I have to offer her, and if she's content — '

'Content! content!' raved Mr. Ackroyd. 'Of course she's content; the silly girl thinks she's in love with you. Oh, you've been very clever — you've made yourself out a sort of hero — and she's taken it all in. Wait till she's lived with you for a week or two; wait till you've dropped this play-acting, and shown her the real man she's tied herself to.

'But you've got to deal with me before you get her, and I'm not a romantic sentimental school-girl, taken in by a rascal with a glib tongue ... I'm a hard-headed business man, and you'll find that you can't get the blind side of me. If you'd had the least spark of decency you'd never have done what you did last night and got her talked about all over the village.

'Such treatment may be good enough for your riff-raff friends from London, but it's not good enough for my daughter. I know a thing or two about you, my boy, and I tell you that if you come near my daughter again after tonight, or try to see her, I'll put the thumbscrews on you till you're grovelling on your knees for mercy.'

'Father!' Norah's voice cut in on his tirade with such a peremptory cry that in spite of himself Mr. Ackroyd was silenced.

His daughter was looking at him with flashing eyes.

'How dare you speak to George like that! You can say what you like to me — but I won't stand here and let you insult him. I love him, and I'm going to marry him whatever you say; and it's — it's cowardly to keep on hinting at all these things and never giving him a chance to defend himself. Why can't you say right out what you mean and let him deny it?'

Mr. Ackroyd laughed bitterly. 'Deny it! He won't deny it, because he can't . . . I'm sorry for you, my girl. But one day you'll thank me; one day you'll realise that you hadn't such a brute for a father as you thought; that I was only telling you the truth, and this man — ' He pointed a scornful finger at the black sheep. 'Look at him!' he scoffed. 'A pretty figure of romance — a — '

Laxton turned suddenly; he took Norah's hand and tried to draw her to the door.

'Go away and leave us,' he said; his voice was harsh and broken; he was at the end of his tether, and he dreaded lest he should break down and do something violent while she was here.

'It's all right,' he added, with a touch of impatience, when she tried to resist him. 'I'm not afraid of your father,' he added scornfully. 'Go upstairs — to please me.'

'I want to stay — I don't want you to have to bear it all.'

He smiled faintly. 'I'm used to being blackguarded,' he said carelessly. 'It's nothing to me.' He drew her out into the hall, and for a moment they were out of sight of the room.

He kissed her and almost pushed her from him, and the next moment he was back in the library with the door shut behind him.

'And now,' he said calmly. 'We can go on with this very interesting conversation. Do you mind if I sit down? I'm rather tired — we walked home.'

He dragged a chair forward and sat down, leaning his arms on the table.

He looked utterly cool and unconcerned, and for a moment even Mr. Ackroyd was conscious of a faint feeling of admiration for him; for a moment he lost his blustering courage and stared at the black sheep blankly.

'If you've quite done abusing me,' Laxton went on quietly, 'perhaps you'll state what are your real objections to me as a son-in-law.'

Mr. Ackroyd leaned over the table on the opposite side, thumping it with his clenched fist to accentuate his words.

'I object to you, in the first place, because you're a blackguard,' he said. 'Because you've got a record which any honest man would be ashamed to put his name to. I object to you because you've nothing but a mountain of debt to offer my girl. I object to you because it isn't in you to make any woman happy, and because you care no more for Norah than you do for ... for a hundred other women.'

The black sheep met his eyes unflinchingly. 'All this is very interesting,' he said coolly. 'But it seems to me that you're missing the greatest point of all, which is that your daughter wishes to marry me.'

'My daughter is no more than an innocent child, taken in by the first glib tongue she's ever heard. She thinks she cares for you because you're the first of your kind she's had the misfortune to meet, and because — ' He broke off, and a little flame lit his eyes; he leaned closer over the table.

'Look here, Laxton,' he said less violently. 'I'll make a bargain with you — I'll give you three thousand pounds down — in cash — if you'll undertake never to have anything more to do with my girl.'

The black sheep sat very still, staring down at the table before him. His face was quiet and expressionless, but he was thinking rapidly.

Three thousand pounds! — a lot of money to some people, perhaps; but to him! He looked up suddenly.

'I consider that offer an unpardonable insult,' he said deliberately. Rodney had been standing with strained attention, waiting; he drew a deep breath now, and passed a hand wearily across his rough hair.

For a moment he had had a very real hope that perhaps this offer would produce some good result; even now he almost expected Laxton to try and drive a bargain — to ask for more — but the seconds ticked slowly away, and neither man spoke.

Then Laxton pushed back his chair and rose. 'It's waste of time to stay here — there's nothing to be gained by further discussion. I'm sorry you've chosen to take this stand against me, but it will make no difference. I shall marry Norah — if she will have me,' he said.

He went out, shutting the door behind him.

The two men left behind looked at one another silently.

'Young blackguard,' Mr. Ackroyd broke out. 'I'll teach him to come his fine airs and graces over me; I'll — Why the devil didn't you put in a word? You make out you care for Norah.'

'Perhaps that's why I held my tongue,' said Rodney roughly. 'If Norah wants him, she'll have him, and nothing you or I can say or do will stop it.' He paced up and down the room slowly; presently he came to a standstill beside his uncle.

'The way to make children loathe the sight of sweets is to give them as many as they can eat,' he said.

Mr. Ackroyd looked up pettishly. 'I don't know what the hell that's got to do with it,' he began, then broke off. 'What d'ye mean, Rodney?'

'I mean,' said Rodney slowly, as if he were weighing his words very carefully, 'I mean that perhaps if she got engaged to the fellow —'

'Hang it all, she is engaged! Didn't you see the ring she was wearing? Well, I did, and I'll bet you a ten-pound note it's never been paid for and never will be. However, go on. What were you saying?'

'Only that . . . if there is no opposition — she might get tired of him; she might find out what he really is. She would certainly find out if he really cared for her, or only for her money.'

Rodney made his explanation haltingly; he wanted to help Norah — wanted her to be happy with Laxton if, indeed, it meant happiness for her to marry him. And yet deep down in his heart the faint hope existed that perhaps if all objection to the match were removed she might slowly grow to discover for herself the mistake she was making and the sort of man Laxton really was.

Mr. Ackroyd said 'Humph!' once or twice. He looked at his nephew searchingly.

'I'd like to wager that she never does marry him, with or without my consent,' he said presently. 'She's no fool, and she's only got to see enough of him — the man's bad to the core; and I know.'

'What do you really know?' Rodney asked interestedly. 'You keep on hinting at something, but you don't tell us anything definitely.'

Mr. Ackroyd grunted. 'All in good time,' he said, with an air of great mystery. 'I'm content to wait, my boy — you wait, too. But give my consent to this marriage I never will.'

Rodney made an impatient gesture. 'If you don't,' he said sharply, 'he'll persuade her to run away with him, and she'll do it.'

His uncle did not answer, and raising his head Rodney was surprised at the distress in the elder man's face.

'Don't say that, Rodney,' he said agitatedly. 'It would break my heart if I thought she'd do that.'

There was no bluster about him now; his usually red face was pale; Rodney knew that this was his moment.

'Well,' he said bluntly, 'I do think so. She's — she's fond of the fellow — it's absurd to try and pretend she isn't; and — and he's an attractive chap in a way — not the way you care about, perhaps, or that I care about,' he added hurriedly, as his uncle showed fresh signs of explosion; 'but women like him — they always have done! Why not give him a run? Let them be engaged and see what happens! It will stop the chattering in the village and put things on a proper footing.'

'Never! I won't consider it — I'm surprised at you for even suggesting such a thing. I hate the fellow — I distrust him. There's no chance of happiness for my girl with a rogue like that.'

'There's always a chance of happiness for any woman with the man she cares for,' said Rodney roughly.

'Confound it all — anyone would think you were holding a brief for Laxton,' Mr. Ackroyd broke out irately. 'What's your game, anyway — I thought you cared for the girl yourself.'

Rodney raised his eyes. He laughed mirthlessly. 'So I do,' he said, 'but I'm not such a selfish beggar as to try and prevent her from being happy.'

There was a little silence. Mr. Ackroyd cleared his throat vigorously. He was touched, in spite of himself, but he hardened his heart to the momentary softening.

'It's all bunkum — this eternal chatter about happiness,' he said irritably. 'Norah will be as happy married to you or any other man as she will be to Laxton — a thundering sight happier if the truth's known too, I'll guarantee. Anyway, I won't have him here — I've put my foot down, once and for all. He doesn't come here again, you understand, and he doesn't marry her with my consent, and so . . . Hullo! What do you want?' he broke off to ask roughly, as Norah opened the door.

He pulled out his watch and looked at it testily. 'Half-past eleven; you ought to be in bed and asleep. It's no use coming down here — he's gone, that precious admirer of yours.'

'I want to speak to you,' Norah said. 'I know he's gone — that's why I'm here. I want to speak to you, and if Rodney doesn't mind going away . . .' She glanced at him timorously.

Rodney turned at once. 'All right,' he said gruffly. He went out and shut the door behind him.

'Now, I'm not going to have any more arguments tonight,' Mr. Ackroyd broke out as soon as they were alone. 'I've had enough for one day. You heard what I said, but in case you've forgotten I'll say it again — you don't marry George Laxton with my consent, and you don't get a penny piece either.'

He looked at her frowningly. 'You understand?' he insisted.

'Quite.' She met his gaze without faltering, then she gave a little quick sigh. 'I'm sorry, Father, because I shall have to marry him without your consent then, that's all.'

Mr. Ackroyd looked at her, and a spasm of pain crossed his face. He had never dreamed that she would take this determined stand.

He half made an involuntary movement towards her, then checked himself and turned his back. 'Very well,' he said shortly.

And the silence fell again.

Norah's face was quivering. She loved them both so much, these two men; it was hard to be asked to choose between them, and yet she knew that her choice was already made.

Mr. Ackroyd took out his pipe and made a great business of filling and lighting it, but in reality he was not conscious of anything except the silence behind him. It seemed an eternity till she moved or spoke.

'I'm sorry,' she said then with difficulty. 'I hoped you wouldn't be so hard, but as you are . . . well, I love him, and I'm not going to give him up — even for — you,' she added in a whisper.

He heard the little quiver in her voice, but did not turn; then he heard her walk slowly to the door, heard her fingers on the handle, heard her whispered 'Good night!' and she was gone.

'Norah . . .' He thought he spoke her name, but in reality no sound passed his lips, he stood dumbly staring at the closed door.

'Let her go,' was the bitter thought in his heart.

He turned away from the door. 'Let her go.'

The grandfather clock in the hall was striking twelve; its heavy booming notes deadened the sound of his foot-steps; then he stopped with a little sharp exclamation, for Norah had not gone to her room — she was sitting there on the bottom stair, her head down-flung on her folded arms, her pretty hair tumbling about her shoulders.

Mr. Ackroyd stood looking down at her with a suspicious moisture in his fierce eyes, then he stooped and gently touched her.

She put her arms round his neck, and hid her face in his coat. 'Oh, I don't know what to do!' she said, sobbing. 'I love you both so much.'

There was a little silence, then Mr. Ackroyd laid his big hand on her tumbled hair, stroking it as he used to when she was a little girl.

'Shall we give him a chance?' he asked presently in a rough whisper. 'Will you forgive your poor old dad if he says he's sorry, and is ready to give the boy a chance? ... I don't promise anything, mind you,' he added, with a touch of his old fierceness as she lifted her tear-stained face; 'but, well, there — if he proves that he's got any guts in him — we'll see, we'll see. No going behind my back, mind you — no runaway matches or nonsense of that kind. It's all to be above board, and straight sailing, and you'll find that I know how to play fair, if he does.'

'Daddy — darling!'

She kissed him and Mr. Ackroyd kissed her in return.

'It's a bitter disappointment to me, and I'm not going to say it isn't,' he said presently. 'But if you care for the fellow, and he cares for you ... well — I married your dear mother for love.'

He blew his nose violently to hide his unwonted emotion.

'Now run along to bed — you look tired out. No; I absolutely refuse to say anything more tonight. We'll talk in the morning, and I'll see Laxton again ... Tush! You'll strangle me. There — there — run along, my pet!'

He kissed her and stood at the foot of the stairs watching till she had reached the top. She turned then, leaning a little over the banisters to whisper a last anxious appeal.

'Daddy — you won't have changed your mind in the morning?'

He smiled ruefully, shaking his red head. 'I'm a man of my word. When I say a thing I mean it. I'll play fair as long as Laxton does. Now run along.'

He waited till he heard the door of her room shut, then he went back to the library and stood for a moment at the window, drawing the curtains aside a little.

The whole world was wrapped in sleep — but over in the direction of the village a few lights still shone brightly through the darkness.

They came from the windows of Barton Manor, he knew, and suddenly he raised a clenched fist and shook it in the direction of the black sheep's home.

'As long as you play fair,' he said, under his breath, 'but, by God! if you don't!'

CHAPTER SIXTEEN

THE black sheep slept badly that night; he was over-tired, and his head ached, and he woke in the morning in a bad temper.

He lay on his back for a long time staring up at the ceiling and trying to remember what had happened last night; the remembrance that he was an engaged man woke him up thoroughly; he got up and began to dress. Meredith came to his door.

'Not dressed! We've had breakfast. The Durrants and the rest of 'em are going back to town today, you know.'

The black sheep muttered something that sounded suspiciously like 'Good riddance!'

'Are you going with them?' he asked ungraciously.

Meredith laughed. 'No, I'm not,' he said, frankly. 'What happened to you last night, by the by?'

'The car broke down and we had to walk home.'

'We?' Meredith echoed quickly.

'That's what I said — I was with Norah Ackroyd.' Laxton laughed rather mirthlessly. 'We were put through our paces properly when we did get home, I tell you.'

'The old man?'

'Yes — not that it makes any difference.'

'Of course not.'

'I suppose there's not much chance of saving Barton Manor, then,' Meredith said abruptly.

Laxton was brushing his hair vigorously; he paused for a moment.

'The Lord only knows!' he said lugubriously.

He threw the brushes down and climbed into a coat.

He looked at Meredith's back. 'I suppose ... you — you haven't heard anything of — of the Hewetts?'

Meredith glanced over his shoulder.

'Not a word. I'm going over to Didsbury some time today — I'll hear something then, I expect.'

Laxton gave a quick sigh.

'Come on — let's go downstairs.' He turned to the door. Meredith did not follow him — he was leaning forward looking down into the garden with sudden interest. When Laxton was out on the landing he called to him.

'George — here! Come here — quickly.'

The black sheep turned; he was yawning wearily.

'What's up now?' He sauntered back. 'What's the excitement?' he asked. He looked over his friend's shoulder. 'Good Lord! my future father-in-law!' he said softly.

Mr. Ackroyd was walking up the drive leading to the house. There was a sort of reluctance in his whole bearing.

The two men at the window looked at one another.

'It is the same Ackroyd,' Meredith said in a queer voice; 'the chap I told you about — the man my father knew.'

There was a sort of excitement in his eyes. 'What do you suppose he's come for?' he asked.

The black sheep hunched his shoulders. 'The Lord only knows! Perhaps he's thought of something he forgot to call me last night. Let's go down.'

He went down the stairs unconcernedly. Mr. Ackroyd was in the hall when he reached it.

'Good morning, sir,' said Laxton. His voice was a little subdued.

'Good morning,' said Mr. Ackroyd. The two men eyed one another suspiciously.

'Won't you — er — come in?' Laxton asked. He led the way to the library, held the door for Mr. Ackroyd to pass, and closed it. There was a little silence.

The elder man looked round the room critically; he had not exercised much taste in the decoration of his own house, but he knew a good thing when he saw it, and he was impressed by his surroundings.

Laxton drew forward a chair. 'Won't you sit down?'

He was decidedly puzzled at the elder man's attitude. There was nothing of last night's bluster about him now; there was even a faint trace of nervousness in his manner.

He ignored the offered chair; he leaned both hands on the carved oak table that stood in the centre of the room, and looked at Laxton with eyes that were somehow pathetic in spite of their fierceness.

'I've come here, Mr. Laxton,' he said abruptly, 'because I love my daughter; and if you can prove to me that you love her, too, and mean to try and make her happy, I'll take back every word I said last night.'

For a moment the following silence was unbroken; the black sheep stared at Norah's father as if he were a specimen of manhood he had never before encountered.

'Are you trying to pull my leg?' he asked blankly.

It was such an utterly boyish question that it would have brought a smile to the lips of a disinterested onlooker, but Mr. Ackroyd was in no mood to smile.

He looked at the black sheep, and his heart misgave him; was it possible that this man could ever settle down? — ever give up his rackety life, and make a good husband for any woman?

He broke out again almost agitatedly: 'I'm a man of my word, and I told Norah last night that I was willing to give you a chance. But you've got to play fair. The girl's fond of you, though you're the last man I should have chosen for her.'

'You told me that last night,' said the black sheep, with a faint show of temper.

'And I tell you so now again,' Mr. Ackroyd answered. 'But there's no accounting for a woman's fancy, or perhaps her mother would never have married me,' he added, in grim parenthesis. He raised himself from his leaning position and looked at Laxton.

'Well, what have you got to say?' he asked.

But for once in his life the black sheep was tongue-tied.

'I don't know what to say,' he stammered at last. 'I don't know what to think. It's — it's an extraordinary thing that after last night — '

The elder man cut him short. 'If you love Norah and mean to treat her well, we'll forget last night,' he said. 'I sowed some wild oats myself when I was your age, though you seem to have beaten all records that I've ever heard of. We'll let that pass for the time being. Well — what do you say?'

The black sheep looked away from his companion's honest eyes; he wondered if he looked as nonplussed and chagrined as he felt. There was an uncomfortable silence, thn Mr. Ackroyd covered the little space between them and laid his hand on the young man's arm.

'You make her happy,' he said, 'and I'll be a good friend to you. Is it a bargain?'

He held out his hand, and Laxton took it. He did not know

what to say; he hated being thrust into this position. In his heart he knew that he would far rather have had this man's enmity than his friendship. He could tolerate the one because he knew that he deserved it; he could not tolerate the other, knowing himself unworthy.

'I don't — don't want you to be misled at all,' he stammered. 'You say you know all about my affairs — perhaps you do; I've nothing in the world but a couple of hundred a year, which was left to me by my mother, and this place — which is to be sold. I'm up to my neck in debt and borrowed money, most of which will be paid off by the sale of Barton Manor. I've had two offers for it already — one from the old Shylock I owe money to and the other from some client of Moffat's — my solicitor. I — I haven't closed with either, because — well ... I suppose one always hopes that something will turn up,' he added forlornly. 'And that's all.'

'And that's how we'll let it stand for the present,' Mr. Ackroyd said. 'As you say — one always hopes that something will turn up.'

He turned away and picked up his hat from the table.

'Will you be coming along my way — presently?' he asked.

'I shall be delighted — if I may — of course.' Laxton was nervous and agitated; for once he had lost his self-control.

He walked down the drive with Mr. Ackroyd. They shook hands at the gate, and Laxton went back to the house feeling as if the end of the world had come.

What was the top and bottom of it all? he asked himself. Experience had made him suspicious of everyone and everything. He could not rid himself of the feeling that there was something behind this sudden change of front.

Meredith pushed open the door and thrust his head round. He grinned when he saw that Laxton was alone.

'I came in to pick up the pieces,' he said flippantly. 'What did the old dog want?'

Laxton laughed. 'He wanted to tell me that he withdrew his opposition. I'm to be recognised — pardoned — acknowledged as his future son-in-law ...'

He threw himself down in a chair and groaned.

'Can you see me playing the part, Hal? Can you see me on my best behaviour all day and every day? Can you see me acting the devoted lover to a girl I don't care a damn —' he stopped abruptly; his face flushed dully. 'Forget I said that,' he rushed on.

'I'm all right — after all, if I behave like a good boy it will save Barton Manor.'

'Ackroyd said so?'

'Not in so many words; but I think that's what he meant.'

'Lucky bounder!'

Laxton laughed mirthlessly. 'Think so?' he said.

Meredith looked at Laxton dubiously for a moment; then: 'I've got something to tell you, George,' he said.

'Fire away then.'

'It's only . . . well — Dolly had a letter from — from Laurie Fenton this morning.'

'Well?' the black sheep's voice had subtly altered. 'Well?' he said again sharply.

Meredith was not looking at him now — he kept his eyes carefully averted.

'Nothing,' he said awkwardly. 'Only — it's all a mistake about her wedding, I mean; it was put off at the last minute — she isn't married. I — I thought you'd like to know. I knew you'd have to hear sooner or later, of course.'

Laxton was staring out of the window. He roused himself with an effort.

'Why do you tell me?' he asked perkily. 'It's no interest to me.'

'No — no, of course, not. I only thought — '

'Well, stop thinking,' said Laxton rather brutally. He turned on his heel and walked out of the room.

The hall was piled with luggage. As he crossed it, Dolly Durrant came running down the stairs.

'Hullo, Georgie, boy!' she said cheerily. 'What are you looking so gloomy about? I've been looking for you to congratulate you. So you're going to turn into a country squire, after all, eh? I suppose you won't be allowed to have us here any more.' She made a little grimace. 'Never mind' — she laid her hand on his arm — 'you'll have to run up to town for a weekend sometimes, and then we'll have some good times.'

'I shall run up to town pretty often, I dare say,' said Laxton rather sharply.

Dolly looked after him with resentful eyes; then she turned to Meredith.

'Have you told him?' she asked. 'About Laurie, I mean.'

Meredith nodded. 'How did he take it?' she asked eagerly. 'Do you think he still cares?'

Meredith shrugged his shoulders. 'I'm hanged if I ever know what he feels,' he said. 'He's such a self-contained sort of beggar. However, it's all fixed up. Parental blessing and all. Barton Manor won't be sold if George plays his cards well.'

'Well, he'll do that all right, of course. Catch George putting his head into the matrimonial noose if there wasn't a jolly big bait.' She sat down and looked at Meredith.

'Are you coming up to town with us today?' she asked carelessly, though there was a trace of anxiety in her eyes.

Meredith shook his head. 'No, I think not; Laxton wants me to stay on here for a bit.'

She flushed. 'You're not generally so considerate for him,' she said jealously.

He looked half-amused, half annoyed. At one time he had seriously thought of marrying Dolly Durrant, but just lately she had got on his nerves a bit; she was so restless and changeable.

He took his hat and went out. He turned in the direction of the Ackroyd's house; he had never been there before, but he knew pretty well where it was from Laxton's description.

He sauntered on lazily; when he reached the end of the lane that led up to the Ackroyds' house he stood hesitating for a moment. He did not want to meet with a cool reception. He had none of Laxton's *sang-froid* and stoicism; he could not imagine himself carrying off an awkward situation with a high hand.

But he wanted to see Norah again; in a chagrined mind, he ranked her amongst his few failures. It would be stealing a march on old George, too, he liked pulling George's leg. He went on up the lane. Suddenly he heard Norah's voice in the garden. And the next moment she came round the path. 'Oh,' she said, 'I thought it was — ' She broke off, smiled at Meredith and held out her hand. He said that he really felt he must apologise for coming, but —

'You see, my father knew your father very well at one time,' he explained. 'I saw Mr. Ackroyd at Barton Manor this morning and recognised him; so I ventured to call.'

Norah flushed. 'At Barton Manor — did he go there? I didn't know.'

'He came to see George.' He paused and looked down at her. 'I'm very glad to hear it's all settled and that you're going to make George a happy man,' he said.

To Dolly Durrant, or any of her friends, his voice would have conveyed that he was bitterly envious of Laxton's good fortune, but it passed Norah by. She was unused to men who spent their time playing at love. She took a speech for its face value.

'Thank you,' she said. 'You're very kind, but — but it isn't really quite settled yet — ' She broke off, with a little nervous laugh. 'I suppose you know that my father didn't quite like the idea of it — at first. It's all right now. At least, I think it will be.'

'George told me a little,' Meredith admitted. 'And I am very glad to hear that things are all right. Barton Manor is a beautiful place to live in.'

She laughed. 'Oh, but we shan't be able to live there,' she said positively. 'I only wish we could. But George hasn't any money, and I dare say we shall just have quite a small house somewhere. I shan't mind though,' she added happily. 'And if I had to do it, I could cook and look after things myself quite well.'

'I'm sure you could,' he agreed.

They turned back together across the lawn.

Meredith looked at her, and realised afresh how pretty, how very pretty she was. Her skin was clear and a little tanned by the sun. He contrasted her with Dolly Durrant, and Dolly suffered; he sighed.

Norah looked up quickly; she did not understand him in the least, but she knew that he made her feel uncomfortable.

They were both silent for a few moments, then Meredith said suddenly: 'You know Laurie Fenton, don't you?'

'Oh, yes; but she isn't Laurie Fenton now — she's married, you know.'

'She was to have been,' he corrected. 'But the wedding was put off at the last moment for some reason or another.'

'Oh!' The little monosyllable sounded rather constrained. 'Are you sure?'

'Positive. Dolly Durrant — one of the girls staying up at Barton Manor — had a letter from her this morning.'

'Oh.'

'Of course, I know Laurie very well,' Meredith went on casually. 'We all used to knock about in a little crowd together last winter — Dolly and I and George and Laurie.'

'Yes.' Another pause. 'I went to school with her,' Norah added.

'Did you really!' Meredith looked interested. 'You know her better than I do then, probably?'

'Perhaps I did, but we were never great friends. I am afraid she thought herself too good for me. She was the prettiest girl in the school,' she added generously.

'She's not my style,' Meredith declared.

'I think she's very pretty,' Norah maintained.

There was a little flush in her cheeks. She wished he would not keep on talking about Laurie; she wished that the mention of her name had not given her that sudden little feeling of apprehension.

The gate clicked behind them, and she turned eagerly, but it was only Mr. Ackroyd.

He came up to them with a little frown on his face; he looked at Meredith with unfriendly eyes. Meredith introduced himself.

'I remember you years ago,' he said. 'You were a friend of my father's, but I suppose you don't remember me? My name is Meredith — Harold Meredith.'

'Bless my soul,' said Mr. Ackroyd blankly; he stared the young man up and down. 'Bless my soul! Of course! But how you've grown — you were only a little boy then.'

'It's a good many years ago, you know.'

'So it is; time flies so, I lose count of it altogether. And what are you doing here?'

'I'm up at Barton Manor — staying with Laxton.'

Norah was bending over Friday, patting his shaggy head, or she might have seen the sudden change in her father's face, the quick look of dismay; but it was gone almost at once, and when he spoke his voice was quite even.

'Indeed — well, I'm pleased to see you. Your father was a good friend to me — many years ago.'

'He used to speak of you — often,' Meredith said.

He was feeling more at his ease now; after all, he wasn't such a bad old boy, he told himself; he pulled out his case and offered Mr. Ackroyd a cigarette.

'A cigarette! Me! Not for the world! Ruinous things — perfect poison. I always smoke a pipe.' He felt in his pockets. 'Dear me — I must have left it in the house. Norah — your feet are younger than mine — just run in and see if I've left it in the dining-room.' He waited till she had gone, then he turned sharply to Meredith.

'You're a friend of Laxton's?' he asked.

'Yes — I've known him for years.'

'Have you told him that you know me?'

'I mentioned it — yes.'

'What else have you told him?' sharply. Their eyes met.

'What else? Oh, you mean . . .' Meredith shook his head. 'No, I haven't told him that. I guessed that he didn't know from the way he's been talking.'

'Good — well, you'll greatly oblige me if you won't mention it — for the present, at least.'

'Certainly; it's no business of mine.'

'I'm much obliged. You know he is engaged to my daughter?'

'He told me — yes.'

There was a slightly amused smile in Meredith's eyes. Mr. Ackroyd watched him closely.

'You like Laxton?' he asked then, abruptly.

'Yes — he's my best friend.'

Mr. Ackroyd frowned.

'And a man doesn't give his best friend away — eh? Is that what you mean?'

Meredith did not answer.

Norah came running back over the lawn. 'I can't find your pipe — I've looked everywhere.'

Mr. Ackroyd drew it out of his pocket. 'I'm sorry, my dear; I had it all the time,' he said rather guiltily.

CHAPTER SEVENTEEN

NEXT morning George Laxton walked leisurely up the lane, and through the Ackroyds' garden on his way to lunch. There was nobody about, and sun blinds were drawn like discreet lids over the windows of the house.

It was a hot day for early May, and Laxton thought regretfully of a hammock slung under the trees at Barton Manor, in which he had left Meredith, with a gin-and-tonic.

He had only been engaged four days — it seemed like a month! He went on across the grass and up the steps to the house. The door was open and the big hall looked cool and inviting.

Laxton went in.

There seemed to be no one about, but the drawing-room door was only ajar — he pushed it open rather impatiently.

Here drawn blinds and coolness greeted him again; there was a scent of fresh flowers in the room, and the long French windows were opened to the lawn.

'Well, here I am,' said Laxton. He tried to speak agreeably. He went across the room to where Norah was sitting, and, bending, imprisoned her with a hand on either arm of the chair. 'Here I am,' he said again. 'Punctual to the — Laurie!'

He broke off with a stifled exclamation, and for a moment there was a silence; then the black sheep raised himself stiffly and moved back a pace.

Laurie was looking up at him with flushed cheeks and parted lips; he could see the quick rise and fall of her breast beneath the white linen dress she wore; she rose to her feet, laughing shakily.

'You didn't expect to see me! No, and I didn't expect to see you — not here!' She spoke almost in a whisper, then suddenly she put out a hand and touched him. 'Oh, it isn't true, is it? Tell me, it isn't true?'

Laxton did not move. He stood staring down at the hand on his sleeve. It was like a dream — he wondered if he waited a moment whether he would wake up and be able to laugh at himself for the torture that was rending him now.

But the minutes ticked by, and he was still there — in the cool, shaded drawing-room, with the scent of flowers filling the air, and the song of birds out in the garden, and this girl — this woman whom alone in all the world he had loved and wished to marry, looking up at him.

Then suddenly he broke away — he put the width of the room between them as if he were afraid to trust himself. He tried to speak naturally.

'I didn't expect to see you — I had no idea you were here — I — ' Then all at once he broke out in a rage. 'Why have you come here? Why couldn't you let me alone? You threw me over — we said good-bye once. If you've come here to torture me again I — ' He stopped, he came back to where she stood and took her hand.

'No, no . . . I didn't mean to speak to you like that. Forgive me, Laurie — but . . . but I can't stand it. It's not fair to me . . . I've been trying to forget you — I made up my mind to forget you, and now you come here . . . If they find out — if they guess — '

His eyes met hers, and she cried out: 'Then it is true . . . I didn't believe it . . . I was so sure — sure — '

He laughed recklessly. 'It's true enough — if you mean my

engagement. You put the idea into my head yourself that day when you came to Barton Manor. You looked after yourself right enough, so why shouldn't I? You threw me up for Hewett because of his money . . . Well — I'm going to do the same. I've got to get something out of life; I've had little enough so far, God knows . . .'

He broke off; he passed an agitated hand across his forehead. 'What are you doing here? Who asked you here? Where is Norah?'

'I don't know; I haven't seen her. I've only just come. George — ' She broke down into weeping; not very bitter weeping — just the tears that a butterfly cries when it finds that the sun is setting, but it hurt Laxton insufferably to see her; he walked away again, his hands rammed into his pockets; presently he broke out hoarsely —

'What's the good of crying? It's your fault. None of this would have happened but for you. I'd have given up everything for you — you know that; and now because some one else has taken pity . . .' He laughed mirthlessly. 'Oh, for God's sake, stop crying. If any one comes in . . .'

'That's all you care for! You don't mind how unhappy I am — you've forgotten you always said you'd love me — you've changed in just this little time.'

'I've forgotten nothing — I haven't changed. You've only yourself to blame . . . Oh, for God's sake! . . .'

His agitated pacing had brought him again to where she stood, her face hidden in her hands.

A pretty enough picture of grief she made, and Laxton, with all his worldliness and experience, was too blind to see that there was nothing behind the picture — no real grief or love for himself, only a sort of chagrined anger.

He looked down at her with passionate eyes. His hands half went out to her. Then he forced them back and went on again with his restless pacing.

'It's not fair,' he said hoarsely. 'Leave me alone, for God's sake! . . . I was beginning to forget — a little. I suppose I can't hope to — quite . . . Norah — she believes in me.' He laughed mirthlessly. 'That amuses you, doesn't it? It would amuse me, only — somehow — it's pathetic . . .' He stopped at the open window, looking out into the sunny garden.

Behind his back Laurie cast an anxious glance at herself in a mirror over the mantelshelf, then she moved over to where he stood and clasped her hands round one of his arms, bending her cheek to his sleeve.

'After all, I love you better than you love me,' she said in a whisper. 'I broke off my marriage — at the very last minute — for you. I knew I couldn't marry any one — but you ... George, it isn't too late. You can tell Norah ... tell her that it's me you love. She must know that you don't care for her ...' Her hand stole down and closed about his.

'You said you would always love me,' she said again softly.

For a moment it seemed as if her voice were holding him — for a moment she thought she had won — then suddenly he wrenched himself free.

'No, no ... it's too late — I can't ... Even I couldn't do such a thing ... It's no use ... Oh, let me go ...'

He broke away from her, hardly knowing what he was doing; he went down through the French window to the lawn below, half blind with misery and his own desire to do as she asked, and take her back into his life.

He went on across the garden through the sunshine, and into the lane; he felt as if he could not put distance enough between himself and this woman. The old misery and restless longing had come back, and yet — in the midst of it all he felt that there was a restraining hand holding him — something keeping him back — something which he in turn dare not let go.

It was Norah — he knew that with a sort of vague realisation; knew that the happiness of her whole life lay with him to make or mar, and though he would have said that she was nothing to him, there was something in his heart to which he could put no name — which would not allow him to go back on her, or break his word.

If Norah had only been here at this moment! — He felt desperately that he wanted someone to stand by him — to give him a hand that would help him through the turbulent sea of his own desire — to make him strong enough to walk on — and not turn and go back to that cool, scented room where the one woman he had ever cared for ...

The memory of her as she had looked in that last moment rose up before him, and he half stopped — and turned his head.

But even as he hesitated — fighting with himself — Norah came running towards him from the high road, with Friday racing in front of her.

She looked up into his white face with laughing eyes.

'We went to meet you — Friday and I! — have you been here long? ... Which way did you come?'

'No — yes ... I came through the village. I'm sorry — I don't know where I missed you.' He tried hard to steady his voice, but it shook badly; a little gleam of anxiety filled her eyes.

'What is it? — oh, is anything the matter?'

'No ... no ... nothing. Don't let's go in yet — walk down the road with me a little way.'

'But I thought you were coming to lunch. I thought — '

'So I am — but we'll go for a walk first.' He tried to laugh. 'Don't look so scared. I want to talk to you; we'll go through the fields.'

He pushed open a gate on the left of the road, and held it for her to pass through. He was recovering his composure. Presently he drew a long breath.

'Well, and how does it feel to be engaged?' he asked with an effort at lightness.

'Marvellous,' she said joyfully. 'It's just marvellous.'

'I wish I could be with you always,' he said, stammering a little. 'I'm — I'm a much nicer sort of chap when I'm with you than I am when I'm by myself, or with anyone else.' He broke off. It was so impossible to explain himself. He did not even know what it was he wished to explain.

'I think you're nice — always,' she said. 'When you're with me I think you're such a dear that you couldn't be more of a dear, but when you've gone ...' She stopped with a little self-conscious laugh. 'Do you feel conceited now?' she asked.

But the black sheep did not answer. He was looking away from her across the fields, and for a moment his face twitched as if in pain. 'Anyway,' he said at last, rather hoarsely, 'you're the dearest girl I've ever met in my life, and I've met a good many,' he added, with a little touch of irony.

She looked up at him flushed and happy, and, struck by something in the hard outline of his face, she stopped and gently disengaged herself from his arm.

'I'm going to kiss you for that,' she said shyly.

She stood on tiptoe to reach him, and for a moment it seemed as if he hung back, trying to evade her, but the next he caught her to him almost roughly, kissing her again and again with a sort of desperation.

They were both a little flushed and embarrassed when at last he let her go.

'Such shocking behaviour!' she said with pretended anger. 'What would the villagers say?'

The black sheep laughed. 'They'd say I had surprisingly good taste,' he answered audaciously; there was a look in his eyes which set her heart racing happily; she loved him so much; she believed in him so utterly.

'I think we ought to go back now,' she said. 'If we keep Father waiting for lunch . . .'

Laxton agreed reluctantly; for the moment he had forgotten who was waiting for them up at the house; his brow clouded.

'Are you as happy as you look, I wonder?' he asked her a trifle roughly.

'Much, much happier, I think,' she said. She squeezed his hand and let it go. 'Now we've got to behave,' she informed him, and they went the rest of the way soberly.

As they turned into the garden, Laurie Fenton came out on the steps. Norah gave a little cry.

'Why, it's — Laurie! . . .' Her voice sounded rather dismayed. She looked up at Laxton quickly. 'I had no idea she was coming,' she added. 'I wonder if . . .' but she did not finish the sentence. She went forward to greet the elder girl rather reluctantly.

Laxton looked on stolidly. Whatever he was feeling there was no sign of emotion on his face. 'We have met before,' he said calmly, when Norah turned to him. 'I went up to the house before I met you, and Laurie was there.'

'You didn't tell me,' Norah said quickly.

Her blue eyes flashed an unconscious query from one to the other.

Laurie laughed. 'Didn't he! How very forgetful! Why didn't you tell her, George?'

He met her eyes steadily. 'I meant to,' he said. 'But . . , well, I had so many other things to tell you — I forgot.'

Norah flushed and the little cloud left her eyes; she was thinking of that moment down in the fields when Laxton had kissed her; she felt quite happy again as they went into the house.

Rodney and Mr. Ackroyd were both in to lunch, and Laurie at once set herself to be charming to them.

She ignored Laxton almost entirely, for which he was profoundly grateful. He hardly ate any lunch; he was thankful when the meal was over; Laurie's voice and light laughter got on his nerves; it was such an impossible position for him to sit at table with these two girls, as if there had been no mad, merry past before he knew Norah — no shattered dreams of happiness.

He gave a quick sigh of relief when the meal was ended; he wondered how soon he could make his excuses and get back to Barton Manor.

Mr. Ackroyd touched his arm. 'I want to speak to you . . . No, no — presently will do. Come to my study in half an hour.'

He turned away and the black sheep went out into the garden with Rodney and the girls

Laurie was walking with Rodney and talking and laughing as if she had not a care in the world. Laxton looked after her wonderingly. It seemed impossible that only an hour ago she had cried and clung to him so broken-heartedly.

'Are you going back to town tonight?' he called to Laurie.

'Am I — well, of course,' she answered. 'I only came down for the day to see Norah — but I'm going to invite myself for a week sometime.' She threw Norah a smile. 'You said I might, you know,' she challenged her.

Norah made no answer. There were some deck chairs in the shade under the trees, and she sat down in one rather wearily. Rodney drew up another for Laurie.

'It's as hot as June,' he said. 'Aren't you going to sit down, George?'

He never spoke to the black sheep if he could help it, and when he did there was a vague unfriendliness in his voice.

Laxton shook his head. 'No, thanks — Mr. Ackroyd wants to speak to me.' Norah did not raise her eyes.

She was sitting, leaning a little forward, her chin in the palm of her hand; her radiant happiness of the morning had faded; in her heart she was wondering why it was that until now she had never realised how much she hated Laurie Fenton.

Laxton strolled away over the grass.

'How tall George is!' said Laurie affectedly. 'I always used to tell him that he made me feel a perfect pigmy.'

Nobody spoke; Rodney coughed deprecatingly.

Norah was looking after Laxton, presently he disappeared into the house. He paused for a minute outside the door of Mr. Ackroyd's study with a faint feeling of nervousness. What was he wanted for? he wondered. What fresh disgrace had he fallen into already?

He opened the door with apprehension. Mr. Ackroyd was sitting at the open window in his favourite armchair; for once in his life he was not smoking; he turned when the black sheep entered.

'That you, Laxton? Sit down.'

Laxton obeyed, and for a moment there was silence, then Mr. Ackroyd said: 'I'm going to tell you something which I wish nobody else to know.' His fierce eyes searched the young man's face. 'Can you keep a secret?' he asked abruptly.

'Yes,' said Laxton.

'Well, I hope you'll keep this one.' He swung round in his chair a little. 'I've never had a day's illness in my life,' he said; 'but yesterday — ' He sighed and shook his head. 'Yesterday wasn't the first time, though it was the worst ... I was in my office — in London, when it came on ... I didn't know what it was then, but I know now that it was a heart attack.

'I've had 'em before, not so badly; but this one ... I went to a doctor.' He paused, and for a moment he looked away into the garden towards the little group under the trees.

After a moment he went on heavily. 'I'm not a dying man — don't think that; but I've got to be careful. He told me straight out that my heart's wrong — badly wrong. I'm an excitable man — you know that, eh?' he asked, with a sudden twinkle. 'Well, he warned me that I'm too old to allow myself to be excitable. I've got to go slow and give the young ones a chance, or he won't answer for the consequences ... Do you understand what I mean?'

Laxton stammered out that he was afraid he did; that he was sorry — very sorry.

'Well, so am I ... I don't want to die yet awhile — I hope I shall manage to hang on for a good many years,' said the elder man more cheerfully. 'But in case anything should happen, I want to see Norah settled down before I go. You think I'm a rum 'un, eh?' he asked. 'After all I've said ... Well, well, perhaps. I'm a dog whose bark is worse than his bite; but it all comes to this: if you want to marry Norah — if you'll give me your solemn word that you care for her and will be good to her for the rest of your lives — well, marry her, and I'll make you a present of Barton Manor and give you an income big enough to keep the whole show going.'

There was a long silence. Laxton sat staring out of the window; one might almost have thought he had not heard. Mr. Ackroyd was watching him keenly.

'Well?' he said at last; there was a sharp note in his voice. The black sheep got to his feet; he felt dazed with the overwhelming shock of it all.

'I — I simply don't know what to say,' he stammered at last. 'It's — it's so amazing ... I — I can't seem to take it in; such overwhelming generosity. I can't find any words to thank you.'

It was quite true; though this was the thing he had been working for, now it had come it left him dumb with sheer stupefaction.

'Well, don't try,' said Mr. Ackroyd shortly. 'I dislike thanks; I've told you before that anything I do is done for Norah, and because I want her to be happy. I suppose you're thinking what a blustering old fool I am — to swear blue murder against you one moment and then go round like a weathercock. Well — perhaps I've my own reasons for the change, Mr. Laxton.'

He rose to his feet; he looked up at the black sheep's flushed face. 'So that's settled, is it? You go and have a talk to Norah — but not a word about the other thing, mind you — you know what I mean.' He tapped his side significantly.

'Of course not; I'm only too sorry.'

'Thanks! I'm sorry myself, but we won't talk about it.'

The black sheep felt dismissed; he half-turned to the door, then came back.

'I feel that I haven't said half enough,' he said with embarrassment. 'I — I feel that it puts me in a very false position. Of course, I know that things have been said in the village about ... well — that it was money I was after.' His colour deepened; he looked again towards the open window. 'I assure you that that isn't so,' he added, with an earnestness that surprised himself.

There was a little silence; then Mr. Ackroyd said: 'Well, well, I'll take your word for it. Let me know when you've fixed up a date — the sooner the better.'

Laxton held out his hand. 'I'll do my best,' he said.

There was the barest possible hesitation before his hand was taken.

'I'm sure you will,' said the elder man.

He stood quite still till the door closed behind Laxton, then his face changed all at once. The kindly expression of his eyes grew ugly, and he raised his fist and shook it threateningly.

'You — young — blackguard!' he said, under his breath. 'You damned young blackguard.'

CHAPTER EIGHTEEN

LAXTON crossed the grass slowly to the little group under the trees. He hardly knew if he were standing on his head or his heels. He still could not rid himself of the conviction that soon he would wake up and find it only a dream.

He sat down beside Norah, wondering if he looked as queer as he felt.

'What did Father want?' she asked.

Her voice was a little constrained; she had had a bad half-hour since Laxton left them; Laurie had told of the old rackety days in London — of the pace Laxton had gone; more than once she began some little anecdote about him and broke off with a conscious laugh as if to suggest that she was treading on dangerous ground; there was a spark of maliciousness in her eyes now as she looked at Laxton.

Hers was only a dog-in-the-manger love at best; she had magnified her feeling for him beyond recognition since the moment when she heard he was engaged to another woman. Had she been able once again to bring him back to the old subjugation she would very quickly have cooled off and tried to hold him at arm's length.

She bit her lip with vexation when Laxton rose to his feet. 'Come and walk about,' he said to Norah; she looked after them with sullen eyes as they strolled away together.

'What did Father want?' Norah asked again.

She kept her eyes averted; she walked a little away from the black sheep; her heart was throbbing with jealousy of that past in which she had had no share — of which she could never know everything.

A cloud had fallen on her happiness, though she tried bravely to dispel it.

Presently he laid a hand on her shoulder, stopping her. 'What's the matter?' he asked. 'I've never seen you walk with your head down like that before.'

His face changed a little. 'What's the matter?' he asked, more gently.

But she would not tell him. How could she admit that she was jealous of Laurie Fenton?

He waited a moment; then, 'What do you think your Father was saying to me?' he asked.

'I don't know . . . '

Laxton put an arm round her. 'He was saying, "My boy, you can marry Norah as soon as you like, and I'll buy Barton Manor and give it to you for a wedding present." '

She moved a little from him. 'It's unkind to say things like that when you know they're not true.'

'They are true. He didn't say exactly those words, but that is what he meant.' He waited a moment. 'Well, I thought you'd at least be surprised,' he added, with a touch of chagrin.

Her eyes were shining now through their tears. 'He didn't . . . it isn't . . . oh, are you sure?'

'Positive — I . . . where are you going?'

'To tell Father that he's just the greatest darling in all the world.' He caught her hand, snatched a kiss before he let her go, and then followed slowly.

Norah was out of sight when he reached the lawn again — Laurie called to him.

'What's the matter? Have you been quarrelling?'

Laxton looked towards the house and laughed. 'No,' he said. 'We've been fixing our wedding day.'

He did not glance at her as he answered, but Rodney did, and he saw the treacherous pallor that crept slowly over her face; it seemed a long time before any one spoke, then Laurie said —

'Really! Don't you know the old adage about "marrying in haste" — '

'The exception proves the rule,' said the black sheep coolly.

He was half ashamed because it had given him such a real throb of pleasure to be able to hurt this woman, even if it was only a hundredth part so great a hurt as that which she had meted out to him; presently Rodney got up and walked away. There was an uncomfortable silence.

'Is Barton Manor to be thrown in?' Laurie asked then in a bitter voice.

'Yes.'

Her eyes dilated. 'You don't mean . . .' He turned his head and looked at her deliberately. She broke into a little, harsh laugh.

'What fools they must be to be hoodwinked by you!' she said shrilly. 'What blind fools — as if they couldn't see —'

He cut her short.

'That's enough ... I can do without these heroics.' His eyes softened unwillingly as he read the bitter jealousy in hers. 'It's your own fault,' he said more quietly. 'If you'd only said one word — none of this would ever have happened. A month ago Barton Manor could have gone to the devil for all I cared.' He shrugged his shoulders. 'Well, it's no use crying over spilt milk.'

She broke out wildly. 'You never really loved me. You couldn't do this if you had ever cared at all, George ...'

The black sheep frowned. 'For God's sake put an end to this scene. Do you think I want every one to know that I was once fool enough to believe in you?' He stopped. 'Here's Norah coming back,' he added urgently.

Laurie rose to her feet.

'I shall go now ... I wish I hadn't come ... I —' She caught her voice on a sob.

'Laurie — for God's sake!' said Laxton.

But he need not have feared; the sob was only a very good imitation, and by the time Norah joined them there was no trace of emotion on Laurie's face.

'I really must be going,' she said sweetly. 'I do hope you'll be happy,' she added.

Norah looked up at the black sheep.

'I know I shall,' she said. The little cloud had quite vanished from her horizon. Laxton flushed a little; he was feeling far from unhappy himself; he was surprised at his own eagerness to get Laurie out of the way; he suggested to Norah that they should walk to the station with her; he was not going to risk another *tête-à-tête* conversation.

They went back to the house to say good-bye to Mr. Ackroyd; they found him in the library with Rodney.

'What's all this about Norah's wedding day having been fixed?' Rodney asked his uncle roughly when they had gone.

Mr. Ackroyd looked up from some letters.

'It's true — I've told them to get married as soon as they like.' There was a little pause; the eyes of the two men met.

'But they never will be married,' the elder man added in meaning parenthesis.

Rodney stared.

'What the devil does that mean?'

Mr. Ackroyd got up and shut the door.

'There's a saying that if you give a criminal enough rope he'll hang himself in the end,' he said. 'Well, I'm just paying out the rope as fast as I know how. You should have heard him this afternoon in here — gave me his word that he'd do his best to make Norah happy! Word! He doesn't know what the phrase means . . . I don't know how I stood here and listened to his lying tongue.'

'But I thought' — Rodney looked utterly amazed — 'I thought it was all right. What's he done now? Surely he's had no time to —'

'No time!' roared Mr. Ackroyd, with a return of his old violence. 'No time! I tell you, this morning — only this morning, mind you — he was embracing that Fenton girl . . . I passed the drawing-room window and saw him with my own eyes — saw him standing there with his arms round her and her head on his shoulder!'

* * *

George Laxton lay asleep in the big hall at Barton Manor, sprawled inelegantly on an old settle.

It was a warm, breathless night, and the black sheep had come in an hour or two ago and flung himself down, where he now lay, with a feeling of utter weariness.

Meredith was still out, and it was nearly midnight.

Presently there was a step on the gravel drive outside, and Meredith appeared in the doorway; he had been hurrying, and was rather breathless; but he stopped short when he saw Laxton and stood for a moment looking down at him with a half-smile on his face.

The clock on the stairs struck twelve.

Meredith glanced up at it, then put out his hand and shook the black sheep by the shoulder. 'Wake up, George!'

Laxton was on his feet in an instant now, his eyes looked a little wild — he stared at Meredith for an instant without recognizing him, then he laughed.

'I suppose I was dreaming. What the devil —'

'Sorry to be so late; I ran up to town this afternoon to see Dolly and lost the train.'

He looked at his friend critically. 'Well — how goes it?' he asked. 'Father-in-law repented of giving his consent yet?'

Laxton laughed. 'On the contrary. Date fixed and everything.'

Meredith stared. 'What do you mean? You're going to be married?'

'True story,' said Laxton laconically; he lit his cigarette, and strolling over to the door flung the dead match into the darkness. 'Fixed for the fourteenth of next month,' he went on; then: 'Father gives us his blessing and — Barton Manor.'

'Rubbish!' There was a sharp note of disbelief in Meredith's voice.

'That's what I thought,' Laxton admitted. 'But, apparently, I am neither mad nor dreaming. We're to have Barton Manor for a wedding present, and I'm doomed for life to live in Sleepy Hollow.'

Meredith was looking at him open-mouthed. 'Well, I'll be damned!' he said at last. 'After all the old man's said; after all he . . .' He broke off, staring hard at his friend's back. 'How did you work it?' he asked interestedly.

'I didn't — I never said a word or did a thing. He sent for me after lunch today and suggested it himself. You might have knocked me down with a pipe-cleaner. But apparently it's all O.K.'

There was a little silence. Meredith walked away a step or two and came back.

'I suppose it's all right,' he said at last uncomfortably. 'No hanky-panky or anything? — I mean, the old man's not playing a double game — eh?'

Laxton laughed. 'What! Old Ackroyd! Bless your heart, he's not nearly clever enough for that. He's only an old gas-bag. He barks a lot, but it ends there — fortunate for me, perhaps.'

Meredith looked somehow worried. He joined the black sheep in the doorway.

'By the way,' he said suddenly, 'Laurie Fenton hasn't been down here, I suppose?'

There was the barest perceptible pause; then — 'Yes, she has; I lunched with her up at the Ackroyds'.' He turned. 'Why?' he asked bluntly.

'Nothing . . . at least, Dolly told me she saw her last night and that she said something about running down here — to see you, I understood.'

'Very kind of her,' said Laxton shortly.

He waited a moment, then: 'What are you driving at?' he asked irritably.

'I'm not driving at anything, only ... well, I took Dolly to supper at Marnio's tonight. We were just leaving the place when a taxi drove up, and Laurie got out with a man whom I could have sworn was old Ackroyd.'

The black sheep laughed. 'What rot! Why, he's been down here all day.'

Meredith looked relieved.

'Well, then, of course, it couldn't have been.'

'No — I know it wasn't. I saw Laurie to the station myself — Norah and I both did. I daresay it's some new admirer she's got hold of,' he added with hard bitterness. He shut the front door with a little slam, and put up the chain.

'I'm going to bed.'

They went upstairs together.

'So you're to be married on the fourteenth,' said Meredith as they paused for a moment on the landing above.

'Yes. I wanted to skip off to town to a registrar's, but the old man wouldn't hear of it. We're to have a peal of bells and a marquee and feast the yokels, and all the rest of the paraphernalia.'

He stood for a moment staring across the wide landing with unhappy eyes, then suddenly he turned away.

'Well, good night.' He went into his room and slammed the door.

Meredith waited a moment; once he took a step forward as if to call the black sheep back again, then he shrugged his shoulders and went on to his own room.

CHAPTER NINETEEN

THE next few days passed away uneventfully enough, though to Norah they seemed like a dream.

Every morning when she woke she counted off one more day before the fourteenth, and told herself that it could not really be true that such a little while was left before her wedding-day.

Laxton was up at the house a great deal; he took her out and altogether behaved in an exemplary manner.

'He's just — perfect,' Norah told herself again and again, with a little thrill of delight to realise how right she had been in her judgment, and how wrong her father had been.

Mr. Ackroyd was in London a great deal, and even when he was at home Norah was too concerned with her own happiness to notice that he seemed to avoid her. Rodney, too, kept out of the way, though sometimes she thought there was a little pitying look in his eyes when they met hers.

But she was to happy for the moment to worry about anything; life was just a wonderful unreality in which nobody counted except the man she loved.

One afternoon they were racing Londonwards in the train.

Norah had been chattering away happily enough, but a little shadow now seemed to fall over her face; she clasped her hands in her lap.

'Sometimes I think I'm really too happy for it to last,' she said, with a little tinge of fear in her voice. If I found that you didn't care for me — any more . . . I think I should die!'

The black sheep caught his breath. 'You're not to talk like that,' he broke out almost incoherently. 'I won't listen — I haven't deserved to be spoken to like that. I . . . I just hate to hear you say such things.'

'George!' She turned her head in amazement; she looked at him with bewildered eyes.

Laxton was quite white; he took his arm from her waist and went across to the other side of the carriage.

There was a little silence, then he forced a laugh. 'It's your fault,' he accused her. 'You started talking nonsense, and I must have caught it from you.' He held out his hand. 'Say you're sorry,' he said more lightly, 'and I'll forgive you. We're nearly in London, and if you look like that . . .'

She laughed at that, and the little cloud melted away.

'I'm not coming round shops with you,' Laxton said when they got to London. 'I'd do a great deal for you, but I do draw the line there. If you'll tell me where you want to go I'll land you safely amongst the dresses, and call back whenever you like.'

'You may come and take me out to tea at four,' she told him when he left her. 'And I shall want a huge tea! London always makes me so hungry.'

She was ready and waiting when he arrived to take her to the Ritz for tea.

'Oh, what a lovely lounge!'

The black sheep laughed. 'Haven't you ever been here before?'

'No — I hardly ever come to London, you know. Shall we sit here?'

'Anywhere you like; I . . .' He broke off; a man had risen from the next table and was coming towards them. 'George Laxton!'

Norah was a little way off; apparently the man had not seen that they were together; he was shaking hands with the black sheep.

'Wondered what had become of you?' he said again; his voice was rather loud and hearty. 'And how's the fair Laurie?' he asked again. 'And when are we to be asked to dance at the wedding?'

Norah was sitting down at the little table, pulling off her gloves. She raised her eyes and looked at the black sheep, all the colour fading from her face.

She had heard every word that the stranger had said to him. Heard, too, a great deal more than those words implied, and for a moment she felt as if all the blood in her body had concentrated in her heart, and then rushed away, leaving her cold and weak.

Laxton stood with his back to her. She could not hear his inaudible reply, but she saw the involuntary silencing gesture he made, and the look of embarrassment on his companion's face.

It was all over in a second, and Laxton was with her again at the table; but she felt in that little space of time as if she had lived through years.

'How is the fair Laurie — and when are we to be asked to dance at the wedding?'

There seemed no other sound in all the world now, except the half-bantering, half-friendly voice of the man who had asked that question.

She was jealous, bitterly jealous. How much was there in Laxton's life of which she did not know?

He leaned across and touched her hand.

'You're eating nothing,' he said.

He could not be sure if she had heard what had been said or not. He was afraid to ask. Norah forced herself to smile. She summoned all her pride to her assistance.

'I'm not so very hungry after all; shopping seems to have taken my appetite away.'

She forced herself to talk and be bright; but it was an effort; she was thankful when tea was finished.

'What shall we do now?' he asked as they left the place. 'Have you had enough of London, or would you like to see some more shops?'

'I think I've had enough; I really am tired; it's hot, too, isn't it?'

She was very silent going back in the train. Laxton asked if she had a headache. When she said 'Yes' he left her to herself. He sat in an opposite corner, pretending to read a paper; above its pages he watched her anxiously. Had she heard, or had she not? He could not be sure.

She opened her eyes suddenly and found him looking at her. 'I thought you were asleep,' he said. 'Is the head very bad?'

'No, thank you.' Try as she did, she could not make her voice sound natural. The black sheep hesitated; then he rose and went over to her.

'Norah, will you answer me something?'

Her eyes were closed again now, and she did not open them.

'Yes,' she said.

'Open your eyes, then.'

After a second she obeyed. 'Well?'

'Did you hear what Clarkson said to me in the Ritz?'

The blood rushed to her face; tears filled her eyes; she tried to keep them back — tried to deny that she had heard, but somehow the words seemed to choke her; she hid her face in her hands.

The black sheep made no attempt to touch her; he sat looking before him with frowning brows. Surely this was the most devilish bad luck! He would have given anything to have wiped out Clarkson's blundering words — to be able to efface them utterly from this girl's memory.

'Look here,' he said at last, with an effort. 'Will you believe me if I tell you the whole story? I've wanted to before, lots of times, but somehow . . .' He caught back a sigh. 'Well, I was engaged to Laurie Fenton — last year I . . . but what's the good of going back over it all? She wanted money, and I haven't got a shilling in the world; she told me plainly that I was no use to her and sent me about my business. That was before I knew you . . . I — oh, for God's sake don't imagine all manner of things that never existed!' he broke out passionately. 'I was rid of her before I ever — ever thought of you. Norah — look at me — '

He tried to draw her hands from her face, but she resisted him.

'You can't love me after her,' she said in muffled voice. 'She's so beautiful . . . Oh, you don't know how I hate her!' she broke out desperately.

'I've tried not to; but somehow — ever since I've known you I've felt as if I could just — kill her! The way she speaks to you . . . the way she looks at you . . .' She turned suddenly and looked at him with such heartbreak that he could not bear it. 'Oh, do you love me better than you loved her?' she asked him.

Laxton put his arms round her. He pressed her head down to his shoulder so that she could not see his face.

'I love you a thousand times more,' he said shakily. 'If — if you chucked me up this minute — I — I should never want to go back to her . . . Do you believe me?'

'I believe everything you say; you know I do. I always shall.'

He raised her head and kissed her. He found his own handkerchief and wiped her eyes.

'Don't cry any more. I hate you to cry; it — it makes me feel terrible. Sometimes I think your father was right — sometimes I think it would have been better for you if I'd cleared out of your life that night in the garden. I'm not half good enough for you.

'I — I'd give my right hand sometimes if I could cut out all that happened before I knew you. It's such an unfair bargain — for you . . . Sometimes I dread that you'll get disillusioned — that you'll see what I really am, and be sorry you ever knew me.' He was stammering; there was desperation in his voice. He let her go, and leaned his elbows on his knees, rumpling his rough hair with a gesture of distress.

Norah looked at him silently for a moment. There were tears in her heart still, and the dull ache of jealousy. Laurie had known this man before she had — had known what it was to be loved by him; nothing could undo that — nothing in all their lives.

She tried to put the thought from her; to remember only that it was all ended and done with — for ever! She laid a hand on his arm almost timidly.

'We won't talk about it any more,' she said. 'I love you, and if you love me that's all that matters.'

But she could not sleep that night for thinking of it. The time that was still to pass before her wedding day seemed all at once interminable. She turned her hot face against the pillow.

'Oh, I wish I had gone away with him and married him when he wanted me to!' she thought passionately. 'I should have been his wife then, and nothing would have mattered.'

CHAPTER TWENTY

NEXT morning there were two letters from old school friends, who had heard of her engagement and had written to congratulate her. They were full of interested enquiries and enthusiasm.

'What is he like? Do send us his photograph to see. And when are you to be married?'

Norah smiled over the words. She skimmed the lines and turned over the page where Laxton's name again caught her eye.

'... How funny his name should be George Laxton! Laurie Fenton — you remember her, of course! — well, she was engaged to a man of exactly the same name last summer! We met them down in Devonshire together one day. He adored Laurie, too! It was quite pathetic the way he used to look at her — just as if he could eat her ...'

Norah dropped the letter to the quilt. She felt as if the foolishly sentimental words scorched her fingers.

Laurie again! Always Laurie! A wave of bitterness swept through her soul. Was she never to be allowed to get away from the past? She felt as if she were caught in the meshes of a net which one day would close about her feet and drag her down from the summit of happiness to despair.

She went into the garden. It was a beautiful morning, but she had no eyes for the sunshine and the flowers. She felt weary and dispirited. She longed to see Laxton, and yet she dreaded their next meeting.

She tried to tell herself that it was unfair to remember things against him that were ended and forgotten, and yet she seemed unable to think of anything else. Could a man's love change so quickly? Only a few short weeks ago he had wanted Laurie, and now! ...

Friday, walking faithfully at her side, stopped and looked up at her as if dumbly understanding that all was not well with her. He whined softly, wagging his stumpy tail.

Norah knelt down beside him on the grass and put her arms round his neck.

'You're the most faithful friend, after all,' she told him. 'You'd never love anybody but me, would you?'

He licked her hands and rubbed his woolly head against her.

'What a very charming picture,' said a voice, and looking up Norah saw Laurie Fenton watching them from the lane.

She rose to her feet slowly, the blood rushing to her face, and for a moment the two girls eyed one another without speaking; then Norah moved forward.

'I was just thinking about you, Won't you come in?'

Her voice was quite unemotional, but her heart was beating fast as she opened the gate.

But Laurie shook her head.

'We were driving through,' she explained coolly. 'And I thought I'd run in and see how you are. You don't look well,' she added critically.

'I'm quite well,' said Norah stiffly. She glanced down the lane towards the high-road. 'Are you alone?' she asked.

'No — a man I know and his sister are down there.' She paused, then added deliberately: 'To be quite frank, I was going to take them up to Barton Manor. It's such a lovely place, I wanted them to see it — I suppose you've no objection?'

'Not in the least — but I don't think you'll find George Laxton there — he was going up to town this morning.'

. 'I know, but I phoned him up before we started, and he said he'd wait in for us.'

Norah caught her breath hard.

It had been a great effort to control her voice at all; she felt now that she was at breaking point.

Suddenly Laurie laughed.

'What's the good of keeping up this absurd dignity with me?' she asked. 'You know, and I know, too, that it's all rubbish — this engagement between you and George. He'd have married me ages ago if I'd been willing, and you know it. You can't be such a little fool as to really imagine that he cares for you? He wanted to save Barton Manor, and apparently he's succeeded, if what one hears is true.'

She shrugged her shoulders. 'If you're satisfied with your share of the bargain, that's all right — only it's absurd to keep up this pretence with me.'

There was a breathless silence; Norah was as white as death, but her eyes blazed.

'Have you quite finished?' she asked. 'Because, if so, will you please — go!'

Laurie shrugged her shoulders.

'Are you going to make a scene? Very well ... You can tell George what I've said if you like, and see if he'll deny it. I tell you that he'd throw you over this minute if I asked him to — but I'm not going to; you needn't worry. He's no good to me unless he's got some money.' She looked at the younger girl, and her tone changed. 'Don't be a little idiot,' she said. 'I'm sure I wish you good luck. George has always been a handful, but perhaps you'll be able to manage him better than I could.'

Norah struck her hand away. 'How dare you?' she panted. 'Oh, I hate you — I just hate you!' Her quick breathing seemed almost to be choking her, but she went on desperately: 'I wouldn't insult him by asking if he ever loved you — you're not worth loving. Perhaps you tricked him into thinking he liked you just for a while — but it's all over and done with now ... Go away — go away, I never want to see you again.'

She was sobbing now; great tearless sobs that shook her from head to foot, but her courage never wavered. No matter if her heart were breaking, she told herself that she would never let this woman know that she had lost faith in the man she loved.

Laurie turned away; her lips were set, and there was a hard light in her blue eyes.

'Well,' she said with a little vixenish laugh, 'you're not married — yet, remember!'

*   *   *

For some time after she had gone Norah walked about in the garden, hardly knowing what to do with herself.

She thought of the words in the letter she'd received that morning; even its writer had known how much Laxton cared for Laurie — even she had noted the way he had looked at her only last summer.

'Hullo, my dear!' said a voice behind her.

Norah started; she would rather have met anyone just then than her father; she was painfully aware that she could not possibly hide her agitation; it threw her into a fresh state of nervous apprehension because he made no comment.

He slipped his hand through her arm affectionately. 'Is the head better? I expect that day in London was too much for you yesterday.'

She felt an almost hysterical impulse to answer: 'It was! It was! Everything is too much for me! I shall die if I can't know the truth — if I can't know once and for all if he really does love me.'

But Mr. Ackroyd seemed to expect no answer; he went on talking unconcernedly. 'Where's George? Not coming up this morning?'

'He said he had to go to London — he was going up by the early train.'

'London!' Mr. Ackroyd echoed with faint astonishment. 'He hadn't gone half an hour ago. I met him down the village.'

She did not answer. She hardly heard. Her one desolate thought was that Laurie had spoken the truth.

'I daresay he'll come up presently,' she said, trying hard to steady her voice.

Mr. Ackroyd looked at her keenly. She was pale and there were shadows beneath her eyes. He released her arm and they went back to the shade of the lawn.

'By the way,' he said presently, 'you must let me know what I am to give you for a wedding present, my dear. Some personal thing I mean — diamonds, or — '

She cut him short. 'I'm tired of talking about the wedding. I didn't think it would mean all this fuss. I wish I'd done as George wanted and gone to London.' She tried to cover the weariness of her words with a laugh, not very successfully.

The morning passed away and Laxton did not come, and at luncheon time his absence was again commented on by Mr. Ackroyd.

'He can't always be here,' Norah said rather irritably; 'and I dare say he has gone to town, after all.'

'I don't think so,' said Rodney unknowingly. 'I think there must be some visitors at Barton Manor. I saw a car in the drive as I came along just now.'

Norah clasped her hands under cover of the tablecloth. She wondered how she sat there without screaming. Her nerves seemed to have gone to pieces all at once. A tortuous imagination had pictured luncheon in the beautiful dining-room at Barton Manor with Laurie — cool and beautiful — and the black sheep ... Who had spoken the truth? she was asking herself desperately. Who had lied to her — Laxton or Laurie and all these others?

She hardly knew how she got through the afternoon. She stayed in her room, unable to settle to anything.

'It's not fair!' she told herself in an anguish. 'It's my home, and I hate her being there!'

She had tea alone; the day seemed like a year; she was just finishing when she heard George's whistle in the garden outside. Panic seized her — she left the table and fled up to her room; she shut and locked the door.

Then a revulsion of feeling set in; she wanted to see him. He would go away and she would have to drag through the night without first having seen him, without even knowing if . . . Then came a knock at the door and a voice, George's voice.

'Norah . . .' She did not answer. He waited a moment, then called again: 'Norah . . . open the door — I want to speak to you — just a minute . . .'

She meant to say no — but she found herself turning the key in the lock. The next moment she had opened the door, and Laxton stood there.

His eyes scanned her face anxiously.

'Is the head very bad? . . . I'm sorry — I meant to have come down this morning, but some people turned up from London, and kept me hanging about.'

His voice implied that he had wished them at the bottom of the sea. Norah's lip curled. She felt as if some demon sprite were at work in her heart, transforming its love and trust into horrid doubt and suspicion.

'What's the matter?' Laxton asked sharply.

'Nothing, only I thought you said you were going to London.'

He answered at once. 'I know I told you so; but it was such a hot morning I decided to skip it and meant to come along and take you out instead. Then these people turned up. I had no idea they were coming. I couldn't be rude; the man was a great pal of mine at one time. He brought his sister — and . . . and someone else.'

Norah raised her eyes then. 'I know,' she said. 'They called here on the way to Barton Manor.'

The black sheep flushed crimson.

'Is that why you're angry with me? I swear I had no idea they were coming. I don't know why they came. I didn't mention Laurie was there because I thought . . .' He took a little quick step towards her and caught her by both shoulders. 'Norah — you're not — jealous?'

She looked at him with flashing eyes. 'Jealous! Of her? How could anybody be jealous of her? She's not worth troubling about. An empty-headed doll. Of course I'm not jealous! What an absurd thing to say!'

George's hands fell to his sides. 'Well, of course, if you don't mind,' he said uncertainly. He looked at her in silence for a moment, and was struck by the drawn expression of her face. His own softened wonderfully.

'Can't I do anything for you? Have you tried anything for your head? Come out in the garden — this room's so hot ... Let me do something for you ...'

'I don't want anything — except to be left alone. Do please leave me alone.'

She did not look at him, but she hoped desperately that he would not take her at her word; if only he would put his arms round her and let her lay her head on his shoulder and cry and cry ... But, manlike, Laxton thought she really meant what she said, and with an almost imperceptible shrug of his shoulders he turned to go.

Norah shut the door and locked it; then she fell in a little miserable heap beside the bed, burying her face in the quilt to stifle her sobbing.

'Oh, I didn't mean to be horrid — I didn't,' she sobbed desolately. She could not understand what had come over her; she only knew that there was a horrid doubt in her heart that she could not kill or even stifle.

And out on the landing the black sheep waited a moment, looking back over his shoulder eagerly as if hoping she would call to him; but the moments slipped away, and the door was still shut, and he went on slowly down the stairs.

Only another ten days to their wedding day. He wished it were all over; he hated the fuss and bother of getting married. He wished Norah had come out with him; that strained look in her face haunted him — he was sure she had been crying. Was it really because her head ached, or was there something else?

He did not think she was the kind of girl to cry for a headache; he would go back after dinner and have it out with her. Perhaps she had been angry about Laurie; but it was not his fault — he had not had the least idea that any of them were coming to Barton Manor.

He could not imagine why they had done so, unless it had been Laurie's wish to upset and annoy him. He scrambled through his dinner, and went down to the Ackroyd's again. He heard Norah's laugh as he went up the path to the door. He found her in the drawing-room perched on the arm of her father's chair, playing cards with Rodney.

They made such a happy group that for a moment the black sheep felt strangely unwanted. Then he went forward.

Norah had heard his step out in the garden, and her heart had begun to race in the old traitorous fashion, but she only looked up with a little nod and a smile, and went on with the game. The black sheep, stood by chafing irritably; her headache had apparently vanished — if ever it had existed, he told himself impatiently; he stood behind Rodney's chair and looked on frowningly.

When the game was finished they started another; he never had a word alone with Norah the whole evening. When he took his leave she and her father walked with him to the gate; she was avoiding being alone with him on purpose, he was sure; he felt lonely and dispirited as he walked away through the night.

He was hanged if he could understand women, he told himself — he had thought Norah different from the rest, but apparently ... he heard running steps behind him — he swung round eagerly.

'George ...'

'Darling ...'

'I didn't mean to be cross — I'm sorry ... No, I can't stay — Father's waiting ...'

'Well — you must kiss me. What was the matter?'

'Nothing — nothing now ... if you still love me?'

His arms tightened their hold. 'Can't you feel that I do without being told? And you're not cross with me any more?'

'I never was cross!'

'Good night, then.'

'Good night!' ...

He waited till her light running steps had died away in the night, then he walked off home whistling like a schoolboy who has been given an unexpected half-holiday.

CHAPTER TWENTY-ONE

'ONLY another three days,' George said one evening when he had walked over from Barton Manor. They were out in the garden together, strolling up and down under the trees in the dusk.

They had both been rather quiet, and Laxton looked somehow subdued.

Norah glanced at him and away again. 'Yes, only another three days,' she said slowly. She gave a quick little laugh. 'It's rather dreadful, isn't it?' she said.

'Dreadful!' He frowned. 'What do you mean?'

'Only that we can't ever get unmarried again, no matter how much we may want to?'

There was a little silence.

'That's not very complimentary to me, is it?' he said. 'Do you think that you'll want to get unmarried?'

'Well, you never know,' she defended herself. 'Lots of people find out after they've been married a little while that they've made a mistake.'

'Then we won't be like lots of people,' he said promptly; he slipped his hand through her arm. 'I hardly know you lately,' he said. 'I can't explain what it is — but you're somehow — different.'

'I think I'm getting afraid,' she told him almost inaudibly. 'Afraid of the responsibility . . . it's for all our lives, isn't it? And if — if it went wrong — '

'We don't want to moralise just now, anyway,' he said, with change of voice. 'What are you going to do tomorrow?'

'Have you to lunch — if you'll come.'

'Tomorrow . . .' He hesitated. 'I was going to town, but — '

'Oh, it doesn't matter . . . if it's very important . . .'

She waited breathlessly for him to answer; when at last he did, his voice sounded constrained.

'It is — rather important; but if you'd like me to put it off . . .'

'Of course not. What is this wonderful business?'

'You wouldn't be interested if I told you.'

There was a little silence.

'I'll see you tomorrow evening, then, I suppose?' she said presently.

He seemed to avoid her eyes, she thought.

'If I get back in time, of course! I may be late.'

Did he love her, or did he not? She lay awake with the same doubt going round and round in her brain like a fiery wheel.

Where was he going tomorrow? Surely it would only have been a natural thing for him to have told her.

She was up early in the morning; she was out in the garden when the postman came; there was a batch of letters for her, but she only looked at the top one — addressed in Laurie Fenton's writing.

She tore it open with angry fingers; how dared Laurie write to her after all that had occurred?

DEAR NORAH,
I daresay you will be surprised to hear from me, but I've been thinking things over since last I saw you, and though you may not believe it, I'm sorry for being such a cat. I've bought you a little wedding present, and hope you will accept it. Couldn't you run up tomorrow and have tea with me? I am leaving London soon, and it will be our last chance to meet for some time. Do come — I wish it so very much.

Yours affectionately,
LAURIE FENTON

Norah rubbed her eyes; she could hardly believe she had read aright; it was so unlike Laurie — such a humble appeal!

And like a flash another thought came to her; this settled her doubts about George at all events; wherever he was going, it was certainly not to Laurie's. Her spirits went up like rockets; after all she could afford to forgive Laurie — she would do as she asked and go. She had an early lunch and went up to town; she was glad to be making it up with Laurie before her wedding day; she hated to quarrel with anyone; she was quite willing to forget the past ... But when she reached the house she began to feel nervous; she almost wished she had not come; when the drawing-room door was opened she felt an insane desire to turn and run away.

But Laurie was there, coming towards her with out-stretched hands; she was beautifully dressed as usual.

'I'm so glad you've come ... it's so sweet of you. I just hate quarrelling with anyone ... I know I behaved like a perfect little beast — but ... well, we won't talk any more about it,' she sighed pensively. 'Lucky girl to be so happy.'

Norah did not answer; she hardly knew what to say; she tried hard to believe that Laurie was sincere, but somehow she could not. Tea was brought, and an uncomfortable *tête-à tête* followed; Laurie talked of the wedding the whole time — what was Norah going to wear? Where was she going for a honeymoon? ...

Norah answered as best she could, but she resented the many questions; she wished again that she had not come.

As soon as tea was ended she rose to go; she said she must get back, that there was so much to see to.

Laurie glanced at the clock with dismay.

'But it's so early — do stay a little longer; I . . .' She broke off, looking towards the door. Outside in the hall were voices and a footstep; a maid entered.

'Mr. Laxton, miss . . .'

There was a moment's unbroken silence; Norah had risen to her feet; every drop of colour had drained from her face; she stood as if turned to stone, staring — staring at the other's beautiful callous face.

Laurie moved forward a step.

'Ask him to wait — show him into the morning-room.'

When the door had closed she turned to Norah; there was something cruel in the expression of her eyes.

'I'm sorry — I had no idea . . . he said he wouldn't be here till five. He begged so hard to be allowed to come and say goodbye. I thought you'd have gone before he came . . .'

Norah was deathly white; there was a terrible look of shock in her eyes; for a moment she could not answer, then she took a little swaying step forward.

'Don't let him see me; don't let him know I'm here. Oh, I beg of you, don't let him know — don't ever tell him. I can go before he sees me . . . Please — please . . .'

Her voice was only a whisper — she was white to the lips.

Laurie hesitated. 'You don't look fit to go alone . . . Hadn't you better . . . Oh, very well — if you really mean it . . .'

She opened the door; there was nobody in the hall, but both girls saw the hat flung down on a chair, and a wave of utter despair swept over Norah's soul.

How many times had he been here? she wondered — how many times had he lied to her and deceived her? . . .

Laurie spoke to her again, but she did not hear; she went out of the door and into the street, blind and dazed with misery.

She never knew how she got home; it all seemed an unending nightmare till she found herself again on Lumsden platform.

It was early evening then. The sun was setting over the fields as Norah walked through the little village. She felt as if there were leaden weights chained to her feet, dragging her down; as if a cruel hand had torn her heart from her body and given her in place a throbbing mass of nerves.

There was no possible excuse to be made for him this time, at any rate. She had seen for herself; she had proof at last.

She almost ran as she passed Barton Manor. She could not bear to look at it. She only wanted to get home — to shut herself up from everyone.

She had turned into the lane when she ran into Harold Meredith. He was sauntering along, switching at the hedges with a cane. He brightened considerably when he saw her.

'George is in town . . .'

'I know.' She summoned all her pride to look and speak calmly; she even smiled at him.

'You do look disconsolate . . . Won't you come back with me?' She did not want him, but the words seemed forced from her.

'Delighted!' He turned to walk beside her.

He looked at her admiringly. 'You look marvellous,' he said enthusiastically. Have you been to town too?'

'No — yes — but not with — with George.' There was a note of constraint in her voice. She looked away from him.

'It's wonderful how things come about, isn't it?' Meredith went on ruminatingly. 'I never thought when I came down here that I should stay on and see George married — never thought, the night of that dance, that I should lose my bet.' He chuckled. 'George has told you all about that bet, of course?'

She forced herself to smile at him. 'No! no, he didn't . . . Do tell me.'

Meredith saw no harm in repeating the story. As a matter of fact, he thought it was rather fine of him to tell it against himself, as it were.

'Well, it was like this,' he began. 'I bet George a fiver he couldn't get you to come to the dance. As a matter of fact,' he added in candid parenthesis, 'I was dead sure he couldn't. I didn't really believe him when he said that it was all fixed up between you two already, or I should never have made the bet. And, of course, he won.'

'Now how do you mean that he told you it was — was all "fixed up already"?' Norah asked. Her voice sounded flat and expressionless.

Meredith looked apologetic.

'Perhaps I oughtn't to have let it out,' he admitted with a little laugh. 'Old George told me the first night I came down to

Lumsden, in fact — that you and he were going to be married — only — er — well, he asked me to keep it to myself, as he said your father wasn't quite as pleased about it as he'd hoped.'

He was too engrossed in the telling of his story to notice the silence with which it was received.

'I always knew Laxton would fall on his feet,' he rattled on. 'Some fellows are made that way. No end of bad luck to start with, and then — hey! everything comes right, like it does in story books. Of course, he made out that he didn't care about Lumsden, and that he was glad he couldn't afford to keep the house up, but I knew it was bluff; from the first it's been his one idea to save the place, and I don't blame him.'

They had reached the front door now. Norah led the way into the hall.

'I expect everybody is out,' she said. 'If you'll just wait while I take off my coat.'

She ran upstairs. She took off her coat and changed her dress. She felt still as if she were moving in a dream . . . 'All along it's been his one idea to save the place . . .'

So she had only been a means to an end. Any other woman with money would have done equally well. She had wondered at his love for her — now she wondered no longer, because it had never existed.

As she stood at the dressing-table brushing her hair a ray of sunlight from the garden caught the diamond of her ring.

She found herself wondering if, perhaps, it was the same ring he had given to Laurie — last summer!

She went down again to Meredith.

'Perhaps you'll stay to dinner,' she said.

'I should like to — like to awfully; but I think I ought to get back in case George turns up. He said he might be late, but I don't somehow think he will.'

Norah gave a queer little laugh.

'I do,' she said. 'I don't think you need expect him to dinner.'

But Meredith would not be persuaded. 'Perhaps if George is strolling up after dinner, he'll let me come along, too,' he said as he bade her goodbye.

She stood at the door till he was out of sight. She felt numbed and lifeless.

George was with Laurie now — he and she were together. She could not bear it — she could not . . .

Rodney and she had begun dinner before Mr. Ackroyd came in from town. He had missed his usual train, he explained.

'By the way, I came down with Laxton,' he said. He seemed to avoid his daughter's eyes.

'Did you? What time was that?'

Mr. Ackroyd looked at his watch. 'We caught the seven-ten,' he said. 'I asked him to come along and have some dinner, but he wouldn't.'

'He'll come along later I expect,' Rodney said.

'No, I don't think so.' Mr. Ackroyd was helping himself to wine. 'He said he was busy — letters to write and so forth — said he should come along tomorrow.'

So he would not come! It seemed the last straw to Norah that he could not even give her this small attention; not that she wanted him — now! — but . . . the day after tomorrow was their wedding day!

She thought of the pile of invitations that had been sent out — the shower of presents that had been arriving during the week, and for a moment the farce of it all turned her sick.

How everyone must be laughing! All those people who had warned her against Laxton. How could she ever face them again — how could she bear it?

After dinner she went and sat out in the garden; presently Rodney followed; he drew up a chair beside her. He heard her catch her breath in the darkness.

'A penny for your happy thoughts,' he said a little wistfully.

'Oh, Rodney — don't!' she said, with such a ring of pain in her voice that for a moment he was silent.

Suddenly he turned to her. 'Norah — if there is anything wrong . . .'

She broke in quickly. 'No — no . . . there's nothing, nothing.'

Her voice was feverish in its anxiety. Presently she got up and left him there alone.

She looked in at the library to say 'Good night' to her father. She excused herself on the old plea of headache. She was thankful that he did not try to detain her or ask questions.

She made no attempt to undress; she sat down in the darkness by the open window and looked out towards Barton Manor.

What was she to do — what could she do?

He did not love her — she knew that now. How, then, could

she go on with this wedding? How could she tie herself to him for the rest of her life?

Down in the garden she could hear Rodney pacing up and down on the gravel path. He stopped beneath her window, and she heard his voice through the night.

'Have you gone to bed, Norah?'

'Yes — I'm tired.' The pacing began again.

Lumsden Church clock struck nine ... only nine! All those hours and hours of darkness to be dragged through.

She leaned her head on the sill, folding her arms about it.

If only she could fall asleep and wake again to find it was not true; if she could only wipe out the past weeks — the hours of her great happiness and these last days of ever-growing disillusionment and misery.

Even yesterday he had lied to her when they came down from London together; he had said that if he were free he would not go back to Laurie — and he had not even waited for his freedom!

She began to cry softly — she did not know what to do. She was afraid of her father — afraid of Rodney, and there was no one else to whom she might turn or in whom she could confide.

It was all over — the wonderful dream of happiness; the thought drove her to her feet and sent her pacing the room. She could not bear it; she could not — she must see him once more — see him tonight.

She leaned from the window and called softly to Rodney. 'Rodney — wait for me; I'm coming down, after all.'

She was breathless when she reached him — she began to speak urgently.

'Rodney — I want to go to Barton Manor — will you come with me?'

'To Barton Manor — now? ... It's so late ...'

'I know — I know ... but I must go — I must.'

'Something is the matter. I knew there was ... Is Laxton —'

'No, no — it's nothing — nothing. He hasn't done anything; but I want to see him. I can't sleep if I don't see him just for a minute. I won't stay — and you can come with me. Rodney — please!'

There was a little silence. He seemed to feel the depths of her agitation, though he could not see her face.

She laid her hand on his. Already she was moving off across the garden, and Rodney followed.

Once she stumbled a little, and he caught her arm. 'Norah — if anything's wrong ... Why can't you tell me? Can't you trust me? You know I'd do anything — anything in the world.'

'I know — I know — but there isn't anything you can do — nothing at all.' But she let him hold her arm — there was a comforting sense of protection in his clasp.

When they reached the high road —

'We'll go through the garden,' she said. 'I know the way — the way we came the night of that dance, when you followed us and were so angry ... Do you remember, Rodney?' She laughed shakily.

'I'm not likely to forget,' he answered gruffly. He fumbled for the latch and pushed the gate wide. 'I think it would be better if you waited till tomorrow,' he said agitatedly. 'Things always look different in the morning, and if you ...'

She broke down then. 'This will never look different — never — never!' she said wildly, then tried to cover her words. 'Oh, I don't mean that — don't ask me, Rodney — I can't tell you anything — I can't ...'

But he still tried to hold her back. 'Norah, don't do anything hasty; there are always two sides to every question. You can't judge George by yourself. If it's anything you've heard or been told ...' He had no more idea than the dead what was distressing her, though he was doing his best to help and advise; but she would not listen.

They went round to the back of the house, it was a warm night and the long windows of a room leading out on to the terrace were wide open, the light from within flooding the garden in straight, slanting rays.

Through the silence they suddenly heard Laxton laugh — such a joyous, spontaneous laugh it sounded, that for a moment Norah's heart died within her. Was she — oh, was she mistaken? Would it be better to do as Rodney said, and go back home? But again throbbing jealousy urged her on — she went up the terrace steps.

They could see into the room now — see the long green billiard table, with its thick mahogany legs and the shaded lights above — see, too, the men who were playing; Meredith, sprawling inelegantly across a corner, preparing to make a stroke, and the black sheep lolling against the mantelshelf, a glass of whisky-and-soda in his hand.

'Bet you a pound you miss it,' he said suddenly. His words

reached the two out on the terrace distinctly. 'Bet you — '

Laxton looked so careless and debonair. He drained his whisky and set the glass down on the shelf behind him; then he took up the chalk and calmly began chalking his cue.

'Another twenty-four hours, my boy,' Meredith said. 'And then — '

'And then I shall be led like a lamb to the slaughter,' Laxton finished for him, with mock tragedy. 'Lord above! Shan't I be jolly glad when it's all over! ... Whew! ...' He ran his fingers through his rough hair with pretended despair.

Meredith chuckled.

'Lot you've got to grumble about,' he said, 'Barton Manor and a fat income, and — ' He broke off, swinging sharply round as Norah stepped into the room through the long French window.

She seemed unconscious of Meredith's presence; her eyes went straight to the black sheep, as for a moment he stood quite still, staring at her in blank surprise; then he dropped his cue with a little clatter to the floor and went forward.

'Norah! ...'

She waved him away when he would have touched her; for the first time she seemed to realise that he was not alone; she looked at Meredith: 'Please — I want to speak to George.'

'All right — I'm going ...' Meredith caught up his coat and beat a hasty retreat through the window, closing it behind him. Norah and George were left alone.

The black sheep took an impulsive step towards her. 'What a surprise — I — Norah ...'

'Oh, please, please leave me alone!' There was a little catch in her voice — her eyes looked wild. After a moment she went on more calmly —

'I'm sorry to bother you — but I — just — had to come. Rodney came with me — I asked him to wait outside.'

'But why not bring him in? Is anything the matter? Why do you look like that?'

Twice she tried to speak, but no words would come; then at last she asked him, hoarsely — 'Will you ... will you tell me where ... where you were — this afternoon?'

'This afternoon? ... You know — I told you — I went to London — I came down in the same train as your father.'

'I know — I know, but ... oh, how you've lied to me!' She broke out with sudden wildness; she hardly knew what she was saying, she had lost all control of herself; her face was deathly white, and her eyes seemed to burn. 'I know where you were, even though you won't tell me — you never would have told me; you think that anything is good enough to put me off with; you thought I should believe you whatever you said ... but I know — I know ... and I'll never believe in you again — ever, as long as I live!'

'Norah — for God's sake ...'

He seemed to realise suddenly that this was tragic seriousness; he caught her roughly by her arms — trying to read her face. 'What do you mean? You must be mad.'

'Mad, am I?' she laughed hysterically; she wrenched herself free of him. 'And if I am it's your fault ...' She stopped for a moment, panting, then went on again, her voice all strangled and broken.

'Oh, I believed in you, in spite of what they all said — you know I did. I'd have done anything for you — anything — I'd have gone with you anywhere — anywhere — I shouldn't have minded being poor — I wouldn't have minded having no friends or anything — if I'd only had you ... and all the time — all the time — you never wanted me — you never cared for me.'

The black sheep stood motionless, his hands were clenched, his eyes fixed on her face. Presently he broke out disconnectedly —

'You told me once that you'd always believe in me — that you'd always love me — whatever people said ... Somebody's been trying to make mischief — telling you lies.'

She turned on him passionately. 'It's *you* who've been telling me lies. You who said you didn't care for Laurie — that it was all over and done with — and I believed you. You said you never wanted to see her again — and you've been with her all this afternoon.'

'It's a lie — whoever told you —'

She looked at him, her face all twisted with pain.

'It's not a lie!' she said hoarsely, and he hardly recognised her voice. 'It's not a lie! I was there — in her house — when you came!'

Laxton fell back a step, and there was a tragic silence. Then he shrugged his shoulders.

'Very well; I've no defence. You say I was with her all this afternoon — and I say that it's not true! I was in the house ten minutes perhaps. If you don't choose to believe me, I can't make you.' His voice changed; he went over to where she stood.

'Norah, what has happened to make you like this? Either you believe me, or you don't. I've never told you a lie yet.' He tried to take her hand, but she struck his away.

'You've never told me the truth; never once! You wanted Laurie, you'd have married her if she'd had any money — you only fell back on me when she left you. Oh, I know, I know! I know why you got me to come to the dance here that night — not because you wanted me — but just for a bet. I know why you asked me to marry you — because you wanted to save Barton Manor. It was never me you wanted — *never me!*' She struck her hands together passionately. 'Oh, I've been a fool — a fool!' she said, sobbing in anguish. 'Why didn't I see — why didn't I guess!'

'Norah, for God's sake listen to me — just a moment — it's not fair — you're not giving me a chance. Oh, I'm not going to touch you — you needn't be afraid,' he added bitterly as she shrank away from him. 'If you'll just let me explain . . .'

'You can't explain — there's nothing to explain — and I don't want you to — now! It's too late — I suppose I oughtn't to have come here, but I couldn't have gone through the night — and not — not known!' Her voice was so hoarse and broken; she stood there twisting her fingers like a child, her face fallen into haggard lines.

The black sheep turned away — he had gone through scenes before with other women, but nothing like this; those others had left him unmoved, but he felt now that he had wilfully hurt a child who could not defend itself.

'If that's all you've got to say,' he said huskily. 'And if you won't listen to me — '

And she answered in a whisper: 'That's — all! except — good-bye . . . and I'm sorry I — ' She could not go on.

Laxton swung round. 'You're not going like this . . . You don't mean that this is the end of everything — that you're throwing me over? Norah — '

There was a sort of agony in his voice; his face was working painfully. 'Oh, my God! you don't mean that! Listen to me — let me explain — if you ever loved me . . .'

His arms were round her now, but she held herself as far away from him as she could.

'If I ever loved you! If you ever loved *me*, you mean; and you never did . . . I can see it now — though I couldn't then — '

'It's not true.'

She looked up at him. 'It is true — even you can't deny it; only the other day you stayed at home to see Laurie because she asked you to — and you wouldn't have told me that, only I found out. When you asked me to marry you — that night of the dance — it was because she'd thrown you over, and not because you cared at all for me — was it — was it?'

Their eyes met, and suddenly he let her go. 'No,' he said hoarsely; 'if you must have it, no, I didn't care then, but now . . .'

She gave a little tortured cry. 'Oh, and I was so sure you did — you let me think so! I believed in you so utterly.'

'It's not my fault! I told you I wasn't worth caring for; I'm not. I never have been, but you've only just found it out.'

She hardly seemed to hear; she went on brokenly: 'And I suppose — I suppose if I hadn't had any money, you — you wouldn't have — wouldn't have — asked me — at all!'

He made a gesture of despair. 'You won't believe me now, whatever I say. It's useless to try and defend myself. After all, what does it matter? I don't care a curse what becomes of me! I was a fool to think you were different from other women — fool to think you . . .'

She interrupted him. 'It's I who've been the fool — I thought I knew best! I might have known they were all right, and I was wrong.'

There was a long silence; then she moved slowly past him to the window, which Meredith had closed behind him when he went away. Laxton heard her fumbling for the latch, and he turned quickly.

'Norah,' he followed her; caught her round her shoulders.

She looked away from him. 'It isn't — me — that you mind losing,' she said bitterly. 'I know that — it's only — Barton Manor — and — and the money . . .'

Afterwards it seemed impossible that it was she who had said this cruel thing — but for the moment she was driven to madness; she was past caring, past realising what she did or said.

'Let me go . . . let me go!' she said again.

He released her at once, and she fell into a chair, shaking in every limb.

Laxton stood for a moment, breathing heavily, then he gave a queer laugh.

'Well — I suppose it's only what I deserve,' he said. 'But somehow I never expected it from you — ' He did not finish his sentence; he went to the window and flung it wide; she heard him call to Rodney.

After a moment Rodney appeared; he looked pale and anxious; but the black sheep did not even glance at him.

'I think you'd better take Norah home,' he said.

He went round the table and picked up the fallen billiard cue mechanically, returning it to its stand.

'What's the matter — what has happened? ... George — Norah?'

Rodney looked flushed and distressed. Out in the garden he had heard Laxton's raised voice and Norah's sobbing.

'Can't I help . . . is there anything I can do?'

He had never felt a spark of sympathy with the black sheep in all his life until now; but there was something about him as he stood there that looked crushed and beaten in spite of his defiant carriage.

Rodney took a little step towards him, half extending his hand. 'Let me help — if there's some misunderstanding.'

Laxton turned sharply away. 'Thanks — but you can't help.' He made a little desperate gesture towards Norah. 'Take her away — for God's sake,' he said hoarsely.

But Rodney did not move. 'I can't go like this,' he said. 'Can't you tell me what the trouble is — Norah — why don't you speak?'

But she only sat there, her face hidden. She looked so little and helpless, all her cheeriness and pluck knocked out of her, that an uncomfortable lump rose in Rodney's throat. He went over to her.

'Come, dear — forgive him — whatever it is. You haven't forgotten how soon you are to be married!'

'Ackroyd — for God's sake.' Laxton was nearly at the end of his tether. His face was white and drawn; he tried to laugh, but it was only a jarring sound.

'There won't be any wedding,' he said recklessly. 'I've been found out at last as the good-for-nothing — the outsider you all told her I was. We've given Lumsden something to talk about with a vengeance this time — something for the gossiping fools to cackle about for a month.' He stopped, panting.

'Take her home — take her home.'

Rodney put his arm round her. 'Come, dear . . .'

He drew her towards the open window and the dark garden

with its soft air and scent of summer. She went unresistingly at first, but out on the terrace she stopped and looked back at the black sheep.

If he had only spoken — only held his hand to her, she would have gone back to him even then; but he stood motionless, leaning against the table, his head held defiantly; and it was impossible for her to know how his hands were gripping the table to keep himself from rushing after her.

She waited a second; then she freed herself from Rodney's hand. She went back, and, drawing off her ring, laid it down on the table. Then she went out slowly into the summer darkness.

CHAPTER TWENTY-TWO

MEREDITH stared at his friend in blank amazement. 'Rot!' he said energetically. 'Rot! Don't stuff me with such rubbish! No wedding! Pooh! I know better than that. Why — '

'I tell you it's all off — finished and done with! Look — if you don't believe me.' Laxton held out his hand and showed Norah's ring.

There was a little silence; then Meredith sat down in a chair helplessly. 'But why? What's happened? What have you been up to? This afternoon when I saw her everything was all right. She said she'd just come back from London.'

'So she had — she'd been to see Laurie.' The black sheep shrugged his shoulders. He gave a bitter laugh. 'That what's done it — she was there when I called.'

'What!'

'When I called, I said. It was Laurie's idea. I wanted my letters back. I know women, and I wasn't taking any risks. She said I could have them if I called. I wasn't in the confounded house ten minutes — I swear I wasn't, and she was glad enough to get rid of me, I can tell you. God! what a fool I've been — what an infernal fool!'

'But, surely, if you told Norah why you were there — '

'She never gave me a chance, and I don't blame her.' He stretched his long arms. 'Well, I know where I am now, anyway. Shylock can have Barton Manor, and anything else he can get hold of. I'm off.'

'Rubbish . . . Look here, George — it's absurd to take it lying down like this. Let me see Norah — let me try and explain things. Damn it all, man the wedding's the day after tomorrow!'

The black sheep turned sharply away for a moment; then: 'I know,' he said slowly. 'I know. It's good of you to offer; don't think I don't appreciate it, but ... but it can't be done. I'm through, I tell you; it's the best way, after all. I shall go up to town first thing in the morning and see Shylock.'

'And leave Norah to face things here alone. Very pleasant for her, certainly.'

Laxton flushed. 'Is it my fault? Can I help it? It's her doing, not mine. How can I stay? I — oh, don't notice what I say — I'm half off my head, I think!'

He dropped into a chair, and leaned his face in his hands.

Meredith stared at the floor; his eyes looked very worried. 'I say,' he said suddenly, 'you don't suppose — you don't think this is a put-up job, do you? Old Ackroyd's a sly old bird, you know, and he might have been playing hanky-panky.'

'Nonsense! The thing's right enough. I've been found out a bit sooner than I expected, that's all. Oh, for God's sake, stop talking about it, there's a good chap.' The black sheep's voice sounded muffled; he got up and began pacing the room restlessly, as if he did not know what to do with himself.

'I'm — I'm sorry,' Meredith said again. 'I only wish I could help — it's rotten luck — rotten! Things were going too swimmingly, and now to end like this — losing Barton Manor and all the rest of it — '

The black sheep turned sharply. His face was white, and when he spoke his voice was hoarse.

'Barton Manor! Do you think I care a damn about that? Shylock's welcome to it, or anyone else for that matter.' He broke off; he looked away from his friend to the open window and the dark night beyond, and suddenly he went on desperately, as if the words were being forced from him against his will. 'It was the girl I wanted — but she didn't believe me, and — no matter what I do — or what I say — she'll never believe me — now.'

Meredith stammered out: 'I'd no idea — I never dreamed ... George — I — I ...'

The black sheep laughed wretchedly. 'Oh, what's it matter?' he said recklessly. 'It'll all be the same in a hundred years' time. Lock up, will you? there's a good chap — I'm going to bed.' He went out of the room, up the stairs two at a time, and presently his door slammed.

CHAPTER TWENTY-THREE

WHEN Meredith came down to breakfast the next morning he found Laxton in the hall making a great business of brushing his coat; he looked up with a careless nod when he saw his friend.

'Hullo, I've had my breakfast; I want to catch the early train to Town. I'll be back tonight some time.'

He hoisted himself into his coat. 'By the way,' he went on, with rather overdone carelessness, 'if — if Mr. Ackroyd comes along, I've sent him a letter, and you might say that I shall be here till the end of the week if he wants to try and spoil my beauty. So long.'

He went through the open door and down the sunny drive without another word or backward glance, but Meredith had seen in those few moments how worn-out he looked, and a sudden desire to do something to help surged through him again.

But the black sheep was not one to wear his heart on his sleeve; he carried his head high as he walked through the village; he answered one or two 'Good mornings' cheerily enough.

He was too early for the train, and for an intolerable ten minutes he had to walk the platform beneath the eyes of a dozen people.

Everyone knew him round Lumsden now, and everyone was interested in the romance of the coming wedding; but although he knew it was highly improbable that as yet anything of last night could have leaked out, Laxton felt he could not bear the curious eyes turned on him.

He was thankful when the train came in. He chose an empty carriage and flung himself into a corner.

Looking back on those moments in the billiard-room last night, he told himself that he should never have let her go — that he ought to have held her against her will till she listened to him — held her in his arms till he had forced her to believe in him. A sigh escaped him; it was too late now; there was something in his nature, some sort of obstinate pride which he knew would never allow him to ask again for forgiveness or approach her in any way.

The only thing was to clear off abroad; to go back to the

wandering years he had left behind — a dreary enough prospect it seemed.

And Shylock would have Barton Manor — would take it as a handsome *quid pro quo* for the pile of IOU's and bills reposing somewhere in his possession under lock and key. There would be some sort of satisfaction, at any rate, in being able for once to defy the old devil and tell him to do his worst.

He took a taxi when he got to London, and drove straight to the City. Shylock, otherwise Thornycroft, would be surprised to see him; at their last meeting, after his engagement to Norah, they had shaken hands over a glass of wine and a cigar, and Thornycroft had expressed himself as highly pleased with the way in which affairs had arranged themselves. This would be a blow for him — the black sheep realised grimly.

He went up the iron staircase slowly. This morning he had only been conscious of a great desire to settle his affairs, and be free to clear out, but now there seemed something horribly final in it all; something that seemed to be closing the door to any last way of escape.

He stood for a moment outside the closed door through which he had passed so many times to stormy scenes, and stared at the brass plate with a sort of horror in his reckless eyes.

He opened the door and went in. The same clerk rose from a chair and came forward; the same little smile lit his dull eyes as he saw Laxton.

'Mr. Thornycroft is out just now,' he said in his flat, expressionless voice. 'But I think you are expected, sir . . . and if you care to see the senior partner . . .'

Laxton said it was all the same to him whom he saw; he did not care.

During the few minutes he was kept waiting he looked round the dusty office with unhappy eyes. In a moment he would walk out through that same door, and everything he had wanted of life would be left behind him here for ever.

'Will you please step this way, sir!'

The same old request, the same few steps across the room, and through the door with its frosted glass panel; the same little click as the door closed behind him, and then — a man rose from the desk where old Thornycroft was wont to sit — a man with fiery hair and fierce eyes that looked their hatred at him — Norah's father — Mr. Ackroyd!

CHAPTER TWENTY-FOUR

THE two men looked at one another in silence across the paper-strewn table.

Mr. Ackroyd spoke first: 'You didn't expect to see me, eh? No ...'

Laxton looked round him with dazed eyes. 'Mr. Thornycroft, where is he? I thought —'

The elder man cut him short. 'My partner is out; I thought I should like to see you myself this time.' The last two words were significant.

The black sheep took an unsteady step forward; he leaned a hand on the table, staring at Mr. Ackroyd's harsh face with incredulous eyes. At last: 'So *this* — is how you get your money,' he said.

He laughed shakily; he groped backwards for a chair and dropped into it; there was a little silence, then: 'Does — does Norah know?' he asked hoarsely.

'My daughter does not know,' the answer came flintily. 'And if you'd played the game I never meant you to know either. I gave you a sporting chance, but apparently it isn't in you to run straight. When my daughter came home last night ...' He stopped, and went on grimly: 'Well, we won't talk of it; she's disillusioned now, and thoroughly, thank God!' He looked at the black sheep with accusing eyes. 'What have you come here for?' he asked.

Laxton looked up. 'You know, without asking. I came here to tell you that you can take Barton Manor, and anything else of mine you can lay your hands on, in exchange for that batch of IOU's and bills you've got with my name on them. The place will sell for more than I owe you.'

He rose to his feet suddenly. 'You say that I can't play fair,' he said with sudden fury. 'Do you call it playing fair to do what you've done? You knew you'd got me in the hollow of your hand — you knew that. My God! I'm half beginning to think there was something in what Meredith said after all, and that this is all a dirty put-up business.'

This was perhaps the hardest blow of all; to know that he owed everything to this man — Norah's father. What would she think when she knew — and of course she would know. Presently he spoke again.

'There's one thing I'm going to say in self-defence,' he began roughly. 'And you've got to listen whether you like it or not. Since I've engaged to your daughter I've done nothing that even you can throw up against me. If I started on the wrong track it was only at first. I admit that right in the beginning I wanted to save Barton Manor, and that I considered that before — before anything else. I ought to be shot for it, but that's the worst you or anyone else can have against me.

'As to — as to this question of any other woman, the whole thing's a mistake which I can't disprove — not that I would if I could,' he added defiantly. 'Give a dog a bad name . . .'

Mr. Ackroyd was leaning back in his chair, his fierce eyes fixed on the black sheep's face. 'You say you can't disprove it,' he said slowly. 'How if I can prove it?' He waited a moment, but Laxton made no attempt to speak, and he went on: 'Perhaps your memory is conveniently short; perhaps you've forgotten a certain morning — not so very long ago — when Miss Fenton was in my house, in my drawing-room, and you — '

The black sheep sprang to his feet. 'I never knew she was there. It was no wish of mine to meet her . . . if you were spying . . .'

'I passed the window and saw you with your arms round her . . .'

'And I say it's a damned lie, and if you've told Norah that you did . . .'

Mr. Ackroyd rose. 'And I say it's the truth,' he said with passion. 'I saw you with my own eyes. Do you take me for a fool?' he demanded furiously. 'Do you think I couldn't judge for myself what it all meant? I knew if I gave you enough rope you'd hang yourself. I knew if I tried to rush things on you'd give yourself away, and apparently you've done the thing thoroughly. I was beginning to fear that you'd be clever enough to carry it through, and I'm more obliged to you than I can say for failing at the last minute.'

'Set a thief to catch a thief,' said the black sheep hoarsely. 'It strikes me that we're a pair, you and I. If you told Norah that you saw me embracing Laurie Fenton I tell you to your face that you're a liar, and if you think that I went to her house yesterday with any thought of dishonour to your daughter . . .'

Mr. Ackroyd laughed cynically. 'You're very plausible, I must admit,' he said. 'But it won't go down with me. I know too much about you. If things had gone right I'd have held my tongue from now till Doomsday rather than have said a word to Norah, but as it is — '

The black sheep broke in hoarsely: 'You mean she knows all this?'

'No, she doesn't,' the answer came sharply. 'I'm not proud of my business, Mr. Laxton, whether you choose to believe it or not. I've kept it from her all these years, and, please God, I mean to keep it from her till I die. As for you — I'm prepared to treat you fairly — even now — if you'll clear out and never show your face in Lumsden again. You've caused Norah enough suffering — you've done your best to break her heart.'

Laxton laughed hoarsely. 'You admit that she cares for me, then.'

'I believe that she did ... Or at least, that she cared for the man she believed you to be; but now she knows you for what you are.'

The black sheep's eyes blazed. 'If you say much more,' he said chokingly, 'I'll go back and make her marry me — I'll never leave her alone — I'll — I'll ... oh, my God! I don't know what I'm saying ...'

He walked away to the window, and for a moment the silence was unbroken, then Mr. Ackroyd spoke.

'I think this interview has lasted long enough; we may as well come to the business side of it.' He pushed back his chair and went over to a small safe at the end of the room; presently he came back with a bundle of papers; he untied the tape which bound them. 'Perhaps you'll kindly look through these and identify them,' he said flintily. 'Or if your solicitor — '

The black sheep turned. 'Moffat can see to it — he's a business man and I'm not. It would be as well, perhaps, to have the thing done properly — seeing who I've got to deal with,' he added brutally.

Mr. Ackroyd looked up — his hands trembled for a moment as he laid the papers on the table; then suddenly he caught them up again. He tore them through and through, and across and across, till the whole bundle was reduced to tiny fragments; then, with a passionate gesture, he swept them off the table, scattering them on the floor at Laxton's feet.

'There are your bills and your IOU's,' he said hoarsely. 'And now get out of my office. I could have taken your last farthing if I'd chosen — I could have brought you down to the gutter; but from what I know of you it'll hurt your pride far more to know that you've been forced to accept my charity than it would have done had I allowed you to hand me over the deeds of Barton Manor. You owe me nothing, do you hear? Nothing! I make you a present of what you've had, and Barton Manor, for what it's worth! It's a big price to pay, but I pay it gladly — to be rid of you. And now go.'

CHAPTER TWENTY-FIVE

WHEN Laxton had gone Meredith wandered moodily about the house. Its silence depressed him after the noise and jollity he had known there. He wondered if anyone had acquainted all the invited guests with the news of the postponement of the wedding; the sight of his own top hat freshly ironed, annoyed him; he had quite looked forward to showing Lumsden how smartly a Town man could get himself up for a wedding. He slept till lunch-time, and afterwards he slept till early evening, when he was wakened by someone roughly waking him; he opened his eyes to find the black sheep standing beside him.

'Wake up, you lazy devil! I've been hunting the house for you. I'm going back to Town tonight — if you're coming, you'd better go and chuck your things in a bag.' His voice was jerky. He turned and walked away without waiting for any reply.

Meredith ran after him. 'Wait a minute. What the hell are you in such a hurry for? What train do you want to catch?'

'There's a fast up in an hour. I suppose you can be ready?'

'I suppose I can,' Meredith grumbled; 'but — '

Laxton broke in irritably. 'I don't ask you to come. You can stay on if you like, but I'm going — I hate the sight of the place. I'm going to have some grub. You can ask questions while you eat.'

But though he sat down to table, the black sheep never ate a mouthful. It was only when he had tossed off a couple of brandies that Meredith ventured to ask questions.

'What have you been doing all day?'

'The Lord only knows,' Laxton laughed recklessly. 'I saw Ackroyd this morning . . .' His face changed suddenly. 'By the way,' he said sharply, 'did you know that he was Yale and Thornycroft?'

Meredith flushed hotly. 'I did — yes ... I should have told you, only he asked me not to.'

'I'm much obliged to you, I'm sure,' Laxton said bitterly. 'Not that it matters, I suppose. Well, I offered him Barton Manor for my batch of bills, and he tore them up and threw them at me.' He laughed again. 'Oh, we had a melodramatic scene, I tell you — he hates me properly, there's no doubt about it.'

He pushed his chair away and rose; he began pacing the room restlessly; when he reached the long window that looked out over the terrace and lawns beyond he stopped.

It had been just such an evening as this when he first brought Norah to Barton Manor; when they stood together in the sunset on the terrace, and the first wild thought came into his mind which had led on to this disaster.

He spoke without turning. 'You haven't seen ... anyone, I suppose?'

'No, not a soul — I haven't been out.'

Laxton looked away.

'It's all over the village, of course; everyone knows. You should have seen the fools stare at me when I came off the train ...' He swung round. 'For God's sake stop eating and let's get out of this cursed hole ...' he half laughed. 'Don't mind me — my nerves are on edge.'

'Oh, it's all right,' Meredith answered; he swallowed a last mouthful of cold salmon. 'I shan't be a minute getting my things together.' He went out of the room.

Laxton looked haggard and ill. It was quite true that he did not know what he had been doing all day. It had all seemed an unending nightmare since the moment when he found Mr. Ackroyd at Thornycroft's desk; he tried to drag his memory painfully back to those moments and remember what had been said.

'George.' Meredith called to him.

The black sheep pulled himself together.

'I'm coming ...'

He went out again to the hall. This was the last time he would ever come here — wild horses would never drag him back to Barton Manor again. He had called it a rotten hole and said that its quietness bored him to death. And yet — now he was leaving it — he stopped in the doorway and looked round the cool, dark hall wistfully.

Meredith glancing at him saw the sudden emotion in his face. 'Come on,' he said with gruff kindliness.

They walked to the station silently. It was only when the train was moving slowly out of Lumsden that the black sheep leaned forward and let the window down with a run.

He looked out at the little village, bathed in sunset, till the last glimpse of the thin church spire and scattered houses had vanished; then he turned to Meredith, who was watching him with kindly concern and vague sympathy.

'Well, that's another chapter of my chequered career finished and done with,' he said flippantly. 'What's the next, I wonder?'

Meredith did not answer.

CHAPTER TWENTY-SIX

MEREDITH had been back in town two days before he suddenly thought of Dolly Durrant. In the excitement of the past week she had been ignominiously pushed into the background, but he was conscious of a distinctly pleasing thrill as he realised that in all probability she would be rather more than delighted to see him.

He told George Laxton where he was going.

The two men were staying together in Meredith's rooms.

George looked up from a paper he was pretending to read. 'Dolly!' he echoed vaguely. 'Oh — give her my love.'

'Right-oh.' Meredith glanced at himself in the glass and jerked at his collar. He did not find Laxton a too cheerful companion in these days, and he was quite looking forward to seeing Dolly. He hoped his reception would come up to expectations.

Apparently it exceeded them, for Dolly jumped up from her chair and so obviously expected to be kissed that Meredith promptly kissed her.

'Glad to see me?' he asked, and was surprised at his own delight at seeing her.

'Of course, we'd thought you'd forgotten us. Hal, where is George? And what really happened? We had a wire to say that the wedding was off, and we've waited and waited and never heard a thing till yesterday, when Laurie told us a little, but —'

'Laurie! Has she been here, then?'

'Yes — she came to tea yesterday,' said Dolly, with a giggle. 'She *was* smart! I should think someone's left her a fortune! She was most mysterious about it, too, and wouldn't say a word. She told us a little about George, because I just insisted on knowing!' Her face sobered suddenly. 'Hal, I can't help feeling sorry for that Ackroyd girl.'

'I know — it's rotten. Poor old George.'

'Poor, indeed! I think he's behaved disgustingly,' she declared. 'But you always have stuck up for him.'

'You'd have stuck up for him, too,' Meredith said warmly. 'I've never seen him so cut-up.'

'Cut-up! When he did it himself! Laurie told us.'

'Told you what?'

'That he'd thrown Norah Ackroyd over at the last moment, and — '

'Laurie's a liar, then,' Meredith said hotly. 'George never threw her over. It was the other way about; and it's my belief that Laurie knows more about the whole thing than she cares to admit. She's a sly cat. I wouldn't trust her any further than I could see her.'

Dolly looked triumphant. 'I always told you what she was, and neither you nor George would ever listen. But, seriously, she told us that George had broken off his engagement, and hinted that it was all for her sake — as I suppose it was.'

'Laurie's a liar!' said Meredith again, with more force than elegance. 'George doesn't care a snap of the fingers for her — and he never broke off his engagement. Norah Ackroyd broke it off herself, because she was at Laurie's, though God knows why! — and George was there — two days before their wedding was to have been. Oh, I don't suppose that was all. There was a lot more he didn't tell me — but that was the last straw, and if Laurie thinks George is going to marry her . . .'

'Oh, I don't say she thinks that. She's flying for higher game now.' Dolly laughed knowingly. 'Give you three guesses, and you'll never guess who her "latest" is!' she challenged him.

'I don't know. Ryan Hewett again, I should think.'

'Good gracious, no! it's not him this time. Do guess!'

Meredith shook his head. 'Give it up. Tell me.'

'Well, it's Mr. Ackroyd — old Mr. Ackroyd — the girl's fiery father.'

'Rot!' Meredith burst out laughing. 'Oh, I say, that's a good one, that is! Tell me another.'

Dolly looked angry. 'It's true, I tell you,' she insisted. 'Mother and I saw them having dinner together the night before last; and

Laurie told us herself yesterday that she was going to meet him again tonight.'

Meredith sprang to his feet excitedly. 'I knew it — I knew it all along,' he said. 'I told George, but he wouldn't listen to me.'

Dolly stared. 'My good man, what are you talking about?' she demanded. 'Do, for Heaven's sake, explain yourself.'

Meredith subsided on to the arm of her chair. 'I'll bet you it's a put-up job,' he said eagerly. 'I sort of felt by instinct that it was. I can't explain it all to you now, but are you going to lend me a hand?'

'But what on earth . . . Oh, for goodness' sake do tell me what you're so excited about; I hate mysteries.'

'All right — I'll explain. It's like this: old Ackroyd is Laxton's Shylock. I forget the real name of the firm, but it's something and Thornycroft.'

Dolly pulled a face. 'Oh, you mean the money-lenders, Yale and Thornycroft; I've heard George swearing about them heaps of times — go on.'

'Well, it's Ackroyd — Norah's father — he owns the show; he is Shylock, in fact.'

'Oh dear!' said Dolly, with a gasp. 'Poor old George!'

'Yes, I know — he never knew till the other morning when he went to the office to square his debts and liabilities. Old Ackroyd was there, and they had a rare set-to from all accounts, and Ackroyd tore up his bills and IOU's and threw them at him. If it had been me I should have stood on my head for joy, but Laxton seems to think it a deliberate insult. He says he'd rather have been sold up than owe the old man a penny. However, that's neither here nor there, the point is, I believe Ackroyd put Laurie Fenton up to making a split in the camp — to choking Norah off and breaking the engagement.'

'Oh, Hal — whatever next!'

'Well, I think so; I know it sounds mad; but such things have been done before, and it would be fairly easy with a woman like Laurie — she'd sell her best friend for money.'

'I think you're crazy.'

Meredith got down from his perch. 'Oh well, if that's all the sympathy I get.' She caught his arm as he was turning offendedly away.

'Don't be silly; go on — tell me some more. After all, it would be rather lovely to see Laurie done in the eye,' she added, with vicious inelegance. 'And she deserves it if she's been playing such a rotten trick.'

'We've got to find out. Can't you suggest something? You know her better than I do.'

Dolly shook her head. 'I haven't seen much of her since last summer; she only came here yesterday because she's got a new hat and wanted me to see it.'

'She didn't tell you where she was going tonight with Mr. Ackroyd, I suppose?'

'Yes, she did — she said they were going to Marnio's, and then to a theatre.' She laughed. 'Well, there's no fool like an old fool, is there? And if Mr. Ackroyd is going to marry her — '

'Don't you believe it, my child; he's far too game; he's more than a match for her. The thing is, how are we to catch 'em?' He took a turn down the room and came back. 'Look here, I'll get him to come along to Marnio's to supper tonight. I shan't tell him a word about Laurie, of course. You come, too.'

'Perhaps he won't come.'

'I'll make him. I'd give fifty pounds to see Laurie's face when she walks in with Ackroyd and sees Laxton. It'll be as good as a play.' He chuckled delightedly.

'I don't see what good it's going to do,' Dolly demurred. 'If George does see her, he . . .'

'It's no good arguing on "ifs", my dear girl; you just doll up and come along and don't ask questions. We'll meet you there — what time did Laurie say?'

'Half past six, I think. Let her get there first, and then she'll see us all walk in.'

She was as eager as he was now. In her heart of hearts she had never liked Laurie, though they had once passed as great friends.

'But supposing George won't come,' she said as a last word.

Meredith laughed. 'He'll have to come — I'll make him,' he said, with a confidence he was far from feeling.

But, to his surprise, Laxton raised not the least objection; he seemed rather to welcome the thought of a diversion.

'Have we got to dress?' was all he asked.

'I suppose so — it's a smart restaurant.'

'What a bore.'

Meredith looked at him consideringly.

'Dolly saw Mr. Ackroyd the other night,' he said then carelessly.

'Oh!' The little monosyllable was casual enough. After a moment Laxton rose to his feet. He stretched his arms wearily, picked up a cushion which had fallen to the floor and pitched it into a chair. He asked no questions, and Meredith let the subject drop, but he began to feel decidedly nervous as the evening wore on.

Supposing Laxton made a scene. Meredith hated scenes. Supposing Laurie did something foolish. He was on the verge of telephoning to Dolly to meet them at some place other than Marnio's. He found himself hoping quite sincerely that Laurie would not turn up, after all.

'I don't know what we're dressed up like this for,' Laxton said from the doorway irritably. He was in his shirt sleeves and struggling into a dinner-jacket. 'What do you want me to come for? Can't you go by yourself?'

'Don't be such a bear. It'll do you good. You've hardly been out of this place since we came here.'

'I shall be out of it for good and out of England, too — before long,' said the black sheep darkly.

He rather dreaded facing Dolly.

'Look here,' he said threateningly, as they left the house together, 'I'm not going to be catechised. If there's anything said . . .'

'There won't be a word said,' Meredith assured him. 'Dolly isn't such a little fool.'

'Is Ackroyd still in London, do you know?' he asked abruptly.

Meredith coloured guiltily. 'I don't know, Dolly didn't say; she doesn't know him to speak to, she just said she saw him.'

They walked a little way in silence. 'Was he alone?' the black sheep asked then with overdone indifference.

'No — Dolly said he had a lady with him . . . but no Norah,' he added hastily.

Laxton turned his face sharply away. Norah!

It was like the voice of something lost and beloved calling him back, tugging at his heart-strings.

He hated this suffering from which there was no escape; hated it because no matter where he was, or what he was doing, his thoughts were never free of her.

'I've told Moffat to get rid of Barton Manor as best he can,' he said presently. 'I shall never go there again.'

Meredith made no comment.

'I shall send a cheque to Ackroyd when it's sold,' Laxton said again. 'If he thinks I'm going to be under an obligation to him he's made a mistake for once in his life.'

They walked on in silence; Meredith was relieved when they reached Marnio's.

Dolly was waiting in the lounge; she greeted both men effusively.

'It seems ages since we were at dear old Barton Manor,' she added thoughtlessly.

'It will be longer before you're there again,' said the black sheep, trying to laugh.

Dolly rushed over to Meredith to hide her embarrassment. 'What a fool I am,' she said vexedly. 'I meant to be so careful not to say a word to hurt him, and now look at me!'

'You look marvellous,' Meredith declared. He squeezed her hand.

'Silly — I didn't mean that — didn't you hear what I said?'

'I did, but George won't mind. He's been talking about Barton Manor himself this evening.' He lowered his voice. 'You haven't seen her, I suppose?' he asked.

'Laurie? — no . . . not yet — we — Oh, here she is! . . .'

She broke off with an excited giggle as the big outside doors opened and a girl in a white, shimmering cloak stepped into the lounge. She was smiling, and apparently on the best of terms, with the man who followed close at her heels.

Meredith gave one glance at them and turned away — his heart was racing — he looked across to Laxton.

Dolly caught his arm. 'Oh, I'm so — *scared!*' she said in a hysterical whisper.

'Don't be silly! She won't hurt us — it's we who are going to hurt her . . . Look . . .'

He broke off sharply. Laurie was close to Laxton now, but she had not yet seen him; she was too busily engaged with Mr. Ackroyd. They could hear her light laugh and sugary sweet voice.

Laxton must have heard them, too — for just as she reached him he turned round slowly and their eyes met.

There was a breathless second — Dolly's fingers closed tightly on Meredith's arm; and they both heard the little exclamation which Laurie gave as she recognised the black sheep — saw the quick involuntary step she made towards him.

'George . . .'

The black sheep's eyes wandered past her to the man at her

side, and back again to her flushed face. For a moment he looked at her coolly and unflinchingly, then he deliberately turned his back and cut her dead.

CHAPTER TWENTY-SEVEN

THE two parties entered the dining-room together. Laxton was stalking on in front, his head in the air. An attentive waiter hurried forward; he cast a speculative eye over the new arrivals.

'Table for three,' said the black sheep curtly.

The room was very full. The only two tables vacant were close together. When Laxton took his seat Laurie was almost facing him at the smaller table which Mr. Ackroyd had chosen.

She was white enough now, and there was a scared look in her blue eyes; her hands shook as she unfastened her wrap.

'It's the loveliest thing I've ever struck,' Dolly told Harold Meredith in an excited whisper. 'It's like a scene from a play — Laurie looks like a ghost, doesn't she?'

The black sheep was apparently by far the least concerned of them all. He was ordering a lavish dinner and talking and laughing as if nothing of import had happened. He knew that Mr. Ackroyd was red and furious, and a little wave of exultation swept through him. He would show Shylock that he was not so utterly down and out. He would move heaven and earth to at least pretend to be enjoying himself for this one evening.

He paid extravagant attention to Dolly. He was the life and soul of the party; he wondered if any of them guessed what a sick heart he was hiding beneath all his forced gaiety.

Long before the dinner was ended he saw Mr. Ackroyd rise and call for his bill — saw the air of relief with which Laurie gathered her cloak around her and followed him out of the room.

And with their departure the black sheep's gaiety seemed to fall from him, and for a moment he leaned back in his chair, pale and silent. For the first time it occurred to him that this would all be used against him; that Mr. Ackroyd would go home and enlarge on the fact that he had seemed so light-hearted and so evidently enjoying himself.

'A perfectly delightful evening,' Dolly said, when presently they rose to leave. 'I don't know when I've enjoyed myself so much. Dear George was so amusing!'

The black sheep's mouth twisted into a wry smile.

'If you'll excuse me, I'll be getting back,' he said when the suggestion was made that they went on to a theatre; 'I haven't been sleeping well; I've got a rotten headache.'

'That's the champagne,' Dolly told him teasingly. 'You shouldn't drink so much.'

She went off happily with Meredith, and the black sheep walked away alone through the crowded streets.

Too much champagne! He wondered if he had drunk a great deal, and if that fact, too, would be used as a further weapon against him. He tried to believe that he did not care; but somehow tonight it seemed impossible.

Only a week had passed since he saw Norah; it seemed like a year.

If only he could make up his mind once and for all to the inevitable; to clear out of England, and have done . . .

He went off to bed before Meredith came in. He felt as if he could not face the storm of questioning which he knew was inevitable. He did his best to avert it in the morning, but Meredith was obdurate.

'Funny thing, running into Laurie last night, eh?' he began as soon as they met. 'And with old Ackroyd, too . . .'

The black sheep did not answer.

'Looks more than ever as if there might be something in what I said about it all being a put-up job — eh?' the other pursued.

Laxton pushed his chair back from the breakfast table.

'Oh, shut up!' he said irritably. 'Why the dickens can't you stop talking about the cursed business? It's over and done with; let it rest.' There was a little silence, broken by some one tapping at the door, and Rodney walked into the room. He hesitated when he saw the breakfast table. He looked from Meredith to Laxton awkwardly.

'I'm sorry; I'm afraid I'm an early caller, but . . .'

'It's we who are late,' Meredith said; 'come in, won't you?'

Laxton had not moved; he had turned rather pale, but otherwise he gave no sign of emotion.

Rodney looked at him nervously.

'I wanted to speak to you, Laxton — if I might have a few moments with you alone.'

Meredith half-rose, but the black sheep motioned to him to sit down. 'You can say anything you have to say in front of Mr. Meredith,' he said curtly.

Rodney shrugged his shoulders.

'If you're going to take that attitude —' He looked at Laxton's hard face, then broke out urgently: 'Don't be a fool, Laxton. I want to do what I can, believe me. If it wasn't for Norah . . .'

Laxton interrupted him angrily.

'Kindly leave your cousin out of the question,' he said roughly.

'I'm afraid that's impossible,' Rodney answered quietly. He drew a letter from his pocket and folded and unfolded it nervously. 'I'm in an awkward position,' he said again, with some agitation. 'Mr. Ackroyd is my uncle, and he's been very good to me; but . . . will you just read this?'

He handed the letter to Laxton. The black sheep took it reluctantly and glanced at the writing, then his face changed.

'I've no wish to read it,' he said stiffly; he threw it down on the table.

Rodney took it up.

'Don't be a fool, Laxton . . . I — I hate interfering, but . . .'

'I've told you I've no wish to read it . . .'

Then all at once his mood changed; he almost tore the letter from Rodney's hand; there was a moment's silence as he read —

Dear Norah,

I dare say you will be surprised to hear from me, but I've been thinking things over since last I saw you, and though you may not believe it, I'm sorry for being such a cat. I've bought you a little wedding present, and hope you will accept it. Couldn't you run up tomorrow and have tea with me? I am leaving London soon, and it will be our last chance to meet for some time. Do come. I wish it very much.

Yours affectionately,
Laurie Fenton

The black sheep looked up; his eyes were furious.

'I don't know what the devil you think this has got to do with me —' he began.

Rodney took a step forward.

'If you look at the date,' he said quietly, 'you will find that

Norah was asked to go to Miss Fenton's house on the same afternoon that you were expected.'

There was a little silence; Meredith pushed back his chair.

'Well,' said Laxton blankly.

Meredith broke in eagerly —

'Can't you see, you silly old bat, that the whole thing must have been a put-up job, to get you both there — for Miss Ackroyd to see you there?'

'Oh, stuff and rubbish!' Laxton threw the letter down again. 'This isn't a confounded Sherlock Holmes story — in the name of heaven what do you two imagine you're going to discover?'

He looked at Rodney.

'How did you get that letter?' he asked.

Rodney coloured; his eyes looked distressed.

'Norah showed it to me — I — I — I can't tell you any more; it's an impossible position for me — Mr. Ackroyd is my uncle, but . . . but I feel that if I can do anything . . . anything to help . . .' He stopped in embarrassment.

The black sheep hunched his shoulders.

'I'm much obliged to you for coming here,' he said stiffly. 'But, as far as I am concerned, the whole matter is just where it was before you came. It's ended, from my point of view — and I shall be glad if you will all stop trying to prolong the agony,' he added, with bitter cynicism. 'I shall be leaving England in a day or two, and then . . .' He broke off — and went on again more quietly: 'You mean it kindly, I know that; but this is my affair, and I'll manage it myself and in my own way.' He waited a moment. 'If that's all you have to say — ' he added.

Rodney picked up the letter without a word, and turned to the door. He opened it quietly and went out, shutting it after him.

For a moment the two men left behind were silent, then Meredith sprang to his feet.

'Well, of all the confoundedly ungrateful fatheads,' he began furiously, 'commend me to you. You say you want the girl — you say . . . The Lord only knows what you do say or mean, for that matter, and yet, now your chance is here, now you've got the whole thing in the hollow of your hand, as it were . . .'

'Oh, for God's sake, shut up,' Laxton broke in furiously. 'When I want your infernal meddling I'll ask for it. A nice sort of fool I should look going off on a wild-goose chase on the strength of such a letter. It's . . . it's damned silly,' he added savagely.

'To imagine that a man like Ackroyd is going to take the

trouble to get round Laurie Fenton, of all women in the world, to be party to a melodramatic trick like this. What the devil do you take me for, I should like to know? There isn't a farthing's worth of proof — and — and even if there were . . .' He stopped.

'Yes,' said Meredith. 'Go on! Even if there were?'

'Even if there were, I've done,' Laxton finished violently. 'If you think I'm going cringing round for forgiveness after what's happened, you've made a mistake — and that's all about it.'

'Well, that's a pity,' Meredith said calmly. 'Because I know for a fact that old Ackroyd offered to pay all Laurie Fenton's debts and give her a nice little present into the bargain if she'd make it her business to see you didn't marry his daughter. *Now*, what have you got to say about it?' he demanded triumphantly.

The black sheep did not move — only after a long silence he looked up at Meredith.

'It's all a trumped-up story,' he said agitatedly. 'You're pulling my leg — I —'

'It's not. I know it sounds like it — but I swear to you, Laxton . . . Lord, man! where are you going?'

The black sheep was half-way across the room.

'I'm going to see Ackroyd and have this out,' he said.

'George — for God's sake!' But a slam of the door was the only answer.

The black sheep went down the stairs two at a time. He hailed a passing taxi and was driven off pell-mell to the City.

It was typical of him that he never stopped to think or calculate his chances. His blood was on fire with what he had just heard. When he burst open the outer door of the offices, from which the polished plate of Yale and Thornycroft stared smugly at prospective victims, the meek-looking clerk backed away from him in alarm.

'Is Mr. Ackroyd in?'

'I don't know, sir — if you'll wait a moment.'

But the black sheep could not wait; he swept the meek little man out of his way and went on to the door with the frosted glass and green curtain, turning the handle without ceremony; then he stopped.

'Oh, you are in,' he said with deadly calm.

Mr. Ackroyd rose from the table where he was sitting, and the faintest look of anxiety crossed his face, but it was gone instantly.

'May I ask the meaning of this extraordinary — ' he began; but the black sheep cut him short. He shut the door and stood with his back to it.

'I've come here to dictate terms to you — for a change,' he said grimly. 'And the sooner you sit down and do as you're told, the better for you. No, it's not a bit of use ringing that bell, unless you want that half-witted youth in the other room to hear me call you all the names you once called me, and a few more which perhaps you haven't heard.' He moved forward a step, standing close to the table. 'If you don't want your — your daughter to know the whole truth of this damnable business,' he said hoarsely, 'you'll sit down here and now and write me an apology. You never thought I should hear the truth, I know; experience evidently hasn't taught you that there are not many women in the world who can be trusted to hold their tongues.'

He was making a random shot; beyond the little Meredith had told him he had no more idea than the dead as to what had really happened; but, coupled with the letter Rodney had brought to him that morning, the whole story seemed to be slowly piecing itself together.

Mr. Ackroyd met his eyes steadily; he showed no sign of flinching.

'I suppose you know the risk you're running — coming here, bullying and blackmailing me,' he said calmly. 'I am not in the least afraid of you, Laxton, and a piece of bluff like this won't come off. Get out of my office.'

The last sentence was a poor attempt at his old blustering authority, but the black sheep did not move.

'If I do go,' he said, 'I go straight to your daughter and tell her the truth; tell her that you've carried your hatred of me to the extent of stooping to pay Laurie Fenton to prevent our marriage.'

Mr. Ackroyd laughed scornfully.

'You can't prove it — the whole story is absurd.' But the words were less confident. 'It's a likely story, too, isn't it? Just because I was dining with Miss Fenton last night. And, by the way, I noticed how soon — how very soon — you've managed to find consolation. No, Mr. Laxton, I'm afraid you'll find it difficult to creep back into my daughter's affections this way. You're too late. I took good care to tell her of our meeting last night, and I fancy . . .'

'You devil, you! My God, if you were a younger man I'd choke the life out of you!'

The black sheep was white as death; his hands gripped the table in front of him to prevent himself from actual violence.

Mr. Ackroyd shrugged his shoulders.

'Violence never served any good purpose,' he said indifferently, 'and as for this cock and bull story — whoever your informant was — it's a tissue of lies. Is it likely for one moment that I should lower myself to ask Miss Fenton — to bribe her, as you suggest, for such a purpose? No, no; you've run your head against a brick wall this time. A very clever attempt, I admit, but these things have to be proved, you know.' He was recovering his jauntiness; he looked at Laxton with a contemptuous smile.

There was a little silence.

'I suppose Miss Fenton's written statement would be considered a sufficient proof?' Laxton said quietly. 'You overlooked one fact, sir, in all this. The fact that if *you* could buy Miss Fenton — somebody else could easily outbid you.'

The two men looked at one another unflinchingly; then Mr. Ackroyd broke out in hoarse fury —

'It's a lie — the whole thing ... I don't believe a word of it ... She wouldn't dare.' He leaned forward, his face crimson — he shook his clenched fist in Laxton's face ... 'Curse your meddling,' he said, choking with fury. 'You've come between Norah and me once — and now you're trying your tricks again. She put her love for a jackanapes like you before her love for me, because you've got a glib tongue and a handsome face. Curse you for your interference, I say! If you try to put her against me ... if you try to ...' His hoarse voice wavered and broke; he stood for a moment staring at Laxton, and a curiously glazed look stole into his furious eyes; then suddenly he swayed helplessly and fell face downwards across the table.

CHAPTER TWENTY-EIGHT

DOLLY DURRANT was yawning over a late breakfast when Meredith sent up an urgent message asking if she would see him. He was in the room almost at once, and had cast himself down in a limp heap of agitation in the most comfortable chair he could find.

'Mercy me!' said Dolly blankly. 'What in the world —'

He looked up.

'I've done it — I've done it properly,' he said with a half-groan. 'If you hear that there's been a murder — if you hear that old Ackroyd's been found with his fiery head smashed in you'll know who's responsible . . . me! me! me!' He thumped his chest with mock tragedy.

Dolly chuckled.

'I don't know that I should blame you so very much,' she said. 'Anyway, what have you been doing, and where's George?'

'Goodness knows — very likely the police have got him by this time. He rushed out about an hour ago, swearing blue murder and all the rest of it — he was gone before I could stop him.'

'Gone! Gone where?'

'To find Ackroyd, of course.' He told her of Rodney's visit, the letter, and George's threat.

He leaned his head in his hands and groaned.

'It was a silly trick, I admit, but I told George I knew for a fact that old Ackroyd had offered to pay Laurie's debts and give her a handsome present if she'd smash the engagement. Of course, I made it up; there may be some truth in it, but if there is it's only a lucky shot, and Laxton went off at a tangent, and if there's murder done . . .'

Dolly laughed.

'What a joke! Good old George!'

He rose from his chair and put his tie straight. 'Well, if that's all the consolation you've got to offer me — ' He looked at her, and suddenly his face changed. He held out his hand. 'Come here.'

She obeyed hesitatingly. Meredith encircled her with his arms.

'Do you think if we got engaged we should make a hash of things?' he asked, with sudden surprising earnestness. 'Do you think you'd chuck me over without giving me a chance to explain if you heard that — that . . . well, that I'd been kissing the house-maid?' He finished with brilliant inspiration.

Dolly smiled and dimpled. 'Supposing we try and see,' she suggested.

It was a very elated Meredith who was whirled up in the lift to his flat a couple of hours later — a Meredith who wore his hat at a jaunty angle and a flower in his button-hole, and who hummed a love song sentimentally as he crossed the stone landing to his own door — a love song which broke off on a little staccato note as he walked into the room and saw the black sheep.

'Hullo!' he said blankly; 'you're — er — you've got back then.'

'Yes.'

Meredith closed the door and went forward slowly. He quite expected Laxton to comment on his jaunty air or the flower in his coat. After a moment of silence he ventured another question —

'Any — er — casualties?'

Laxton laughed drearily.

'Yes — one . . .'

'Good heavens . . . You haven't . . . George, you silly fool — you might have known I was only kidding. I never thought for a moment you'd take it seriously.'

The black sheep stared. 'What do you mean? . . .'

'It wasn't true — what I told you about Laurie and old Ackroyd — I made it up — I had my own ideas about it all — but I only said what I did to wake you up — and now . . .'

They stared at one another blankly; then the black sheep began to laugh.

'For heaven's sake — if you've done anything rash,' Meredith implored.

Laxton dropped into a chair; he drew a long breath and ran his fingers through his rough hair.

'Well, this beats the band,' he said at last. 'Because it's true! The old man as good as admitted it when I taxed him with it. Oh, it's true, right enough,' he said again, with heavy bitterness. 'I've had my goose properly cooked, and by the woman I once thought marvellous.' He made a little gesture of despair. 'It only shows what a fool I've been, what a ghastly fool!' He dropped his head in his hands.

Meredith laid a hand on his shoulder. 'Well, well?' he asked nervously. 'Go on! What happened? what did you do?'

'Do! I didn't do anything except swear a bit, and try to bluff. It came off, too. He changed all at once — practically admitted everything, and then — just as he was cursing me to all eternity, he went down in a sort of faint — a heart attack, I suppose. He told me he suffered with them. I haven't altogether believed him lately, but apparently it's true. Anyway, he's ill, and if anything happens to him I suppose they'll try to add murder to the list of my other crimes.'

He rose and began walking restlessly about the room.

'My God, I'd never have believed Laurie capable of it,' he broke out passionately.

'I would,' Meredith said complacently. 'She told Dolly Durrant and her mother that you'd jilted Norah the night before the wedding — she hinted that it was all for her sake — oh, you know — the same old tale.'

'Did she! She took good care not to tell them about the scene we had when I went for my letters, I suppose. I told her straight out then that I'd made a mistake — that all along I'd — I'd — Well, let it go. Nothing can put things right again now.'

'But, my dear George, when Norah knows the truth —'

Laxton turned. 'And do you think I can ever tell her?' he asked hoarsely. 'Do you think it would do me any good to blackguard her father to try and save my own hide? Is it likely she'd believe me, for a start? He's got the pull all along — he told her that I was with Dolly last night — that I'd soon consoled myself. If he lives or dies, it's all the same — he's put the lid on me once and for all.'

'But you'll see Norah — surely to heaven! In common justice to yourself — it's the only thing you can do.'

The black sheep shook his head.

'The only thing I can do is to clear off abroad and stay there. I've nothing to offer her, even suppose ...' His voice broke a little, and for a moment he was silent, then he went on in his old flippant manner: 'So it's all settled and done with, my son! A third-class berth to America, and then —'

Meredith looked horribly distressed.

'Rot and rubbish,' he said violently. 'You'll do nothing of the kind.'

Laxton was lighting a cigarette; he looked up, shielding the flame with his hand.

'It's done already,' he said briefly. 'I went down to Cockspur-street on my way home just now, and I'm off on Monday.'

Meredith attempted no argument; he knew it would be useless.

The two men had a silent lunch together, at the end of which Meredith broke the news of his engagement.

As a preliminary he cleared his throat loudly. 'I — er ...' he began, 'I've got something to tell you.'

The black sheep laughed drily.

'Don't trouble. I guessed as soon as I saw you.' He paused and smiled his congratulations. 'Well, I hope you'll make a better do of it than I have. Good luck, anyway!' He rose to his feet. 'Don't mind me if you want to be off.'

He took a cigarette and lit it. 'I'm going down to Lumsden tomorrow,' he said, with rather overdone indifference. 'Oh, you needn't look so darned knowing,' he broke out wrathfully, meeting Meredith's eyes. 'I'm only going to fetch the Jag. — it'll have to be sold, as I'm off on Monday.

'Bet you a bob you don't go on Monday, or any other day,' Meredith said calmly. 'Bet you a fiver, if you like.'

'You're too ready with your fivers,' Laxton said, bitterly. 'I haven't forgotten the last occasion, yet . . .'

'Neither have I — you never allowed me to pay that.'

The black sheep laughed mirthlessly.

'You'll be able to pay this one, my son. Give my love to Dolly.'
He went out, shutting the door.

From the window Meredith watched him go swinging down the street; and there was a little pucker of thought between his brows.

'I should like to win that fiver,' he told himself as the black sheep turned the corner out of sight. 'Now — I wonder!'

CHAPTER TWENTY-NINE

It was late afternoon the following day when Laxton got down to Lumsden.

It was a hot, sleepy day, and the little village street looked deserted as he left the station. One or two people stared at him with interested curiosity. He walked with his head held high, looking neither to the right nor left.

It was just as he was leaving the village behind him and getting to the long stretch of country road that led to Barton Manor, and on further still to the Ackroyds' house, that a big, woolly sheep-dog came bounding round a corner towards him.

Laxton flushed up to the eyes. For a moment his heart seemed to be throbbing in his throat. It seemed so certain that in another moment he would see Norah that with a mighty effort he braced himself for the inevitable cut he was sure he would receive, but it was only the gardener who turned the corner and whistled to the dog. He saw Laxton at the same moment. He touched his hat with a sort of embarrassment.

'Afternoon, sir.'

'Afternoon.' Laxton wondered if the man noticed how shaky his voice sounded; he stooped and patted Friday's shaggy head to hide his agitation.

'You remember me, then!'

Friday was wagging a delighted tail.

There was an awkward silence, then Laxton straightened himself.

'I've just come down for a last look round,' he said, with a lightness he was far from feeling. 'I'm off to America on Monday — er ... everybody well, I hope?' he added jerkily.

'Yes, sir — I believe so, sir ... but Miss Norah and Mr. Rodney are still in London, sir. We heard this morning that the master is ill — hope it's nothing serious, I'm sure, sir.'

Laxton looked away.

'Yes, I hope not,' he said stiltedly; he wondered what this man would say if he told him the cause of that illness. 'Well, I must be getting along. Good day.'

'Good day, sir, and a pleasant voyage, sir.'

Laxton almost laughed; a pleasant voyage! It struck him as being distinctly humorous.

And so Norah was still in London. He knew now that he had hoped to see her — that the excuse of fetching the car had been only an excuse to cover that hope. He walked on with dragging steps.

Behind him someone was whistling shrilly — a gruff voice was calling angrily.

'Friday — Friday! Come here!'

Laxton turned; Friday was following closely at his heels; he looked at the black sheep as if asking not to be sent away.

The gardener came up, flushed and embarrassed. 'I never saw as he was following you, sir.' He grabbed Friday by the collar.

Laxton laughed. 'Oh, I don't mind; let him come along if he wants to; I promise I won't run off with him.'

The man looked dubious.

'If you're sure you don't mind, sir.' He turned away, and Laxton walked on with the dog clamouring beside him.

Once they were in the grounds of Barton Manor, they went on to the house; the windows were all closed and the blinds drawn; the caretaker who answered Laxton's ring stared at him with blank eyes; she did not even know who he was — she had been put in charge by Moffat, the solicitor; even when Laxton gave her his name she seemed suspicious; she admitted him reluctantly.

The hall was dark and smelt somehow disused, though it was not yet a fortnight since Dolly and her friends had run riot there; Laxton went on to the library and flung the windows open.

The caretaker watched him from the doorway. 'If you was wanting a meal, sir,' she began deferentially.

The black sheep laughed. 'No, nothing, thanks; I've only come down to fetch my car — I'll get something to eat in the village.'

He went from room to room restlessly. Norah had only been in the house twice, and yet the big, silent rooms seemed filled with her presence. Friday followed at his heels patiently, wagging a feathery tail as if in silent approval every time Laxton spoke to him.

They went out through the billiard-room on to the terrace. The sun was just disappearing behind the belt of dark trees — long shadows lay aslant the lawn.

The black sheep looked at it all with a new sense of shame and heartsickness. He would never stand here again. The place would have passed from him long before he came back to England — if indeed he ever came back.

He went down the terrace steps to the garage at the side of the house; the sight of the car sent an odd sort of pang to his heart; so many times he had driven it with Norah beside him; it had seemed such an important factor in their short-lived romance.

If only one might have things over again! Just a day! Just an hour! He had wasted so many of them — he had never told her how much he cared — never told her that she had given him the only real happiness of his reckless life; she would always think of him with contempt — she would be ashamed because once she had thought she loved him.

Friday gave a sudden little yelp of delight, and the black sheep lifted his head. Then he stood like a man turned to stone, all the colour fading from his face, as he saw Norah standing in the doorway.

The sunset light was behind her, and for a moment Laxton thought he was just imagining it all, that it was just his own longing to see her that had conjured her image.

There was a moment of absolute silence, then she spoke: 'May I — may I come in? I went to the house, and they told me . . .'

She could not go on; just stood looking at him helplessly.

The black sheep found his voice somehow.

'Is it — is it Friday you want? I'm sorry. He followed me. I was going to take him home before I went back to London.' He stopped. 'They told me you were in London,' he said roughly.

He had wished to see her, and yet now she was here it was almost more than he could bear. He could not trust himself to look at her. 'They told me you were in London,' he said again, with a sort of anger.

'I was. I only came down this evening. I saw Hal Meredith this afternoon, and he told me you'd come down here; so — so I came, too. I wanted to see you, and — and he told me you were going — away — on Monday.'

'Yes, I am.' He did not mean to speak curtly; perhaps a disinterested onlooker could have guessed that it was all he could do to keep from breaking down, but Norah only saw the hardness of his face — the way he avoided looking at her.

After a moment: 'I hope your father's better,' Laxton said. 'Of course, he told you that I was in the office — that it was I who upset him and made him ill?' He moved past her to the door. 'I can't breathe in this place,' he complained. 'I am sorry you've had the trouble of coming here. I was going to take the car out. May I drive you to the station, or — wherever you're going?'

She did not answer, and Laxton turned his head and looked at her. Her face was quivering, and there were tears in her eyes.

'Oh, for God's sake, don't cry!' he broke out hoarsely. 'I can't stand any more . . . Tell me what you want me to do — anything . . . anything . . .'

She hid her face in her hands.

'Oh,' she said brokenly, 'oh, I want you to forgive me!'

'I! — forgive — you! — Norah!' He could hardly speak. 'You don't know what you're saying — you don't understand. If you knew the truth . . .'

She looked up. 'I do know,' she said piteously; 'I do know the truth.' Her voice dropped almost to a whisper. 'Father told me — last night — and . . . and . . . I thought I couldn't let you — go — without — without asking . . . Will — will you forgive me?'

For a moment they looked at one another in silence; then the black sheep went across to where she stood.

'I've nothing in the world to offer you,' he said roughly. 'When Barton Manor is sold every penny will go to pay . . . the man I told you about. If things were different . . .' His voice changed suddenly; he turned away. 'Oh, if things were different, I'd tell you how much I love you; I'd tell you that I'd give my soul to have my chance over again.' He stopped abruptly, trying to laugh. 'But as it is — I think you'd better let me take you home,' he added hoarsely. 'I've got a pretty tough hide as a rule, but somehow — I can't — can't stand . . . this . . .' He walked a few steps away from her and came back again. 'Well,' he said jerkily, 'are you ready?'

'Yes.' She followed him back into the garage. It was quite dusk in there now; he seemed to keep as far away from her as possible, she thought; but somehow now it did not seem to matter; she felt as if she had suddenly been lifted up into sunshine, and her heart was singing . . . singing . . .

'I'll back the car out.'

When he had done so he stood by her.

'Let me kiss you — just once! — for the last time. I don't suppose I shall ever see you again. I'm going away on Monday. Oh, my dear, let me kiss you — just once . . .'

He was trembling in every limb; she could feel how his hand shook as he laid it on her shoulder.

She looked up at him, her face quivering.

'If you go — you'll have to take me too,' she said sobbing. 'I shall die if you leave me behind.'

Laxton caught his breath. 'I haven't anything to offer you; I'm not worth a thought.'

She lifted her arms and clasped them round his neck.

'I love you — and if you love me . . . Oh, do you love me?' she asked him tremblingly.

But the black sheep could not answer.

CHAPTER THIRTY

It was Friday who brought things back to the normal again; Friday who, tired of being neglected, stretched his furry feet and yawned dismally.

Norah half turned in the circle of the black sheep's arms and laughed shakily.

'Poor old Friday, he's so tired of waiting.' She looked up at Laxton with a smile. 'It must be ever so late.'

'I don't care what time it is; I've got so much to say to you. Norah — if I go to America on Monday . . .' He broke off. He looked down at her, and suddenly his arms tightened their hold. 'No, no — don't look like that — I don't mean it. I'll never leave you again.' He kissed her quivering lips with a passionate remorse. 'Don't, darling — I'm not going — I didn't mean it.'

She raised her eyes. 'If you mean to go abroad I'll come with you. I don't mind being poor. I don't mind having to work hard, because somehow, whatever happens, I shall always think it the best thing in the world to belong to you.'

'Oh, my dear!' said the black sheep huskily ... Presently —

'There's just something I want to tell you, and then we won't speak of it ever again. That day — when I went to Laurie Fenton's ... no, no; just let me tell you' — as she made a little hurried gesture — 'I wasn't in the house ten minutes. I only went to get my letters. She's nothing to me — nothing! I thought — once — but you know ... and then suddenly I found that any feeling I had for her was changing.'

His voice was rough and ashamed.

'I really think we ought to be going home,' she said, 'if you want to drive me to the station.'

A little flame filled Laxton's eyes.

'I'm going to drive you to London. It's a beautiful night, and we can do it in an hour. We shall be there by half past nine. Well, what do you say?'

'I shall love it!'

'Jump in, then.' But when she passed him he caught her in his arms.

'I'm so happy to have you again,' he said in a whisper. 'I've wanted you so much, Norah when will you marry me?'

She leaned back a little, looking at him with tears in her eyes.

'George, there's Father. I — I can't — oh, it nearly broke my heart to see him last night! He told me everything; about — about Yale and Thornycroft — too.'

The black sheep flushed hotly.

'I should never have told you. I should never have said one word.'

'I know — I was sure — I told him so.' She smiled now. 'So you see I didn't hate you so very much,' she told him.

'You're so much, much too good for me, Norah.'

She lifted her face and kissed him.

'Father wants me to live at Barton Manor ... with you.'

Laxton released her almost roughly.

'Never with me ... It's impossible; after all that's happened, I couldn't take his charity . . . I'd rather empty dustbins . . .'

She refused to take him seriously; she laughed.

'You'd do it so badly they wouldn't keep you a day!'

'You think I can't do anything . . . perhaps you're right.' His voice sounded miserably dispirited.

She snuggled up against him, trying to see his face.

'That doesn't sound like you,' she said wistfully. 'I should hate to think that you're never going to put your head in the air again and tell someone to go to — well, you know . . .'

He bent and kissed her fiercely.

'I can't quite get back to myself yet,' he said rather huskily. 'But some day — when I've safely married you . . .' He broke off, and this time even Friday, sitting patiently at Norah's feet, realised that the best thing to do was to give up trying to attract attention to himself and go to sleep.

THE TOP NAMES IN ROMANTIC FICTION ARE IN HODDER PAPERBACKS

Below is a selection of bestselling titles:

RUBY M. AYRES
- [ ] 12798 8   THE THOUSANDTH MAN 20p
- [ ] 12966 2   THE LOVER WHO LIED.................... 20p

DENISE ROBINS
- [ ] 14985 X   THE UNTRODDEN SNOW 20p
- [ ] 12792 9   CLIMB TO THE STARS 20p
- [ ] 12784 8   RESTLESS HEART 20p

IRIS BROMIDGE
- [ ] 12968 9   ONLY OUR LOVE 20p
- [ ] 12947 6   AN APRIL GIRL......................... 20p

HERMINA BLACK
- [ ] 12801 1   STRANGE ENCHANTMENT 20p
- [ ] 12791 0   CALLING DR. CARDROSS 20p

ELIZABETH CADELL
- [ ] 12797 X   THE GOLDEN COLLAR 20p
- [ ] 10881 9   LETTER TO MY LOVE 20p

All these books are available at your bookshop or newsagent, or can be ordered direct from the publisher. Just tick the titles you want and fill in the form below.

....

HODDER PAPERBACKS, Cash Sales Department, Kernick Industrial Estate, Penryn, Cornwall.

Please send cheque or postal order. No currency, and allow 4p per book to cover the cost of postage and packing in U.K., 5p per copy overseas.

Name..

Address...

....

....